MW00561480

QUEST FOR A NEW WORLD

DONALD M. EDWARDS

Copyright © 2019 by Donald M. Edwards

All rights reserved. This book or any portion thereof may not be reproduced or transmitted in any form or manner, electronic or mechanical, including photocopying, recording, or by any information storage or retrieval system, without the express written permission of the copyright owner except for the use of brief quotations in a book review or other noncommercial uses permitted by copyright law.

Printed in the United States of America

Library of Congress Control Number: 2019916220
ISBN:Softcover   978-1-64376-475-7
eBook   978-1-64376-474-0

Republished by: PageTurner, Press and Media LLC
Publication Date: October 24, 2019

To order copies of this book, contact:

PageTurner, Press and Media
Phone: 1-888-447-9651
order@pageturner.us
www.pageturner.us

PROLOGUE

THERE HAD TO BE SOMETHING DONE!

The Earth's resources were depleting at an astonishing rate. There existed two primary conflicting thoughts about the way to save the world and humanity, as we have known it....

"We must put more pressure on the large world corporations," said Thomas McFarland, the chairperson of the Environmental Advisors, an organization intent on destroying the international corporations. The E. A. had been boycotting the corporation's manufacturing and transportation centers located throughout the European Federation after attempts to influence the World Court had failed.

The E. A. was exceptionally vocal about the European Federation's backing of the International Mining Corporation's intent on expanding their mining interests beyond the asteroid belt. The I.M.C.'s plans were to include the moons of Jupiter. They had been successful in recruiting the disenfranchised to help in the fight against the large corporations. Toward the end of 2024, the Environmental Advisors organized a protest in Frankfort Germany, led by the European coordinator, Anton Harloff. The people were weary of corporate promises, they wanted to revolt against the corporate world's control and the E. A. seemed to be an avenue worth pursuing. It was for this reason that the Environmental Advisors were growing in popularity worldwide.

In the late fall, the E. A. organized a protest at the Washington D.C. mall in opposition to the money-hungry CEO's. The protest developed into a rebellion and a newly developed security force assisted the local law enforcement personnel in putting down the riot. The law enforcement officers and the security team used rubber bullets and water from fire hoses to control the rioting. The ensuing trampling of the demonstrators caused three protesters to lose their lives in the process of fleeing the bullets. The protest movement that martyred their deaths expanded worldwide.

The E. A. continued sowing discontent among members of the Asian Federation by promoting the idea that the European Federation was threatening the takeover (maybe by force) of the existing energy sources now under the control of several corporations. McFarland and the E. A. were in the process of attempting to establish a connection, that common thread which exists between so many of the world's top corporations. Thomas was convinced that the corporations had something in common; all of the top corporations seemed to have a universal business plan. The problem was - who or what controlled them.

In the ten years following 2024, Thomas McFarland's organizations continued the attack on the corporate world but were unable to have a significant effect. The E.A. secured enough materials to construct several neutron-flux weapons with the intent to detonate them at various strategic locations in Asia, which the Asian Federation would consider as an attack by Europe, thus thrusting Europe and Asia into war.

Most corporations survived the war and improved the working conditions by employing many of the jobless to help rebuild Europe and Asia. Improvements in research and development also occurred via large allocations of corporate funds; however, the E. A. was not satisfied that these measures had brought about sufficient change.

The E. A. concluded that the common business plan followed by most large corporations must be the work of a solitary financial organization. The E. A. began an investigation of the world's wealthiest people but was unable to connect any of them directly to any of the corporations. Thomas had no knowledge of the depth of their involvement-but he was about to learn.

Joseph Merrill called to order the third annual meeting of 'The Twelve', a clandestine organization of the leading world corporate financiers.

"For the record, this is January 15, 2024 and all are present except Akalina Vasin," Chairperson Joseph Merrill said as he addressed the ten men and women that surrounded him in a château located in a remote area in the Alps near the Swiss-French border. "We have some imminent decisions to make that have the potential of having a major influence on the world's economy. I, as well as all of you, have been following the activities of 'The Environmental Advisors' and their agenda to destroy our efforts to stabilize the world's economy. Jacqueline, please give us an update on their activities."

"There are wide spread protests in Frankfort, Germany over our planned mining expansion beyond the asteroid belt," Jacqueline Bernard commented. "The Environmental Advisor's founder, Thomas McFarland, claims responsibility for the unrest in the Asian Federation. There are rumors that the E. A. is very disturbed that the European Union mining interests have annexed the Jupiter Trojans as their property. If this conflict leads to a war between Europe and Asia it would definitely have a major effect on our mining efforts and would have the potential of generating a devastating blow to the already weak world economy, especially if the Americas side with the Asian Federation."

"Jacqueline, you have been closely following the activities of the environmentalists. You have a contact within their organization, have you been able to discover any hidden agendas?" the chairperson continued. "There seems to be more than just a concern over our mining enterprises, am I correct in assuming this?"

"You are correct in your assumption, Joseph, yesterday I spoke with my contact," Jacqueline replied. "He told me that there were rumors that the Environmental Advisors were in the process of developing a plan to attempt the takeover of many of the large corporations and redistribute the world's wealth. Their strategy is to boycott products and to stage protests that would disrupt not only the financial institutions but also production and distribution. They are not opposed to the use of force and they are gaining public support. We must impede their efforts now before they become fully organized. I make a motion that we organize a security force within the corporations capable of confronting this protest movement by whatever means necessary to insure our interests."

Edward Mitchell spoke up. "World economy will be the least of our worries if one of the near earth asteroids disturbs the earth-moon system by a direct collision or by creating enormous tidal forces if there is a near miss. We should be focusing our attention on the disaster that would accompany such an event. Since 2014, there have been too many near misses. We need to develop an immediate plan and put it in place for such a catastrophe."

"One thing at a time," the chairperson responded. "We already have a motion on the floor. With no objections, Jacqueline, will you organize a meeting with the CEO's of our European companies and the heads of their security? We should develop a procedure to combat this growing threat of the E. A."

"Edward, now will you please give us a report on the threats of the near earth asteroids," Joseph Merrill said as he continued the report session.

"In addition to concentrating on the asteroid dangers, we need to expand our search for new mineral resources," Edward continued. "With the growing danger of a war over mineral rights, along with the threat of a collision from one of the near earth orbiting asteroids, I propose that we search for a planet outside the solar system and explore the possibilities of colonization and future exploration."

"That is a lofty goal," Nicola De Luca commented. I do not think---

"Before you say no, hear my proposal." Edward Mitchell interjected before Nicola had a chance to continue. "We have several companies that are experimenting with designs of ships to travel outside the solar system. We could have the companies that we finance further develop the new engine, which they designed, to allow us to explore the moons of the outer planets. The engines have the capability to travel into interstellar space, which would cut the travel time to the outer planets to only a few weeks. And with the engineer's design they could further develop the engine to extend flights into deep space."

"If we decided to build such a ship we would need a very secure location away from the prying eyes of the environmentalists and protesters," Nicola continued, as she began showing more interest in Edward's proposal. "We would also need to be very selective in the engineering and construction teams that we employ in developing a 'starship'. We would need to utilize the same secrecy, which surrounded the development of the stealth technology, as well as the first atomic research. How would we be able to achieve such secretiveness with our present day surveillance systems? Our private conversations have continued to be monitored and we have had to employ scrambling devices to maintain any privacy."

"We could develop a manufacturing center in space," Tabor Shakiba added. "Why not use one of the Lagrange Points and secretly construct a manufacturing center there. We could have complete control without interference from organizations that will want to put our companies out of business. We could eventually develop a complete colony with all of the amenities of a five star resort in conjunction with living quarters for the workers and a separate facility for manufacturing. This colony could eventually offset the original development costs."

"The development of a space resort is a great idea, but back to my suggestion," Edward continued. "My proposal was to colonize a planet outside our solar system. We all agree that we have consumed many of the natural resources on earth at an exponential rate and are beginning mining efforts on many of the asteroids. Eventually, we would need to look elsewhere, especially since an asteroid hit is a very real possibility. This would be an urgent situation; therefore, we would need to begin our plan now."

"From the sound of our discussions several are in agreement with Edward," the Chairperson said, summing up the ideas. Are we all in agreement that this initiative is worth further investigation?"

The Committee, feeling the effects of the recent war between the European and Asian Federations, decided to advance the development of their plans to build a manufacturing facility at the L5 Lagrange and anticipated using the facilities as a construction site for the proposed colonization ship.

CHAPTER I

The Naval Academy offered me an appointment immediately upon graduation from high school where I was voted the most likely to succeed. I charmed my way through high school but I expected the Naval Academy would be a little harder and not as likely to respond to my charm. My dream had always been to fly the latest version of a supersonic aircraft and the Navy seemed to be the way to achieve my goals so I readily accepted the appointment. I graduated in the top 2 percent of the class of 2043 at the Naval Academy, but do not think of myself as smart, I just wanted to fly and someday maybe fly into space. After graduation from the Academy, I accepted a position to flight school and became a naval test pilot. It seemed that the Navy was willing to open doors for me. After flying experimental aircraft for a few years, the Navy decided that I should attend the Naval Post Graduate School in Monterey, California, where I became fluent in Russian and several Chinese dialects and became a part of Naval Intelligence. The Navy had developed a program designed to train Naval Officers to become employable in the private sector as a cover for a special operation involving suspected improprieties in international naval procurement, in other words I would become a corporate spy. My 'chosen' career field was International Public Relations. Now I have a position in what the industry calls a corporate recruiter. My friends call me Grant Wickham.

Burns, West and Associates, an exceptionally successful Wall Street Public Relations firm is now my employer, while I am also working under-cover for Navy Intelligence. Having been a major player in the firm's success, now I am on the fast track of becoming a full partner. Although some of my colleagues at Burns are a little envious of my success, they show me a great deal of respect. Several other Wall Street firms have wined and dined me, trying unsuccessfully to persuade me to join their firms.

Spring of 2057

Thursday afternoon, and I was happy this week was about over. I had just gotten home to my 5th Avenue apartment after a demanding day of work at Burns and Associates and a thirty-minute harrowing New York City taxi ride through maddening traffic when Max, a two-year-old black with gray stripes Manx cat, greeted me at the door of my apartment. Max curled up on my lap as I sat down on my cozy chair with a drink to unwind and I began to put the final touches on the speech that I planned to give later at the annual international company-client evening dinner meeting.

Phil, the building's door attendant, a rotund, gray-haired, good-natured man of about sixty years of age, called over the intercom.

"Mr. Wickham, a messenger is here with a package for you," Phil said.

"Send him up," I answered.

I signed for the package, tipped the messenger, and when I got back inside I immediately set it on my desk and opened the package; the contents somewhat intrigued me. When I looked inside I found that it contained 500 new thousand-dollar bills, a first class ticket on a supersonic flight to Geneva, Switzerland, and a note containing a request for my presence at 'a top secret meeting'. The note also contained some information about this meeting and informed me that an additional one million dollars would be on deposit in a Swiss account in my name upon attending the meeting.

I was quite curious about the contents of the note. *What is this about? Could it be Naval Intelligence calling me back for another job? Why would the Navy be paying me 1.5 million? Is it some foreign power or some secret organization that might be in need of my expertise? Who could send such a request? It has been several years since I have had any contact with the Seal's or with N, I.* The million dollars is certainly an incentive!

The note informed me that I must decide whether to accept the offer within 24 hours and it contained instructions as to how to notify the sender. In addition, the note warned me that I was to tell no one about the offer or there would be consequences. *I asked myself, what consequences; I do not take kindly to threats. I could just keep the 500,000 dollars and not get involved.*

Having a very curious but somewhat suspicious nature, I put all these thoughts aside for now because I needed to concentrate on the speech that I would be giving at the dinner meeting at eight this evening. In preparation for the night's dinner, I dressed in my freshly cleaned and pressed tuxedo and prepared for a pre-scheduled meeting that I had set at seven o'clock to discuss a client with Henry Schroder, my boss and colleague, every bit a professional and suave man. I locked the 500,000 dollars and letter in my desk drawer, put the key in my pants pocket, and called for a taxi. As I waited for the taxi to arrive, my thoughts were on the speech and on the before dinner meeting with Henry.

"Henry, I have been thinking about Mr. Whitman's proposal to open an office for his company in London. What are your ideas on that location?" I asked.

"I think that it is a first-class idea," Henry replied.

After further discussion of Thomas Whitman's proposal, Henry mentioned that we have Alexis Lambert working in our London office. She could help co-ordinate our business enterprise there.

The name Alexis brought back fond memories of the time I spent at the Naval School in Monterey. While attending school I met a girl, Alexis, who was the most beautiful girl that I had ever seen. She had flowing medium length red hair, not the fire engine red or carrot top red, but darker, almost auburn with strawberry highlights. She was about 5 foot 6 inches tall with full breasts, narrow waist and long shapely legs. Alexis was attending the University of California, Santa Cruz and our first meeting was over a latte at a quaint little coffee shop not far from the campus. We became friends almost immediately and spent the rest of that day enjoying the entertaining circus atmosphere and the pleasant, cool ocean breezes at the Santa Cruz boardwalk. Later that evening Alexis and I drove down the coast to Moss Landing to have dinner at an unusual seafood restaurant, which served the most delicious cioppino we had ever eaten. After dinner, we walked along the sandy shoreline that lies a few hundred yards behind the restaurant, talking and becoming acquainted. That was the first of many wonderful times spent with 'Alex' - a great two years.

She called me her handsome six-foot-three Navy man. I worked out regularly trying to maintain my well-toned college athletic build. As I said earlier, I did not think of myself as exceptionally intelligent but Alex thought that I was. She liked my dark-brown eyes and straight-dark-almost-black hair. She even liked my unmanageable cowlick and occasionally played with it by twisting it around her fingers.

My mind came back to the present and I looked up and saw Alex, dressed in an alluring black, off-the-shoulder-chiffon formal dinner dress and gracefully walking toward the banquet hall on silver three-inch stiletto heels. As she waited in line to enter the banquet hall, I made eye contact with her, smiled, winked and made a mental note to look her up after the dinner. My mind immediately flashed back again to our dating days and the good times we had in California. Unfortunately, after her graduation we lost contact with one another and went our separate ways although later I would learn that Alex had attempted to contact me several times but I missed her texts due to secrecy of the location of my Navel assignment. Once I returned to a 'normal life' l attempted to contact her but learned that she was seriously involved with someone in London.

I supposed Alex was in New York to attend the company's dinner meeting and she knew that I was the scheduled speaker for the evening. Henry mentioned to me that Alexis had never been married, and that she had just broken off a serious relationship with her fiancé in London. I was hopeful that she would be interested in renewing our relationship; perhaps that was one reason that she came to New York! I had dated several women but none of them seemed to be right for me.

My presentation seemed well received by those attending and I was especially pleased to receive congratulations from the associates with a promise that my partnership was in the works. Presently, I was working on the Whitman project and Mr. Whitman and his executives did not want their identity or their company's identity made public. I expected a full partnership if I did well on this project.

After the dinner was over and the banquet hall was almost empty, Alex approached me with a curious expression. Alex had overheard her name mentioned during the conversation between Henry Schroder and myself before dinner. Being a very motivated individual, she was curious about why Henry and I were talking about her. She was also curious about my seemingly secretive project and my private meeting with Henry before the dinner. Alex was still the very attractive, slender redhead with an outstanding figure that I so fondly remembered. Additionally, she still had the down-to-earth good looks that she had back in college. I was exceptionally pleased that she had not changed much since her graduation eight years ago. Alex was as beautiful as ever, and her appearance was completely dazzling. She appeared to me to be extremely successful.

"What brought you all the way here from London? You didn't come all this way just to hear me speak, did you?"

"I thought that you knew that I am employed at Burns and Associates. I was curious when my name was mentioned while you and Henry were talking before dinner." Alex replied.

"I didn't know that until Henry mentioned that you were working out of the London office," I said. "Tell me what you have been doing for the last eight years."

Alex responded. "After I graduated I lost contact with you. I attempted several times to contact you but you never responded to any of my texts. I traveled a lot after graduation and continued to text you but finally I finally gave up. My dad died of cancer and I inherited a great deal of money from his estate. After I saw most of Europe, I moved to the west coast and attended UCLA were I received a Masters of Arts in Public Affairs. From there I settled down in London and started working with Burns and Associates. The memo I received inviting me to this evening's dinner meeting listed you as the main speaker. How did you become aquatinted with Burns and Associates?"

"I am sorry to hear about your dad's death," I said sympathetically. "I did not know him well but I admired him for raising such a wonderful daughter. You already know most of my story, I am, however, still single and after graduation from the Naval Graduate School, I continued in the Navy for five more years doing some special assignments for them. My parents have been dead for four years and I have not seen my older brother since their deaths, you may remember my telling you that we were never close. After completing my career in the Navy, I resigned my commission and joined the Naval Reserves. That is when I became an associate with Burns and Associates and I have been with them ever since."

"Are you staying here at the hotel?" I asked. "We would be more comfortable at my apartment and could continue where we left off eight years ago."

"I would like that," Alex replied.

I pulled Alex close to me as we got into the taxi for the short ride to my apartment and said. "We've had some good times together and I can vividly remember our picnics on weekends when we didn't have a lot of homework due the next Monday."

"Yes," Alex commented. "And, do you also remember the hikes on the trail along the rocky shore overlooking Monterey Bay and the stops at 'Lover's Point' and the great dinners we had at that little seafood restaurant near the Naval School?"

"Certainly, and I remember the moonlight drives in your midnight blue 2020 Thunderbird hard-top convertible during spring break and the refreshing dips in the ocean. I can still remember the cold chill after a swim. I have never been so cold. We had to cuddle closely and roll up my UCSC dorm room blanket."

We walked hand in hand through the lobby and I got a wink from Phil as we entered the elevator.

"I expect you have had many girls up here. I saw that wink from the door attendant," said Alex.

"Not really, Phil is just being nosey."

I held Alex closely as the elevator moved up to my floor. Once in the apartment we kissed and I snuggled against Alex's neck, much to Max's protests. I put on some soft music and we continued reminiscing about the good times we had back in college.

"What were you and Henry talking about before the dinner?" Alex asked. "As I said before, I overheard my name mentioned in connection with London. If London is involved then I should also be involved."

"Henry and I were just discussing some future business possibilities," Grant responded.

"Grant, you are being very illusive," Alex said. "You are not going to tell me, are you?"

"Not just now," I said wishing to get back to discussing us. "We still have a lot of catching up to do."

I put my arm around Alex's shoulder and began rubbing her arm allowing my hands to explore her body. She was resistant, not welcoming my advances, seeming to have business affairs on her mind. As I got up and went into the kitchen to get us another drink, I put my hand in my pants pocket and felt the key I had put there earlier. My thoughts brought me back to the present and I remembered the money and letter that were in my desk drawer and the decision that I must make within less than twenty-four hours. I had already decided to go see who was willing to pay for my services. Whatever these people have in mind they must feel that their offer will be very appealing to me and that I will not turn it down. I had decided to call the firm in the morning and tell Henry that something urgent had come up that needs my immediate attention and that I needed to take off for a couple of days.

Returning to the sofa, I said. "Alex, I have to leave on a business trip early tomorrow morning. Are you going to be in New York for a few days?"

"No," Alex replied. "I am scheduled to return to London tomorrow afternoon but I would like to spend more time with you and learn more about what you have been doing. Also, I am still curious about the London project that you and Henry were planning."

"I would like to spend more time with you too but I have to be at the airport by six for my eight o'clock flight out of JFK and it is already one o'clock. I also have to arrange with Phil to take care of Max while I am gone.

"Where are you going?" questioned Alex.

"Switzerland," was my reply. "I have a few days of vacation coming. I will call you and we can meet in London on my way back. I'm looking forward to us spending more time together."

CHAPTER 2

I traveled in first class and had a relaxing flight, falling to sleep shortly after takeoff. I went to sleep thinking of my time spent with Alex and eagerly looking forward to renewing our relationship. The flight attendant awoke me shortly before landing and I pushed my seat back to the upright position, buckled my seat belt and prepared for landing. I was anxious to find out the particulars of this intriguing invitation so I hurriedly retrieved my carryon from the overhead bin and was among the first to exit the aircraft. Two brawny men, wearing trench coats and dark glasses, that looked much like secret service personnel, met me at the gate upon my arrival in Geneva. Immediately I was suspicious!

"This way, Mr. Grant," said one of the men. "Your luggage will be taken care of."

They greeted me with a brief handshake and the two men promptly ushered me through the crowded terminal, bypassing customs. This caused me to have an even higher level of suspicion.

The two men escorted me from the airport to a heliport and then we traveled to a magnificent country estate secured in a remote mountain valley somewhere in the Alps. The helicopter was a standard turbo prop with two seats up front with a separate passenger compartment. I was alone in the passenger compartment with all the windows blacked out. I was somewhat surprised that someone with what appears to be unlimited resources would use such standard equipment and not one of the newer hovercrafts.

"What is this place, where are we and who are you? I want some answers, at least give me your names." I stated firmly upon landing and as I looked around at the impressive old castle.

Neither of the men responded to me but they escorted me into the chateau's large entrance hall through a set of three-meter massive hand carved doors. After passing several other massive oak doors and what looked like original oil paintings lining either side of the hall, we approached a set of double oak doors and my two 'guards' ushered me into a sitting room. Sixteen comfortable looking leather club chairs surrounded a large, highly polished mahogany table, and a large monitor mounted was on the wall at the head of the table. I named my escorts G1 and G2 because they felt more like guards than escorts. They were a constant annoyance when they were present. I felt like a prisoner rather than a guest. When I sat down in one of the chairs nearest to the monitor, G1 turned on the monitor and twelve individuals appeared. They were all dressed in non-descript black suits, much like an executive would wear, and their faces were digitally obscured. They were all sitting at a large semicircle table.

The individual nearest the center of the table said, "Mr. Grant Wickham, welcome to Switzerland. You are probably wondering why we sent you the package with the note inviting you here. You are probably also wondering why these secret service personnel are shadowing your every move."

"All of this has given me some concern," I stated. "I want to know who you are. Furthermore, yes, the 'body guards' are annoying. What can be so important that you would be willing to pay me a half million dollars?"

"Your concerns will be addressed in good time, Mr. Wickham. You may call us 'The Committee'. Any contact with us must be made through our security staff."

"Whom will I ask for when contacting you? I want a person's name. I am not accustomed to working with total strangers."

"Because of the increased unrest brought on by protesters and the recent war, we must keep our identity as well as the comments that we are about to tell you confidential," the spokesperson said. "We are venture capitalists and we represent most of the World's wealth. We have done a complete background check on you and have knowledge of your security clearance documented on your military record and we feel confident that you are qualified and capable of accomplishing the task that we are prepared to present to you. Are you interested in continuing to hear our proposal?"

"I am very interested in what you are proposing and I am very curious to find out just who you are and what your motivations are," I answered. "And, how do you think that I can help and how have you obtained information from my sealed military records?"

The spokesperson continued. "You are aware of the growing threat of over-population. The current estimate is that the World's population could double every fifty years even with the present birth-control measures, and that the Earth's population will reach 11 billion by the end of the decade. The World's oil supply and mineral resources are in decline and China, India, as well as Latin America, have doubled their consumption of these resources."

I asked. "Why not use more electric vehicles rather than the older fossil fuel vehicles and I am also under the impression that new mining operations outside of Earth are expanding, is this not correct?"

"Electric vehicles are becoming more popular but most of the World's population cannot afford them. We are sure that you have been watching the news reports lately related to the mining efforts in the asteroid belt by the 'European Federation' and the unrest caused by the protesters. We have received information that this mining effort has changed the orbits of some of the asteroids. We are also sure that you are aware of the activity in the asteroid belt. There is a growing threat of a possible collision between the Earth and one of the straying asteroids as well as the Trojan-like asteroids in our own system. If this happens, or maybe it is better to say *when* this happens, it could change the entire economic structure of the World." The spokesperson continued, "This treat of an asteroid collision, along with the dramatic reduction in our oil and mineral resources, could drastically modify humanity, as we know it. Grant, do you agree that all of these points are valid reasons for concern?"

"Yes I do, but what can I possibly do to help solve any of these problems? I still don't understand what you think I can accomplish or why I have been brought here."

"Grant, The Committee has been working on a plan for over thirty years and now it is time to involve someone outside of our organization to execute things that we cannot accomplish. We have selected you because of your innovative efforts at Burns, West and Associates and your talents of persuasion. Our proposal is for you to select four young men and four young women to serve as an exploration team. The team is to establish a human colony on a recently discovered Earth-like planet and prepare for the future colonization of that planet. Once the team establishes the colony, we will notify all of the world leaders about this and then the leaders can develop a colonization plan. Grant, your mission will be to select the candidates from a set of very specific guide lines that we will provide for you."

"Where will I find young people that would be willing to go on such a challenging mission?" I asked. "They would have to leave everyone they know and everything that is familiar to them. That would be asking a lot of anyone. An Earth-like planet would mean one outside of our solar system. The team would have trouble communicating back to Earth."

"A set of guidelines will be provided that will help you in the selection. Let me continue. A spacecraft is currently under construction and is near completion at the L5 Lagrange point between Earth and the Moon. As you know, the private sector has been financing the space effort for the past twenty to thirty years; therefore, it has been very difficult to keep the construction site secure. The construction crews live at the site. They are isolated and have no communication with Earth. We chose them because they are very specialized artisans. The spacecraft's propulsion system consists of an array of highly efficient plasma engines with an extremely large thrust and an extended specific impulse. Liquid fuel rockets will assist in the initial blastoff. A nuclear fusion reactor provides the power. A biosphere, equipped with everything needed for survival in an Earth-like environment, will be complete with laboratories for the selectees to continue their individual research. A state of the art HQ-3000 super-computer controls all the systems on board the spacecraft."

I asked. "Will I be given the spacecraft's specifications to study as background information when trying to convince these young people to be deprived of their family and friends and go on a voyage never to return home?"

"A very specific set of guidelines for selecting this specialized group of young people will be provided." The Committee reemphasized, "Grant, you are to tell no one about this meeting or even the very existence of The Committee. You are to have no contact with anyone other than the security team and that security team will escort you at all times. We expect your answer within twenty-four hours. Your personality and social profile makes you an ideal candidate for this assignment and we are very confident that your answer will be 'yes'. If your answer is yes, an additional one million dollars will be transferred into a Swiss account in your name and everything you need will be provided."

The monitor turned off and the two security men came into the room and escorted me back to the helicopter. We flew back to my hotel, landing on the hotel's roof-top-heliport. The security team 'body guards' escorted me to a suite on the top floor of the Inter-Continental Hotel and after doing a second audio sweep of the suite and disconnecting all of the communication devices; they searched me and removed my personal communicator.

I felt isolated not being able to talk, hear or see what was happening outside the suite. All I had now were my thoughts. *I thought about the meeting with The Committee, what a strange group of people! Do I believe what they proposed? I am not sure. How can I convince young people to give up everyone and everything they know? I would have to find candidates with no family ties or at least weak family ties. Then I thought about the 1.5 million dollars promised if I accepted the offer. The Committee did not mention what happened if I were not successful. However, they did say that they were confident I could accomplish what they proposed. On the other hand, I could say no and walk away, go back to Burns and Associates and continue with my life. It has not been such a bad life. I would make partner very soon, that is, if I still had a job. From the looks of the two 'body guards' I could have problems leaving, knowing what I already know. The Committee seemed very intent and determined.*

In my aloneness, my mind began to wander, I thought about Alex and our meeting at the Burn's dinner and my hopeful evening in my apartment afterwards. We had a good time back in college. Alex was very charming but could be quite egotistical at times.

I thought about the challenging mission that The Committee had outlined and seemed confident that I could accomplish the assignment. They gave the impression that they were certain that I was the one. The complexity of the search for a team left me wondering. The search would certainly be easier if there were two working together.

I decided to communicate with Alex and ask her if she would like to be my co-adviser. I reached for my communicator but remembered that I had to hand it over to the security team.

CHAPTER 3

Meanwhile, Alex was trying to communicate with me, but all she could reach was my home page. The security team monitored all of my incoming calls. Alex's name appeared on the caller ID, and one of the security men knocked on my door.

"Do you know a pretty redhead by the name of Alex?" one of the security men asked.

I was puzzled that Alex's name would concern the security team. *What kind of background search are they conducting?*

"Alex is a long-time friend and colleague," I replied.

"Her name and image appeared on your caller ID," responded the security person that I had dubbed, G1.

"I want to give her a call; I need you to return my communicator," I replied. "I will require assistance if I take the assignment which The Committee has outlined. Alex would be my first choice as a co-advisor on the project."

"We will need to get an approval for you to make a call," the security person that I had named G2 replied. "You do remember the guidelines outlined by The Committee, do you not!"

The security team awakened me at five A.M. the next morning and asked me to get dressed. I complied and met the two security men in the hall outside of my room. They escorted me to the roof where the helicopter was waiting. The three of us returned to the chateau where I had met with The Committee the night before. The monitor was on when I arrived and The Committee spokesperson reminded me that there was to be no communication until I gave The Committee my decision. I explained that the job they were asking me to do needed a collaborator and that Alexis Lambert was as qualified as I and that I would require her expertise if I were to accept the challenge.

The monitor went blank and I found myself alone in the room. After a few minutes, a young blond-haired woman in her early twenties, dressed in a white tailored blouse and neatly pressed black slacks, entered the room. She was pushing a mahogany food cart laden with fruits, berries, several varieties of cheeses, cold cuts and hard-boiled eggs and accompanied with an array of homemade muffins and croissants. The cart also contained a variety of fruit juices, coffee and teas. She served this bounty of European-style breakfast fare on elaborate antique place settings, along with ornate silver utensils.

I commented to the young woman that I would not be able to eat this much food in a week but that I would give it a 'Yankee' try! She flashed me a charming smile without returning a word and left the room. I ate alone but became frustrated waiting for the security men to return me to my hotel. When I decided to try opening the door and leave, the monitor blinked on and The Committee spokesperson told me that they had completed the background check on Alexis Lambert and that she could assist in the mission project. The security man, G1, returned my communicator and I immediately gave Alex a call.

Alex answered her video-com on the third ring and I said, "You look beautiful this morning. I have an interesting proposition for you;

can you meet me in Geneva by tomorrow evening? I will arrange to meet you at the airport and when we get to my hotel, I will tell you all about it. Trust me; you will be excited to hear about this."

"I can meet you in your hotel lounge in an hour," answered Alex. "I will explain when you get there."

The security team escorted me back to the hotel and, accompanied by them, I went to the lounge. I was completely puzzled that Alex was already in Geneva, and especially at my hotel. How did she know where I would be and why in the world would she be here in Geneva! I looked for her in the lounge and saw her sitting alone at a table near the entrance.

"What are you doing here in Geneva?" I asked. "I understood that you were supposed to be in London."

"On my taxi ride back to my hotel after the company dinner," Alex replied. "I thought more about your trip to Switzerland and that it probably had to do with the London client that Henry Schroder and you were discussing before the dinner. I was a little resentful that I was not included in the discussion since I work out of the London office. When I returned to my hotel, I used the complimentary guest data input and looked up the flights to Switzerland. I discovered that one flight departed at 7:45 A.M. to Zurich another at 8:00 A.M. to Geneva. I immediately called the airline, booked a coach seat on the Geneva flight, and trusted that I would not bump into you at the airport, but instead I wanted to surprise you at the hotel. I followed you here with hopes of becoming a part of your business plan. I was concerned when I observed what looked like secret service personnel escorting you past customs and through a door labeled 'secured area - airport personal only'. When I finally cleared customs and exited the air terminal with my luggage, I had lost visual contact with you. I thought that I caught a glimpse you and your escorts while I waited for a taxi, but I was not sure. I realized that this was no ordinary business meeting. I wondered in what you had gotten yourself involved. I asked the taxi to take me to the nearest hotel. I again utilized the complimentary data input supplied by the hotel and contacted several Geneva hotels, using my communicator with the visual component turned off, until I found the one where you were registered. I determined that you were a registered guest at the Inter-Continental and I communicated with the front desk and asked to speak to Grant Wickham. The clerk asked if I wanted to leave a message. I did not give my name but simply ended the call. I caught a taxi to the Inter-Continental and approached the front desk looking and acting like a bride-to-be. I told the front desk clerk that I was Grant Wickham's fiancée and that I wished to surprise you. The hotel clerk informed me that you had not yet arrived and for security reasons they could not allow me to enter your room without your prior consent. I reluctantly left the desk and went to the lounge. I spent most of the night here in the lounge; but, I finally gave up and went back to my hotel."

When we got to my suite and left my security detail posted outside, I ordered room service and a bottle of Champaign. While enjoying a late lunch, I told Alex about meeting with The Committee and about what they had proposed to me.

"This morning I met with The Committee and told them that I would need you to help with the mission project and the team selections," I explained. "Would you be willing to give up your career with Burns, West and Associates for one and one half million American dollars? I have previously received an amount of 500,000 dollars as an incentive to meet with The Committee and hear their plan. They promised to deposit an additional one million dollars into a Swiss account upon my accepting their assignment. I assume there may be more money when the selection is complete."

Alex was excited about the possibility of working with me on the project and about the million plus dollars in the bank.

"I will be willing to assist in the selections," she said. "What happens when we are done? Just how are we going to make the selections? What does The Committee really want?"

"You know all that I know," I answered. "We will have to meet with The Committee and get a number of details clarified. By the way, I am still puzzled that you happen to be here in Switzerland! I did not communicate explicitly at my apartment about my travel plans after

18

the company dinner in New York City. I am very sorry I had to be so blunt but my letter from The Committee had warned me not the tell anyone of the meeting which they had requested me to attend."

"Well, I was jealous at first," Alex returned. "After all, Henry should have consulted with me; I do work out of the London office, you know. Therefore, I decided to take a few days of vacation before heading home and followed you to see what the two of you were planning. I had no idea Henry was not a part of your plan, I can now understand why you were so willing to get rid of me after the company dinner. I am sorry I acted so assertively by assuming to follow you here, but now I am glad I did. Will you forgive my actions?"

Alex convinced me that she understood why I rushed her out of my apartment. Since learning about The Committee's proposal and the opportunity to be my associate on the project, she was motivated to accept the mission assignment.

I found the two security men in the hall just outside my suite and asked them to arrange a meeting for Alex and me with The Committee the following morning. I informed the security team that I wanted some privacy for the night. I had plans for the evening; as I entered my hotel suite romance was on my mind.

Alex, however, had other plans. She let me know that the job opportunity was more important than my romantic plans for the evening and that she was not ready for another relationship at this time. She told me about her last relationship that she was involved in while living in London and that her fiancée, Tyler, had wanted more than she was willing to give.

"Grant, we had a great time back in college," Alex remarked. "We were young then and didn't have the responsibilities that we now have. When we finish this assignment, we can see what direction our romance takes."

I reluctantly agreed with Alex, we ordered room service, had a pleasant dinner, and finished the champagne from lunch. After dinner, we talked more about The Committee's proposal and after a goodnight kiss; we went to the separate bedrooms of my two-bedroom suite.

The next morning Alex and I ordered a continental breakfast and a pot of French roast coffee from room service and while eating breakfast we prepared for our meeting with The Committee.

"What are the parameters for the selection process?" Alex asked, as she sipped on her second cup of coffee. "We will probably need a team of professionals such as MD's and psychologists to help us evaluate the selectees. They must be physically and mentally stable and have average or above physical and mental abilities."

"Now you see why I wanted you to help in this process," I said. "I still need some details about the ship and more information about the colony the selectees are to establish. I will have to focus on their egos in order to be able to convince them to leave everything. They will need to understand that they will be able to shape their own future by developing their own form of government, which will allow them to have personal freedoms with the lack of interference. This is much like God's call to Abram to leave his family and friends and to go to a far country. I am afraid the selectees may not have the faith of Abraham."

The security team, stationed outside my hotel suite, accompanied us to the arranged meeting with The Committee. Alex and I went to the meeting with several questions still unanswered.

CHAPTER 4

After I introduced Alex, we informed The Committee about how excited and elated we were to have such an enormous opportunity but that we had several concerns.

"To begin, we will both have to either resign or be allowed to take a leave of absence from Burns, West and Associates," I informed The Committee. "Therefore, Alex will need the same compensation that was agreed upon for me. Burns, West and Associates promised me a partnership and if I take this assignment, it will certainly affect my future. We will probably both have to resign because I cannot see Henry agreeing to a leave for either of us, which brings up the problem of what we do after our assignment is finished."

Alex and I had previously discussed these issues and had agreed on these points of concern and after negotiating with The Committee, they decided to give her the same stipend that they had offered me. They also gave Alex and me the assurance that after we had satisfactorily completed the assignment, we could apply for a position in one of the companies in which they had a controlling interest. They also informed us that they could assure us that our old jobs and positions would be available if we choose that avenue. After a brief conference with each other, Alex and I agreed to sign a written contract that contained provisions for guaranteed employment and satisfactory compensations after our assignment was completed.

The helicopter returned us to the hotel and Alex and I spent the rest of the day discussing how to accomplish our project. What approach would be the best for the selection process? How would the selectees combat boredom? After several grueling hours of throwing ideas around, we both agreed that we needed to have much more information.

By evening, I invited the security team into the hotel room in hopes of achieving a better working arrangement with them. Our relationships with the security team became much more casual now. The one I had named G1 told us to call him Tom and G2 told us his name was Mike. We were now relieved to have names although Alex and I wondered if these were their real names. We were now actually able to have a conversation with the security team. I asked Tom to set up a meeting with The Committee for the next day.

At ten o'clock, the next morning, after Alex and I had a quick breakfast of bagels, cream cheese, juice and coffee, our security personnel, along with Alex and myself, boarded the helicopter on the hotel roof for the short flight to the estate. The meeting lasted for an exhausting six hours, with a short break for lunch, and Alex and I had all of our trepidations calmed, and our questions answered, well, at least most of them, and they explained the guidelines for the selections. The guidelines stipulated that we were to select students who had earned a BS or MS degree in the graduating class of 2057. Each candidate would have an intelligent quotient of 170 or more. The candidates would have a high degree of mental and physical stability, being psychologically sound and physically healthy. The only real animal protein that would be available on the ship would be fish, although laboratory-generated protein would also be available; therefore, it would be preferred if the selectees developed a vegetarian life-style. Each candidate would possess a wide range of interests and be moderately sociable, no antisocial tendencies, (no nerds or geeks)! They would all need to become self-governing and able to think creatively and resourcefully. Lastly, each candidate would be able and willing to populate the colony and develop a successful society in preparation for the future colonists.

I received a set of the ship's specifications that I had requested. We discussed a few other concerns we had such as where to recruit the candidates. Alex suggested that the top ten universities would be the appropriate place to search. Alex and I discussed our concerns about our abilities to determine some of the candidate's qualifications. After discussing these concerns with The Committee, they agreed that we would need a team of professionals to help us screen the candidates. As we prepared to leave, the spokesperson gave us three months to complete our initial selection and told us that they were impressed with the methods we had developed for the selection process.

The security team returned us to Geneva; but this time, the helicopter did not land at the hotel heliport but rather atop a small nondescript office building not far from the hotel where we had been staying. Tom and Mike informed us that there was an office and living space established for us on the top floor. Tom also told us that he was assigning additional security personnel to protect our privacy and provide protection against intruders who might protest our involvement with the project. Tom admonished us again that we should not speak to anyone concerning our mission, especially from the press or the media. Because of his admonition of secrecy, my mind went back to the recent rioting, caused by the unrest over concerns of diminishing Earth's resources, which had recently been taking place in Germany and several of the Asian countries as well as the hostility in the Asian Federation. Tom told us that he and Mike would continue to be our contacts with The Committee.

Alex looked around our new home and started mentally rearranging the furniture. The apartment consisted of two bedrooms separated by a single bath, a living space large enough for two desks, bookcases and files. At the other end, there was a small dining table. Beyond the dining area, a waist high partition separated it from a small galley. Alex asked for my opinion but I told her that whatever she decided would be fine with me; all I needed was a table or desk, a chair and a bed. Before evening, Alex, along with the help of some of the assigned personnel, arranged the apartment to her specifications and decorating style. Alex certainly had the ability to make decisions and carry them out in an orderly fashion. I was constantly reassured of my choice of a co-advisor, and my thoughts kept going to the prospect of my pursuing her as a wife in the near future!

Realizing there was no food in the apartment, we ordered dinner delivered from a local café and settled down for the evening. Tom and Mike no longer had the guard assignment outside our door. They, along with the entire security team, occupied an office space on the second floor of the building and were available twenty-four hours per day. Tom gave each of us a dedicated communicator to contact the security team whenever we needed them. The first floor housed an office front with several small office spaces to serve as dorm rooms for the students that we were to select. A foyer separated the offices, and a large conference room was located beyond the foyer. In appearance, it was no different from all the other offices in the area.

Alex and I spent a comfortable evening in our new apartment, which was an improvement over the hotel suite, even though the furnishings were not nearly as plush as those in the hotel suite were, but it had a feeling of home. I got ready for bed and suggested that Alex join me. She did not agree with my idea but gave me a kiss and told me to be good and to get some rest so we would be ready to start work the next day.

I had hoped that Alex would soon start to think the same way about me as I did about her. An outsider would think that we were married, and sometimes I think we act like a married couple; I definitely did not think that would be such a bad idea, but she had not yet indicated such to me. It was getting more and more difficult to concentrate on the assigned task having her in such close proximity.

The next morning we awoke and after remembering we had no food in the apartment and that there was no room service, we decided to walk to the café where we had eaten the night before.

"We are going to the café down the street," I informed Tom as we passed through the second floor. "We don't have anything to eat upstairs. Alex and I have made a list of things we need. Would you please arrange for someone to purchase these items for us?"

After returning from breakfast, we settled down for another long day. Alex began to compile a list of the leading universities from North America; South America; Europe and Asia. Meanwhile, I began studying the specs for the ship. Alex shared her list with me and I suggested that the list should also include universities from Australia. After adding Australia, her list consisted of the top twenty universities of the World.

"We have two months before most major universities have their spring graduations," Alex said. "Did you know that the California Institute of Technology and Stanford are among the top ten universities in the world? They are in close proximity and that's not far from our old stomping grounds."

Alex sent the list of the top universities to The Committee by a member of the security team with a request to have the school presidents compile a list of the top graduates that met the intelligence requirements and to designate the top engineering and science students, along with the top students in the various medical fields. These students should also have minors in the liberal arts.

Alex studied the list of candidate requirements given to us while I continued to examine the ship's specifications. Alex interrupted my study of the ship with several ideas concerning the process of selecting members to serve on our elimination-interview team.

"It will be necessary to assemble a team of highly qualified professionals to help evaluate the mental and physical stability of the candidates," Alex said. "We will need psychologists and medical specialists on the interview team. We will definitely require The Committee's input and influence in the formation of this team of specialists."

"How do we measure sociability?" I asked. "And, how do we decide a student's ability to self-govern and think creatively? In addition, how can we determine which ones would have the ability to coexist for a large portion of their lifetimes and keep their sanity intact as well as not killing one another?"

"We may need to add a sociologist to our interview team," Alex commented. "Also, maybe even an economist. As far as a person's ability to think creatively, I would think a person having an IQ of over 170 should not have a problem. To measure someone's sociability, I thought that being a member of an academic club or being involved in school events would be a good start. I first thought that membership in a sorority or fraternity might be an indicator but these students are probably not socially involved in that sort of thing."

We continued bouncing ideas back and forth, as we were formulating lists and criteria for the candidates as well as for those who would assist us as a selection committee. It seemed that each time we discussed our options; we arrived at a better working plan.

I contacted Tom and asked for a meeting with The Committee to discuss the formation of the interview team. Tom, our faithful escort, accompanied us to the office heliport the following morning.

"Tom, I have flight training with helicopters, was a test pilot for the Navy and could easily fly back and forth from here to the estate," I commented, thinking that the frequent trips were a waste of Tom's time, however, he did not respond to my comment.

On most of our flights to the estate, Tom was the pilot. Mike went along for the ride but he also could pilot the helicopter. Tom always was the one that arranged our meetings with The Committee and he seemed to know his way around the estate.

"Tom," I said, "would you ask permission for us to meet with The Committee without an escort?"

"The Committee will not agree to give you access to the estate," Tom said, "at least, not yet.

"Understood," I reluctantly replied! "I only thought that it would free you for other duties since we will need to make several trips for consultation in the near future."

CHAPTER 5

The Committee was waiting for us as at the chateau when we arrived and took our places at the table nearest to the monitor in the familiar assembly room. Tom turned on the monitor and The Committee greeted us with a very pleasant, "hello".

The spokesperson asked. "What can we do for you this morning?"

"We have received the information that we requested from the university presidents and we are in the process of making the initial selections," Alex said.

"We will need a team of specialists, medical doctors, psychologists, and other professionals to help us establish the mental and physical stability of the candidates," I replied.

We explained our progress in the selection process and further discussed the need for a group of specialists to help in the procedure. The Committee agreed that they would use their influence in assembling the specialists for the interview team. The Committee assured Alex that they would complete the selection of the special interview team before we were finished choosing the initial selectees. Alex discussed the list of the leading universities that she had sent to

The Committee. She further asked them if they would contact the universities' administrators to request that they send her a copy of the students' records.

Tom returned us to the office building and after our first lunch in our apartment, we spent the rest of the day relaxing by taking a long walk and discussing our future while waiting for Alex to receive a copy of the student records.

"One thing we need to agree upon is who is doing the cooking and house chores," Alex stated.

"I agree, Alex, and how about if we share all of the household duties, it will be more fun if we do them together," I returned.

"I was hoping that you would agree to make them a joint effort, Grant", Alex added. "It is amazing to me that we seem to be agreeing on a unified arrangement in most that we do."

"What will we do after the selection is finished?" Alex asked.

"We will be essentially unemployed," I said. "We could start our own consulting firm, or we could talk to Henry about giving us back our old jobs although I am not sure he would talk to us, even though The Committee assured us that Henry would let us return to our old positions at West. Or, we could take The Committee up on their offer of employment."

"You mean we could become partners?" Alex asked. "I think it is time that we become more than just business partners."

I quickly got the hint and asked, "What are you suggesting?"

When we returned to the apartment, Alex went to relax on the cozy, chocolate brown leather sofa, I stretched out with my head resting in her lap, and we continued discussing our future as Alex playfully ran her fingers through my hair. Our 'together times' were beginning to feel very relaxed; however, they were becoming more exciting and exhilarating. I looked forward especially to these times, my love for Alex was continuing to grow, and I expected that Alex was beginning to feel the same toward me.

Early in the morning the day after our meeting with The Committee, Alex received the records that she had requested. We studied the students' records and the initial selection yielded 133 students with IQ's of 170 or above and of those, 105 students appeared to have above average social interaction as determined by the community activities in which they were involved and in their participation in student- body events. Alex and I were both pleased that so many intelligent, socially active and community-minded students qualified in the first selection phase. We could now breathe a sigh of relief and realized that surely, we could narrow it down to eight from the 105 qualifying students; however, this was still a daunting task.

We contacted each of the 105 students via electronic courier with the guarantee of a fully paid doctoral program if they agreed to meet with us. Another stipulation was that they met the qualifications to participate in the private study we were offering. The Committee sent each student a round-trip ticket to Geneva, Switzerland, with arrangements to arrive in one week; also, each student received 1000 Euros.

The security team met the students at the airport as they arrived and escorted them to the office where they assembled in the first floor conference room, which now served as a dining/ conference room. All of the students had arrived by noon and after we had lunch, I introduced Alex and myself and congratulated each of them on their recent graduation. I informed the selectees that we represented a private group of wealthy individuals who were interested in preservation projects, as well as being associated with many other enterprises.

"You have been selected by your universities to participate in a special study," I announced. "In appreciation for your participation and if you qualify; all of your advanced studies will be paid for, including meals and accommodations. Each of you, if selected, will receive a small stipend of 2000 U.S. dollars per month. The program will authorize specialized vocational training to prepare you for the specific nature of a future employment opportunity the program may offer. The study involves a very important project and it may require some of you to select very specific fields for your doctoral programs. Your outstanding scholarship is the foremost reason for your selection to participate. We will be looking for those among you that show an aptitude for leadership with a strong background in the sciences and arts. You must also submit to some extensive psychological and medical examinations. If you meet all the requirements of the study, the program leaders will offer you the graduate stipend. We are very hopeful that the incentives are great enough that you will agree to all of the terms of the study."

After a rest break and afternoon refreshments, Alex assembled the young men and women in the conference room and started the selective process by giving them an interest-inventory test prepared by the psychologists that had agreed to be members of the interview team. The test helped us to determine not only what the individual selectees were most interested in, such as hobbies, art, music and philosophy, but also more importantly, it served to determine the closeness of their family ties.

The inventory test took two hours, and after a 15-minute rest break, we sequestered the students in the conference room. Every one of the students looked tired and bewildered after the rigors of the inventory test. It was time to give them enough of a break to rest, renew and refresh!

The little restaurant that we used on our first night in our apartment catered an early Swiss dinner consisting of cheese Fondue and a fresh green salad, followed by Pastetli as an entrée and Basel cookies served with a variety of teas and coffee for desert. During dinner, we overheard many discussions among the selectees about who had invited them. Many of them expressed confusion about the entire process. They also conversed about what the potential reasons were for inviting them. The most prevalent comment was that the reason had something to do with the new hiring incentive that The International Mining Corporation had been advertising. They all had heard rumors of the corporation's exploration and possible expansion to the outer planets. The selectees agreed that this must be the reason that they were invited but what did all the testing and secrecy have to do with IMC.

After dinner, I called everyone together and Alex explained the results of the tests. The tests had determined that 21 of the 105 students selected either did not have family or did not have close relationships with family members. I explained that the study we were conducting would require the separation from their families for a very long period. Of the 21 students, there were five selectees estranged from their families and the others' parents were deceased; therefore, I recommend that these 21 students continue in the study. We directed the 84 remaining students to sign a waiver of silence before they received 2000 Euros each and we supplied them with information about future employment with some of the companies under the oversight of The Committee. I thanked them for their interest, told them of the necessity of not revealing to anyone what they had witnessed during this time and the security team took the remaining students to the airport to await flights back to their individual schools. Our team was coming together. Now, for the next phase.

CHAPTER 6

Security directed the 21 remaining students to the dorm and assigned them double occupancy per room in the converted office spaces on the first floor of the office building. I gave them instructions to relax and enjoy the provided snacks and drinks for the rest of the evening and told them that we would meet them for breakfast the next day at 8 o'clock. Alex and I were able to monitor conversations in the dorm rooms and public assembly areas courtesy of the surveillance equipment placed in the rooms by security. This supplied us with insight into their feelings and views.

Two of the students, Eric Deville and his roommate, Fabian Granville, invited the other students to their room that evening. Among the students were Rachael Lebedev and Mirjam Wadekar.

"What do you think about this offer?" Eric asked the group, "What can be so important to justify all this security? It doesn't seem logical that the International Mining Corporation would have all these safety measures."

"I cannot comprehend why IMC would pay for our education," replied Fabian with his cultured French accent. "It is widely known that engineers are standing in line to work for them."

Fabian Granville was a very handsome young man with dark brown hair, cut short, and hazel, almost brown eyes. He was almost 1.8 meters tall and had a solid build. He had an appreciation of art and an outgoing personality. He had developed a sense of empathy, having survived a tragic accident, which took the lives of his younger sister and both parents. His sister lay in a coma for several days as he lovingly watched over her until her death.

Rachael Lebedev spoke up in Russian but quickly switched to very good English. "What do you presume Grant and Alex are really seeking in us? I agree with Fabian, IMC would not have difficulty finding engineers, Grant and Alex must have something more to propose."

Rachael had a great amount of self-confidence and sophistication. She had a petite, slender build with long brown hair covering her shoulders and large-almond brown eyes. Her passions were art and dance.

"Why would they be willing to pay for our doctorate?" Eric replied.

The students in Eric and Fabians' room continued discussing various scenarios but could not verbalize a logical rationale for their invitation.

"They are searching for individuals in very specific fields of study," Eric began to summarize. "Grant said that they selected us because of our outstanding scholarship. Why would IMC be interested in the arts and philosophy? Why would our family ties be of interest to IMC, unless they are planning an outpost, off the main trade routes, very isolated, and without communication being readily available?"

The discussion of these and other possibilities continued for another hour or so. Eric noticed a very attractive petite young woman sitting in a chair by the window. She had her raven hair cut in a short bouncy style that magnified the beauty of her large, almost black eyes. She was dressed simply in a white sweater, jeans, and wearing elegant pearl earrings. She had been scrutinizing the discussion but had not yet expressed her thoughts. Eric went over and introduced himself.

Eric Deville was slightly over 1.8 meters tall with a well-developed upper torso, which he obtained during his college days of playing tennis and participating on the Yale rowing team. He had thick, slightly wavy blonde hair and sky blue eyes. He had a very friendly personality and was at ease around other people.

"What is your name?" asked Eric.

"My name is Mirjam Wadekar, but my friends at school called me Jam. I really don't like that moniker very much, it reminds me of what you smear on breakfast toast," she replied.

"O.K, Mirjam will be what I call you then," replied Eric. "What do you think of Grant and Alex's proposal so far?"

"I do not know," she answered. "The fact that they chose us to continue because we do not have close family attachments makes me believe that we possibly will be asked to help establish a mining colony somewhere past Saturn."

"You perhaps may be right but I imagine it involves much more than that," Eric responded. "Seeing that you do not have close family attachments, where do you call home?"

"I was born in Delhi and attended a private prep school and then went on to the University of Oxford. My father is a retired mechanical engineer and my mother was a nurse. She died several years ago from hepatitis which she contracted by accidently puncturing herself with a needle while drawing blood from a patient. She had received the vaccine but in spite of this, she developed the disease and consequently died. My father has never recovered from my mother's death and is now living with my older brother and his family. I am considerably younger than either my brother or his wife. After my mother's death, I drifted away from the rest of the family. I customarily see them once every two or three years. I received a degree in bioengineering and plan to work on a doctorate in the field. I have told you my life's history; now, Eric, tell me about yourself and why you are interested in this invitation."

"I also attended a prep school, I was born in Philadelphia but my parents sent me to Connecticut were I was accepted to Cheshire Academy after my 13th birthday. My mother is a teacher and is very influential at the state level. She was instrumental in convincing the academy to accept me to the boarding school at such a young age. I was always larger than most of the kids my age were, so I had no trouble fitting in. My father is an industrial engineer, who holds three industrial patents, and he promised a sizeable donation to the school, which also helped seal my acceptance. I graduated from the academy at an early age and enrolled at Yale the next term. I graduated from Yale with two degrees, one in history and the other in applied science. My degree in applied science involved doing research on new energy sources. I finished the course work for a master of physics and plan to continue my research in innovative energy sources, but now I would like to see what Grant and Alex have to offer."

"What about your family?" Mirjam asked.

"My younger brother died of leukemia many years ago before a satisfactory treatment was found. Like your circumstances, my parents had problems accepting the fact that he is dead. I haven't seen my father or mother since I entered college."

"It is getting late," Mirjam said. "I too, am interested in why we were invited here. We should have our questions answered tomorrow. I am going to leave now since everyone else has already gone. It has been interesting talking with you, Eric, and I hope we stay in touch no matter what tomorrow brings."

"I hope so too, it seems we have a lot in common. May I see you at breakfast? I plan to arrive there a little before eight. Good night, Mirjam."

After she had left, Eric said. "Fabian, I had the most interesting conversation with Mirjam Wadekar. She was the attractive raven-haired girl setting over by the window. I think I am in love! In fact, I want to give notice to the rest of you gentlemen that Mirjam is 'hands off'".

"How do you know that you are in love?" Fabian replied, "How many times have you been in love? "I met that pretty Russian girl, Rachael Lebedev. Remember, she was the one that agreed with me about the IMC connection. As well as I, she also is interested in art, so after breakfast tomorrow we plan to visit The Museum of Modern Art, that is, if we have any free time and if it is permitted."

Alex and I arranged for the breakfast the next morning in the dining room, again catered by the local restaurant.

"How long do you feel we will be expected to arrange for the meals?" Alex asked, as we were having our first cup of morning coffee.

I replied. "I suppose for as long as we are here, after all, this is part of what we are getting these big bucks for."

"How much information should we divulge and how do we set up the interviews with the professional interview team?" Alex questioned.

We decided to wait until after the results of the interviews before we gave the students full discloser.

By seven-thirty in the morning, many of the students were starting to gather and by eight o'clock breakfast was ready to be served. Eric entered the dining room a little before eight, as scheduled, and looked disappointed.

"Perhaps I was too inquisitive and forward with Mirjam last night," Eric muttered aloud.

Just as he sat down, he looked up and saw her entering the room looking for him. When Mirjam saw him, she smiled and walked over and sat beside him.

I welcomed everyone and told the students that I hoped everyone had a restful night. I informed them that we had arranged for a team of psychologists, sociologists, medical doctors and other professionals to interview each one of them to see who would be best suited for the available positions indicated by the study. Alex and I posted a list of the scheduled interviews on the bulletin board by the door. I told them the interviewing process would start immediately after breakfast and that the interviews would involve both today and tomorrow. I also told them that breakfast would start at seven o'clock tomorrow due to the time constraints of the interviewing process. While they awaited their scheduled interviews, I told them to feel free to take in the sights of Geneva and that they should consult with Tom, the head of security, who would assist them with arranging their transportation. While out of the compound, you will need to use the communicators which we assigned to you earlier.

Fabian and Rachael checked the schedule and noticed that their interviews were for the next morning so they decided to keep their date to visit the art museum. They recognized from their previous night's conversation how much they had in common and how much they enjoyed each other's company. They checked with Tom and arranged for transportation.

"We have spent two hours and we have managed to explore only one of the rooms in the museum", Fabian said to Rachael. "Would you like to take a break and have a latte and discuss the paintings we have just examined?"

"That would be wonderful," Rachael replied. "It sounds very refreshing."

"Is that not Tom arriving in the van?" Rachael mentioned to Fabian, as they were leaving the coffee shop and heading back to the museum. "I think I recognize the person stepping out of the van. It looks like Jabbar Bishana."

"I thought that I noticed familiar faces," said Jabbar, as he waved and joined them as they walked back to the museum.

"What did you think about the interview?" inquired Fabian. "What sort of questions did they propose to you?"

"I was the first scheduled for an interview and it lasted for one and one half hours," Jabbar replied. "The first hour consisted of questions about what I think about different governments, did I like my parents, how many friends I have, did I date and whom and how often. They also included a series of questions dealing with my ability to cope under stressful situations. I had to sign an agreement not to divulge specific questions but I am not telling you anything specific. After the oral interview by the psychology team, I striped and put on an examination gown and went into another room where a medical team gave me a *very* thorough physical exam as well as a series of inoculations, which I am thinking may have included neurological receptors. I am definitely pleased that ordeal is all completed."

"What do you think all of this involves?" Fabian asked.

"I do not know what to think. I am of the opinion that it has nothing to do with IMC, replied Jabbar."

Jabbar was between 1.7 and 1.8 meters tall with a slender build and had the appearance of a long-distance runner. He had short black hair and very penetrating black eyes that drew you into him. He had a short black beard and mustache, which were neatly trimmed. He was immaculately dressed in tan slacks and a black squared-tail shirt. He was very friendly and polite and spoke with a slight Middle Eastern accent. He was also an accomplished musician on his Tanbur, a long-necked-three-stringed instrument dating back to 1500 BC, a gift from his great-grandfather.

CHAPTER 7

By four o'clock on the first day of interviewing, Mirjam finished her interview and met Eric in his dorm room. He had finished his interview earlier that day. They spent the next hour in Eric's room analyzing the interview questions and furthermore trying to decide exactly who the wealthy individuals were and what their agenda was. They were sitting on the floor next to the window where Eric had first noticed Mirjam. Eric put his arm around her shoulders and tenderly pulled her very closely to him, she laid her head on his shoulder and looked up at him with her large radiant ebony eyes.

"I recall the psychologists questioning me at length about whom I liked and whom I have dated," Mirjam commented. "That was difficult to answer because I have not dated a lot. I told them about you and that I would like to date you."

Eric gently stroked Mirjam's hair and pulled her face close to his. She did not resist. He kissed her check and she shared the moment by kissing him sweetly.

Fabian, Rachael and Jabbar returned from the museum around five-thirty, just in time for dinner. After they finished dinner, Fabian,

Rachael, Mirjam and Eric met back in Eric and Fabian's dorm room to exchange ideas about what the program leaders' secret agenda could possibly be.

Mirjam asked, "Fabian, you and Rachael have your interviews tomorrow, correct?"

"We signed a sworn statement promising not to divulge any questions asked during the interview," Eric said, "but, I don't see any harm if we discuss ideas in general. They asked me several questions about my family, what my interests are, how many friends I have and for how long we have been friends, how heterogeneous my mix of friends are and, more fascinating, whom I have dated."

"My interview was very similar," Mirjam added. "I can't say for sure, but, whatever the agenda is, it must be something we would never imagine. We will have to be patient and wait for the selections to be announced and then we may find out the answers to our many questions."

"Did you like the art museum?" Mirjam asked Rachael, "Eric and I plan to visit the museum tomorrow."

"Yes, both Fabian and I appreciate art very much, however, our time spent in the coffee house was the most enjoyable part of the day," Rachael responded.

As Mirjam and Rachael were leaving to go back to their dorm rooms, Eric gently put his hand on Mirjam's arm and told her that he would see her at seven for breakfast. She flashed him a very pleasant, sweet smile.

After breakfast, Eric and Mirjam planned a visit to the art museum that Fabian and Rachael had visited the day before.

"I am not overly found of modern art," Eric admitted on the way to the museum. "You will have to enlighten me so that maybe I can be taught to appreciate modern art."

"I would be very happy to be your teacher, I could teach you several things," Mirjam replied. "Eric, I do not know how many people Grant and Alex are going to need for this project which they are supervising, there are only 21 of us left. If Grant and Alex chose you for the project, I would definitely like them to select me also. These last few days have been wonderful for me and I would certainly enjoy being a significant part of your life."

Eric smiled and replied. "I feel the same way; in fact, if you are one of the ones chosen; for me, it would be both of us or neither of us."

As he and Mirjam were spending the morning viewing a few paintings and discussing their youth and hopes for the future, Eric said, "I have been interested in nature and all of its intricacies for most of my life. Before I entered Cheshire I won a high achievement award in the state science fair with a project involving fuel cells, I tried to make them smaller. While working on my masters at Yale I directed my research to involve micro fuel cells."

"I also have an interest in nature. Growing up I had a keen desire in following my mother's career in the medical field. I wanted to be a medical doctor but my father influenced me in the physical sciences. Therefore, I decided to please both of my parents and make them happy by getting a degree in bioengineering. I am not sure that my father knows what I have done or if he even cares."

"I am sorry you have so little contact with your father, but I can understand," Eric replied.

"I am not terribly interested in continuing our visit at this museum," Eric said. "How do you feel about leaving now, Mirjam?"

"We could visit the coffee shop which Fabian and Rachael mentioned that they enjoyed yesterday," Mirjam suggested. "It is hard to find a place to be by yourself, we are so cramped in the dorm. It is so nice just for the two of us to have some time alone."

Leaving the coffee shop, holding hands, and strolling for several blocks around the museum, Eric said. "It is time to call for the ride back to the dorm and check in to see if any new information is circulating among our fellow students, don't you agree?"

"Yes," replied Mirjam. "It is getting a little cool and you are probably getting hungry."

It was 6:15 when Eric and Mirjam returned from their outing at the museum. They found Fabian and Rachael talking at a table in the dining room drinking a cup of tea and waiting for dinner. They joined them for tea and learned that no new ideas were circulating so the four of them continued to discuss the study, which the program leaders were conducting, and in what way they were considering involving the selectees. The four of these curious selectees were developing a close-knit friendship and Alex and I were very impressed with their camaraderie and had spoken together that this could carry over into the project years. This sort of developing friendship was what we were hoping to see.

After dinner, Fabian and Rachael excused themselves and headed for Fabian and Eric's dorm room. Fifteen minutes later, Eric and Mirjam finished their dinner and headed to Eric and Fabians' dorm room. Upon arriving, they found Fabian and Rachael already there.

Slightly embarrassed, Mirjam said. "I do not have a roommate so my room is empty."

Eric excused Mirjam and himself. "Fabian, carry on and we will see the two of you at breakfast in the morning."

Eric and Mirjam politely left and headed back to the dining room.

"That was embarrassing." Mirjam said, "I am glad we didn't take any longer at dinner."

Eric said, "I would like to be alone with you but there is too much uncertainty to get more serious at this time."

They talked until 10:00 o'clock when Eric saw Rachael leave his and Fabians' dorm room. Eric and Mirjam held each other tenderly and kissed each other good night.

The next morning as everyone was gathering in the dining room, Rachael saw Mirjam and smiled but did not say anything about the night before. Fabian gave Eric a wink and mouthed the words "thank you for last night."

Alex and I greeted everyone at breakfast and announced that after the interviews 13 students would remain to continue the process. I told the remaining eight students that our benefactors were very thankful for their interest, the time spent in this intensive process, and that they would receive a stipend to cover the first year of their graduate work at an institution of their choice. This pleased the eight and they each thanked both Alex and me for this amazing experience. Tom and the security team shuttled them to the airport.

By mid-morning, I assembled the 13 remaining students in the dining room where coffee, tea, juice and sweet rolls were available.

"I can imagine how you are feeling and what thoughts may be going through your minds," I said, "both Alex and I had some of the same thoughts when we were first approached. What you are about to hear and see cannot be discussed with anyone outside of this group."

"I am certain each of you will be delighted with the offer our employers are going to present to you," Alex remarked. "Your interviews indicate that your personalities are ideal for the assignments our employers have. I have some non-disclosure forms for you to sign. As I have previously mentioned, it is of upmost importance that this project remain a secret; therefore, if any of the information you are about to receive leaks to the press or media or to anyone else your stipends will be revoked immediately!"

CHAPTER 8

The thirteen students were beginning to take on the appearance of a unified group. They all seemed genuinely interested in the proposition of exploring new worlds. The length of the journey was still a lingering concern but did not seem to present an insurmountable roadblock. Alex and I were very pleased with the cohesiveness of the team. They all were 'take charge' individuals; however, Eric usually spoke first and usually spoke for the entire group. It appeared to Alex and me that Eric was a natural born leader and would be a good choice for leadership, although, that decision was one that the team members would have to make. No one had officially accepted the assignment but everyone seemed very interested in learning more. We were confident that they would accept the challenge. Alex and I were very proud of all of them.

I went into details explaining to the remaining selectees that The Committee's plan was to send a colonization team of four men and four women to a planet of a nearby star. The Committee was very concerned that the depletion of Earth's resources was making it necessary to look elsewhere for an inhabitable environment for humankind. Their plan was futuristic in its infancy but now it was becoming an ever-increasingly imminent necessity. The companies, financed by The Committee, were presently developing mining efforts in some of the outer planets; however, our solar system could only continue to supplement a limited amount of our diminishing resources.

The remaining five selectees would develop and organize the recruitment efforts in support of the plan designed for future colonization. All selectees would work directly with our employers who would give the specifics at a future time. For now, the assignment was on the selection of the eight for the initial team. I explained to all of the 13 selectees that each one would have an equal opportunity to be one of the original eight.

I further explained that their responsibility was to establish a working society not necessarily structured after any social order or government now in existence. I told them that their abilities, self-reliance and human spirit were factors in their selection. The interviews indicated that they each desired a better world and that each of them demonstrated a certain degree of humility. They each also indicated a desire for personal achievement but had a compatibility ratio of between 96 and 99. This would be the bravest exploration ever undertaken by humankind. The team would be the world's present day 'Noah'.

"Each of you will go down in history," I explained. "The Committee that we represent will provide everything that you will need in preparation for your departure provided you accept the offer. You will represent the smallest nation on record, a community of eight, on a monumental journey. You have the opportunity to develop a government that will insure personal freedoms and lack of governmental interference. Your lack of dreams and energy are the only limits to accomplishing all the personal achievements that you desire. This endeavor is a team effort and keeping your humility is paramount in your successes. Your future and that of your children will go beyond what has been known to our world."

I continued to inform the selectees. "New developments in long-term suspended animation make it possible to be in a sleep mode for up to two years at a time. By the time of your departure, scientific advances should make it possible to extend the sleep time. The aging process will be altered by enzyme injections so that you will still be young men and women when you land in the new world."

Eric spoke up and asked. "What is the expected length of the journey?"

I replied. "I am told that thirty years is the expected time of travel. With a life expectancy of ninety plus years and intermittent sleep cycles, this should not be a problem. The design of the ecosystem allows it to function for much longer than thirty years. The system has been designed to last indefinitely if proper maintenance is routinely preformed and it will accommodate up to thirty people."

"How can you be confident in the ship's ecosystem design, has it ever been tested," quizzed Eric.

"The designing engineers have been working and tweaking these plans for a little over twenty years and the design has been tested by a human colony now living on Mars and the colony's existence has not been released to the press or the media at this time," I answered. "Negative public opinion and recent opposition to the deep space explorations has prompted the silence."

"I am still uncomfortable about our survival," Serena stated. "What provisions are available to minimize boredom?"

Serena Li, a petite, pretty, young woman, lived with her family in the Zhejiang Province of China until their deaths five years ago. She had a very attractive smile but was somewhat shy, especially around men of her own age. She completed a bachelor of science in organic chemistry from The National University of Singapore. Serena had been very active in the University Philharmonic Orchestra where she was first chair violinist.

"You could teach music," replied Jabbar, with admiration.

"That is a great idea," I said. "Each of you will be involved in the everyday operation of the ecosystem. You will need to learn how to be farmers, custodians, repairpersons, and be able to perform any other tasks where life skills are required. There will be extensive laboratories, which are elaborately equipped, for you to continue your work. As you can see, life on the ship will not be much different from life here on earth. However, you will be a community of only eight."

Eric asked. "Where and when are we going to learn these life skills?"

"You will have specialized tutors to train you in these skills," I told them. "This training will occur after you receive your doctorates."

I explained the general ship layout to the group utilizing a made-to-scale holographic model beginning with the living quarters and recreational facilities, located on deck A on the first ring. I pointed out the eight separate living quarters arranged in clusters of two. The construction of the living-quarters utilized lightweight polycarbonate three-meter long laminated panels. The panels, designed for easy reattachment to one another, made rearrangement possible. I demonstrated this method by rearranging various configurations by using my stylus. Each apartment would have its own lavatory, galley module and data retrieval units. The common area contained a viewing screen with computer access and a spacious lounge area. The arrangement of these areas was in an open space that also contained areas for golf and tennis as well as beach volleyball. Storage compartments were located around the perimeter of the enormous living space. The laboratories, farming area, water purification system, and air generation and purification systems, along with equipment storage, were located on decks B, C, D, and E of the second ring. A coupling structure separated the two rotating rings.

"How can we be assured of the authenticity of The Committee of which you spoke?" Eric asked. "How do we know that they are trustworthy and able to accomplish what you are telling us? After all, if we agree to their proposition we will be putting our lives at risk."

"These are legitimate questions for you to ask," I replied. "I have prepared a set of documents confirming the authenticity of the committee and sworn to by members of The World Court."

The group continued to study the ship's plans that I had received earlier. They enjoyed 'playing' with the hologram and, I suspected, that their minds were racing with ideas and excitement. By that evening, they all agreed to the terms set down by the committee and each signed the documents. I congratulated the group on their decisions and I arranged with Tom for transportation for all of us to meet at the estate where I would introduce the group to The Committee. At noon, we gathered in the dining room for lunch and after we finished eating, Alex and I excused ourselves and went to our apartment allowing the team to have some time alone to discuss their futures.

The group finished eating and sat around the table in the dining room discussing what the future could possibly involve.

Serena was the first to speak. "What have we gotten ourselves into?"

"We will be responsible for populating a new world," Rachael added. "What an awesome task that will be."

Mirjam said. "We, or at least I, have not had a lot of experience dating much less being a wife or having children."

"I do not know anything about raising a family or how to be a father," Fabian replied.

"Yeah, neither have I," Eric commented. "I have not had an example of what family life is like. How am I supposed to know how to be a family man and raise children?"

"What are we going to do?" Serena added. "Most of the people I know from college are either already married or they are planning a wedding after graduation."

Mirjam said, "We are going to have to grow up. Most things will come naturally. Let us dwell on all of the positives of this adventurous and awesome undertaking. I am getting chills just trying to imagine all the possibilities our future can hold."

CHAPTER 9

Alex and I were walking hand in hand to our apartment as we left the dining room. As we topped the stairs on the second floor, where the security team was located, we noticed that they were gathering up their equipment and getting ready to leave. We saw Tom and asked him why everyone was leaving. He told us that not all of the security team would be needed now but some of them would stay to secure the property while Alex, the 13 remaining students and I were present. Tom told me that he had arranged for a large transport vehicle to take us to the estate at 10 o'clock the next morning. He stated that he would use the vans to take us to the airport where the transport vehicle was located. Tom would continue to be our contact person until the assignment was over.

After we began to relax in our apartment, I commented to Alex. "The reality and scope of the mission seems to be evident to all of the students. They seem energized at the immensity of the undertaking realizing that you and I, along with The Committee, feel that they are capable of the task. For now, I think that possibly the foremost thing on their minds is the all-expense paid doctoral program and with that hurdle out of the way they can begin concentrating on the mission ahead of them."

I walked over and gave Alex a big hug and kiss.

"What was that all about?" she asked.

"I want to thank you for agreeing to help me with this assignment; I could never have accomplished it without your help. It took a lot of courage for you to leave Burns, West and Associates. We both were on a fast track to become one of the associates. However, we each now have a good bank account so it is not so bad, is it? It's not such a bad day's work!"

"I left because you asked me to," Alex remarked. "We could combine our accounts and start the agency that we have discussed previously."

"I have also been thinking about starting that agency, I replied. "We work well together as a team. Where do you have in mind for the location of an agency?"

"I don't know, maybe London," replied Alex.

I said. "I believe we have successfully fulfilled all points outlined in our agreement with The Committee, I hope that they agree when we meet and introduce the team tomorrow morning."

"I suppose our assignment will be over when we present the team to The Committee tomorrow," Alex remarked. "That is, if they agree with our selection."

We both sat there quietly for a moment just gazing into each other's eyes, but not saying anything.

Finally, I said. "We have grown very fond of the students. I feel that they will continue to need direction, guidance and counseling. After all, they are just kids, very smart and grown kids, but kids just the same. They will need assistance with everyday problems. I feel responsible for their safety and wellbeing. I also am of the opinion that they will occasionally require parenting and some moral guidance. At least I need them to need us; I am not ready to say good-bye."

"I agree with you, Grant, I have grown very fond of each of them; possibly we could continue to be a part of the team until they depart on the mission," Alex replied.

"I will make that suggestion when we meet with The Committee tomorrow," I said. "This is perhaps already in their plans. We are just assuming that they will tell us that we have completed the assignment."

Alex and I snuggled on the sofa with my arm around her shoulder and her head on my shoulder. We sat quietly for several more minutes before either of us said anything.

"If our assignment is all but over," I finally said. "I would like for us to think about what we plan to do then."

"I thought we had just decided to look into an agency of our own," Alex remarked.

"Uh, that is not what I mean," I replied with delight in my voice. "I mean about us, you and me. We have been a working team, a good working team; I want to be more than just that."

"What do you propose," Alex replied. "We need to set a good example for the team. We cannot just start living together. I want a commitment before I start a family. I am not sure that us sharing this apartment is setting the right example even though we have separate bedrooms."

I added. "As I said, we are a good team. I am willing to make a commitment. What kind of commitment do you have in mind? Most couples do not have formal weddings these days."

After a few moments of quiet, Alex got up from the sofa and headed for her bedroom. Turning her head toward me and smiling, she suggested that I give her a few moments to herself to reflect on our discussion.

When Alex returned, she agreed to my proposal and we decided promptly to have a simple gathering with the team. I asked the team to meet us in the dining room at 6 o'clock for a little celebration before dinner. I asked Tom to take me to the judge that had helped draw up the documents that the students had signed. I had no trouble obtaining a certificate of marriage. It helped to know people in high places!

When I arrived back at the apartment Alex was in the shower. Her bedroom door was open and a very gorgeous white dinner dress was lying across her bed. I hadn't seen the dress before; I didn't realize that she had packed evening dresses when she met me here in Switzerland. Later I learned that she had asked Mike to take her shopping. Alex finished her shower and came into her bedroom drying her hair. She had nothing on but a towel. I stood there for a moment taking in the scenery; she was a very beautiful woman.

"Your bedroom door was open, I saw the dress on your bed and came into the room to look at it," I said as I turned to leave.

"I went shopping while you were gone," she said pulling the towel around her body.

"I have invited the team to meet us in the dining room, they are to arrive at six," I remarked somewhat shyly. "I told them we are having a little celebration. Tom has arranged to have a cake after dinner tonight."

At six o'clock, I met the thirteen selectees in the dining room, which Tom and his wife, Ann, had decorated simply but beautifully with white Calla lilies tied with red and white satin ribbons and placed in tall-square-clear glass vases, which they arranged on the dining tables covered in white table clothes. All of the team had taken special care to dress as smartly as possible considering the limited amount of clothing, which they had brought with them to Geneva. A few moments later Alex entered the dining room attired in her new white dinner dress. She looked dazzling. I, on the other hand, was simply dressed in a pair of black dress slacks and an azure blue long-sleeved dress shirt (no tie) that I had packed for the first meeting with The Committee. Tom and Mike arrived a few moments later with their wives. They introduced their wives to everyone and we began the evening with relaxation and casual conversation. Mike had thought to pipe in some beautiful romantic music. After a brief time had lapsed, it was time for me to say something!

"I would like to make an announcement," I said. "Alex and I have asked all of you here to help us celebrate our marriage. As you can see, we are not having a large gathering, just all of you, Tom and Mike and their wives, Ann and Jessica. Neither of us have family except for all of you; we have adopted each one of you as our family. We will exchange our commitments to each other."

I handed Alex a single long-stemmed red rose, tied with a white silk bow, took her hand and whispered, "You are beautiful". We stood holding each other's hands.

"I love you Alex. I will take care of you; I will honor you, respect you, and be faithful to you. Alex, I make this commitment to you."

"I love you Grant. I will take care of you; I will honor you, respect you, and be faithful to you. Grant, I make this commitment to you."

We sealed our marriage commitment with a long romantic kiss. Alex and I signed the marriage document and Tom and his wife, Ann, witnessed the signatures. Tom informed us that he was a signature guarantor for the World Court on behalf of The Committee. He convinced us that all was in order and that he would electronically transfer the marriage document to the hall of records when he got back to his office.

We enjoyed the gourmet dinner, which Tom and Mike had catered for us. Their wives had chosen a special dinner consisting of beef tenderloins, baked potatoes, salad with all the trimmings and with cake and champagne to finish off the meal. For the vegetarians, their choice would be portabella mushrooms in a white wine sauce. We ate the vanilla and raspberry-filled wedding cake and drank champagne until all of the bottles were empty. After thanking Tom, Mike and their wives for the beautiful celebration and every one for joining us, Alex and I left everyone in the dining room enjoying his or her after-dinner coffees and anxiously went to our apartment.

I held Alex, pressing her very closely to me when we got to the apartment. I placed my hands in the small of her back slowly moving them down to her hips and pulling her even closer to me while kissing her deeply. Alex responded and passionately returned my kisses. She started unbuttoning my shirt and at the same time, I unzipped her dress and allowed it to fall to the floor. Alex nibbled on my ear, took my hand, and led me into her bedroom where I hugged her tightly, kissed her lips and unsnapped her bra, which floated to the floor. We slowly finished undressing each other and she lay across the bed inviting me to join her. Sometime later during in the wee hours of the morning I awoke with Alex kissing my chest and exploring my body. The warmth of her naked body next to mine made me realize just how much I loved this woman.

The next morning we both awakened refreshed, invigorated, happy, and ready to meet the day. We were confident that The Committee would agree with our selections. In addition, we were unsure of our future involvement with the team, but we certainly anticipated that we would continue to be connected. We showered, dressed and prepared for breakfast. After eating with the team, I explained to them that our plans were for them to meet our employers.

CHAPTER 10

"Rachael, that was a very charming ceremony," commented Mirjam after Grant and Alex had retreated to their apartment. "I am not surprised that they decided to commit to one another; I have been noticing the way Grant looks at Alex and when he is near her, they are always touching one another."

"Haven't they been sharing the same apartment?" Rachael questioned.

Gabriele Morgan entered the conversation. Gabriele had sparkling aqua blue eyes and straight dark-red shoulder length hair. She was 1.6 meters tall and had an attractive figure. An enormous alluring smile invited everyone to get to know her; otherwise, she was a soft-spoken young woman. Both of her parents were dedicated medical professionals and consequently, as a child, her main companion had been her nanny. She attended boarding school during her early teen years and later studied at Oxford where she majored in biology and pre-med.

"Alex told me that she and Grant had separate bed rooms separated by a common bath and that the apartment was furnished by their employers," Gabriele added. "She had set down guidelines, no sex until they had a commitment."

"Now that they are married this will change tonight," Mirjam added.

"Where does this leave us?" asked Serena. How do we know what a man is thinking or what he wants or what makes him happy? I feel very much unprepared in the process of attracting a man or of starting and having a relationship. I have had very little close contact with men my age but I have read and heard that sex and food are the way to make a man happy; however, I would not know this from experience. I suppose I am going to have to improve my cooking skills."

Mirjam said. "I think it takes quite a lot more than that to please a man. We can have a girl talk with Alex in a few weeks and get some pointers from an 'experienced' wife. She has always seemed very open with us and I feel as though some girl talk will come naturally with her, after all, they said we were their family now."

"We do not need to please men other than the seven sitting over there," Gabriele interjected. "Our destiny and our happiness depend on our romancing the special one for each one of us, that is, assuming that we can allure those men and have agreements that once someone has 'chosen' their special man, that the remainder understand he is 'hands off'. I have read novels that make courtship sound fascinating. A fulfilled and lasting relationship should be our goal and each one of those men seems to have wonderful and desirable qualities. Our dilemma is to consider carefully the special one we want to have our entire lives revolve around and with which to have our families."

"Only six are available, Eric is already spoken for," Mirjam said as a reminder to the other women. "We need to go over and talk to the male members of the team. I think that they are possibly as uncertain about their futures as we are ours."

"You are no doubt right; there are only thirteen of us," Serena agreed. "We do not have many choices; it is much like our parents selecting our husbands for us. It is like the old-fashioned arranged marriages our grandparents and great-grandparents tolerated when they were young. If I fall in love with one of the men in the group and The Committee chooses to send only one of us that would be most disappointing."

"Eric and I have agreed that both of us will go or neither of us will go," Mirjam said. "You are correct, The Committee will pick only four couples and I think it reasonable that couples that are serious about each other will be the ones chosen, at least that is what I hope for. We have had several discussions involving what we would like our lives to be like and even have talked about a lasting relationship and having children."

"Eric is a handsome man," said Rachael. "The two of you are lucky. Fabian and I have a lot in common, he is fun to be with but I have not considered any long-term commitment. I am not sure he is the one and I do not know how to determine this. We have not talked about such things; I do not know how he feels, I suppose, as time goes along, we will have opportunities to work our 'womanly wiles' such as the heroines I have read about in novels and see in older movies."

Gabriele spoke up. "I think all of the gentlemen in the group are very nice looking, well built, polite, smart and resourceful. I could learn to like any one of them but when are we going to have the time to develop a real relationship? School will consume one to two years of our lives and we probably will not be at the same schools, maybe not even in the same country. Time and money will prohibit a lot of travel."

"You can always video-text on your personal communicator but any romantic relationship will have to wait until after graduation," Mirjam commented. "Getting involved with someone outside the group will be unproductive if we are serious about the commitment Grant and Alex presented to us. I hope that Eric and I will be assigned schools close to one another."

Rachael said. "Mirjam, I agree with you, becoming a loving couple will be to our advantage. Remember, Grant said that we would have life skill training after graduation, whatever life skill training entails, we should all be back together by then."

The women moved over to where the men were sitting and overheard Makoto saying, "I do not know what to say when around a women my own age or how to carry on a conversation with her. My tongue does not cooperate with my brain."

Makoto had wide shoulders with a lot of upper body strength because of his gymnastic training during his youth. His black hair was styled in a military buzz cut. He was quiet by nature but could join into the conversation when he felt that he had something significant to say.

"You men seem to be having the same kind of concerns and conversations that we have been having," Mirjam commented as she and the other women approached. "We must share some of the same anxieties and concerns that you do."

As the men noticed that the young women had moved into their midst most of them stopped talking, feeling uncomfortable and a little embarrassed having an honest and serious conversation with the women around, especially since they were all near their same age. Eric suggested that they ask the women what they felt was most important in a long-term commitment.

"List the most important things that you want or need from a relationship with a man," Eric suggested to the women. "I suggest that you men to do the same, list the most important things you want in a relationship."

Mirjam said. "I believe a relationship needs to have a serious foundation based on affection and being able to depend on each other is a very close second."

"I agree with you Mirjam," Rachael said. "I feel that a male companion should be willing to protect and offer a since of security."

Fabian said. "My list has sexual fulfillment near the top."

"I agree." Makoto said shyly. "I also feel that companionship is very important."

"Is sex all that you men think about!" voiced Gabriele. "Sex is important but I think that the approval of a mate is also important."

"No," Fabian replied. "Respect and admiration are very important to me also."

"I too think that a relationship should offer security and affection," commented Serena. "I appreciate a sentimental thought or gesture; I think this is motivated by my love of music. Also, group and personal acceptance is very important to me."

"I am a very visual person, I gain inspiration from beauty," announced Jabbar. "I would like my mate to be attractive, as well as smart and talented. All of you women are very attractive, but I have already especially noticed one of you!"

Mirjam interjected. "I think that a man for me would show kindness, warmth and tenderness, all wrapped up in a lasting emotional attachment."

"I think all of the things Mirjam has just said are very important," Eric added. "But, girls, don't forget, men also desire embracing, kissing, caressing, etc. It seems to me that we will have good working relationships and personal relationships from the conversations we have just had. We need to realize that some differences of attitudes and situations may come up and we will have to be able to be open-minded and be acceptant of each one of our varied personalities. We will need to be cognizant of each of our strengths as well as our specialties and not allow jealousies to alienate us."

During the dinner hour, their conversations continued and the more everyone talked, the more their individual differences and likenesses became evident. Before the evening ended, the team started to group themselves in pairs and as their discussions continued, everyone began to relax and they felt comfortable talking to one another. They began some teasing and joking around about the possibilities that lay ahead for them. They all agreed that communication and openness were essential and that there were no reasons that anyone should feel uncomfortable discussing any topic with each other. The conversations continued for a while until someone noticed that it was getting late and that tomorrow was going to be a full and complex day. Everyone was excited and motivated about the events of the day and looked forward to the meeting with The Committee tomorrow.

CHAPTER 11

Summer of 2057

At breakfast, everyone was in a very jovial mood, especially us newlyweds. I thought Alex was especially gorgeous and knew I was a very fortunate man. The team seemed more content and relaxed, they were in groups of one or two couples and very involved in conversation as Alex and I entered the dining room. After the team applauded us, we had a leisurely breakfast of toast, scrambled eggs, jam, juice and coffee or tea.

"Enjoy the eggs; there will be no opportunity for real eggs on the journey," I said. "After we finish breakfast everyone should gather back here by nine thirty. We may be spending the night at the château so bring a change of clothing, etc. Tom and Mike will meet us out front, where we are going to be shuttled to the airport for a short ride to the estate where you will meet our employers. They are a very select and secretive group and our meeting will be by way of a telecom. Alex and I know very little about them other than that they are extremely wealthy and insist on remaining incognito. They have always responded to our requests in a very timely manner. I am assuming that they will want to talk to you as a group. Alex and I have every confidence that they will accept our choices of all of you. You may address them as The Committee."

The team seemed excited now that they were finally going to meet the masterminds behind this monumental undertaking. Eric and Mirjam appeared to be very serious about each other. They sat to themselves with their heads together before breakfast, and during breakfast Fabian and Rachael joined them. After eating, Eric and Mirjam left the dining room holding hands. Fabian tried to show Rachael the same kind of attention but I am not sure about that relationship since she did not seem to have the same responsiveness to him as Mirjam did to Eric. The others seemed content just getting to know each other better.

Tom and Mike drove the vans up to the front of the building, parking along the curb and Eric, Mirjam, Fabian and Rachael traveled in the van with Tom, and the rest of us rode with Mike. Eric and Fabian both demonstrated very courteous manners as they helped Mirjam and Rachael board the large transport helicopter. The excitement heightened for the team as the estate came into view.

The team was in awe with the château's appearance as the impressive three-story mansion with its giant square spires anchoring each corner came into view. The structure as a whole appeared to be as large as a soccer field. Between the spires, there were lavishly decorated windows on the second and third levels. Huge mahogany doors flanked by large cathedral windows made of several hundred small glass panes dominated the ground level. High rugged peaks protruded through a heavily forested area, which served as a fitting backdrop for such an exceptional edifice.

We circled the estate two times before losing enough altitude to land on the pad located a few hundred meters from the front entry. Other security personnel met Tom and Mike as we exited the helicopter. The security personnel escorted us through the front doors and into the large entrance hall that led to the conference room where I had met with The Committee during my first visit to the estate, Déjà vu! Alex and I had been using a different entrance during our many trips to the château over the past several months. While waiting for The Committee to appear on the monitor, we sat in the leather club chairs and the same young woman that had previously provided me with a meal, now served us with coffee, teas and teacakes.

The Committee appeared on the monitor and the spokesperson graciously greeted Alex, the team and me.

"We are pleased with the selection you and Alex have structured," the spokesperson said. Addressing the group, he said. "Your advanced knowledge and personal traits make you the most ideally suited individuals for the success of our mission."

The Committee chair explained that in 2054, scientific breakthroughs in cryogenics and long-term hibernation (cryohibernatics) made it possible for extended space flights and for the past two years, extensive research and continual experimentation indicated that these processes would be very reliable and have had great laboratory success in our Mars' experimental station. The processes consisted of four steps: first, thoroughly cleaning the body of keratinocytes and hair and then submerging the body in an enzyme/aqueous solution in order to keep it hydrated. Secondly, through intravenous injection, controlled by the supercomputer, the body would go into a state of dreamless suspension and would remain in this state for the duration of the hibernation. Thirdly, at a previously determined time, the supercomputer would slowly place the body into a dream-sleep and then finally the body would regain consciousness. The supercomputer would control the ship during hibernation and environmental sensors would alert the supercomputer if human intervention became necessary. If this occurred, the supercomputer would prematurely awaken you. The cryohibernatics process has been tested and proven reliable for a two-year period of sleep. Current research has made, and continues to make, progress to extend the sleep time and the developers have assured us that this would happen before your scheduled embarkation. You would still need to agree on a sleep schedule that would meet the needs of the group.

The deck A ecosystem would consist mainly of a tropical climate with areas consistent with the growing conditions of various fruit trees such as apples, oranges and stone fruit, as well as a large variety of nut trees. The scientists have genetically miniaturized all of the trees. The design of the ecosystem would accommodate 30 people comfortably. There would be ponds, beaches, running streams and wetlands. Your destination would be an Earth-like planet. Spectrometry studies of the planet's atmosphere assured us that it consisted of nitrogen-oxygen-carbon dioxide percentages much like Earth's atmosphere.

"Again, allow me to welcome you on behalf of The Committee, the chairperson continued. "It has been a pleasure talking with such a distinguished group. Your idealism and your self-reliance is what will make your venture successful. The Committee has full confidence that you will accomplish this task. If any of you have further questions speak with Grant or Alex. Tomorrow there will be a breakfast at nine o'clock followed by interviews with some of the designers. Follow Tom and Mike to the dining hall for some lunch, when you have finished lunch, they will show you to your accommodations. After you settle into your rooms, please take advantage of taking a stroll on the grounds around the estate and relaxing for the remainder of the afternoon. We will be serving dinner at six o'clock. Frank and Geraldine are the head chefs at the estate and Sonya, their daughter, is visiting with them for a few weeks and will be assisting them for this evening's meal."

Mirjam, Rachael, Eric and Fabian had rooms next to each other. After settling into their gorgeous five-star rooms, the four met with the others in the hall.

"My room is fabulous; it has a very large bed, big enough for all of us," Mirjam said. "It surely is superior to the dorm-sized beds we have been sleeping on. I could become very fond of this."

"My room has two toilets," announced Eric.

"Honestly, do you not know what a bidet is!" chuckled Fabian.

They all agreed that the rooms were spacious and very modern. Every one paired up for an afternoon walk in the palatial gardens surrounding the main structure of the estate. Well, almost everyone, Daniel, Michelle and Robert stayed in Daniel's room visiting.

"The gardens seem to go on forever," Mirjam commented after she and Eric had walked several meters. "I could get accustomed to living in a palace like this."

After walking a short distance further, they came upon a small pond and sat on a garden bench near the water's edge.

Taking Mirjam's beautiful face in both of his hands and drawing her very closely to his face, Eric said. "I, too, could become accustomed to this type of living. I will build us a beautiful house when we get to our new home. All of my dreams involve having you as my life partner and raising a family together. My hope is that you are dreaming this same dream."

"Eric, of course, my dreams are for us being together," Mirjam said to him, as she was becoming more and more infatuated with the prospects of their future and their new life and home together.

Fabian and Rachael came up the path just as Eric was about to kiss Mirjam.

"I overheard what you were saying about building a beautiful house," Fabian said quizzically. "How do you plan to accomplish that task?"

"We are not leaving our knowledge of technology back here on Earth," Eric replied. "We are intelligent, we will figure things out. It is just a matter of applying what we know and adapting that knowledge to the new world."

"You are right, Eric!" Fabian returned. "But it will be a long while before we will be able to cut stone for a house like this."

Eric added. "We will be approaching middle age when we arrive. With a life expectance of ninety or more years, we will have several decades to adjust to our new home, raise our families and watch them grow."

"There are a lot of things to do and a lot of uncertainty in our lives," Mirjam interjected. "At first it is going to be strange living our lives with such a small group of people. It will take a great deal of compromise and adjustment."

"I know how you must be feeling," Eric said reassuringly. "We will all need to trust one other and rely on each other's strengths. Mirjam, you can count on me to comfort and protect you."

"Fabian and I heard that, Eric," Rachael said. "Are you proposing to Mirjam?"

"That is defiantly in my plans," replied Eric. "But our immediate future is so uncertain. We may not go to the same school, but we have agreed that we will continue in this project only as a couple."

After dinner, as Sonya cleared away the desert plates, I went over the schedule for tomorrow's arranged meeting with the supercomputer and environmental designers. I also announced that The Committee arranged with Stanford and California Institute of Technology to oversee the future educational plans. Those students whose disciplines dealt primarily with life sciences, including medicine, were: Mirjam, Internal medicine and animal biology; Jabbar, organic chemistry, pharmacy and biochemistry; Gabriele, pediatrics and neurology; Rachael, pharmacy and plant/micro biology; Richard, internal medicine; Susann, plant biology; therefore, they would attend Stanford and the neighboring University of California, San Francisco medical facilities. Those students whose disciplines dealt with the physical sciences and engineering were: Serena, electrical and computer engineering; Makoto, chemistry and industrial engineering; Eric, mechanical engineering and applied physics; Fabian, geophysics and environmental engineering; Robert, particle and solid-state physics; Daniel, mechanical and industrial engineering; Michele, chemical and electrical engineering; therefore, these students would attend California School of Technology.

The next morning, after breakfast, we met with the computer designers. Serena was especially interested in the new developments in computer designs. The HQ-3000 no longer used 1's and 0's in the traditional way but rather it used qubits (quantum bits), a process that controlled the rotation of atoms. The qubit and the qubyte could process the 0's and 1's simultaneously by super positioning. The quantum computer used nanotechnology, parallel processing and magneto-resistive random access. The HQ could interact with humans and was fully capable of controlling the guidance and environmental systems aboard the ship. This was all well above my realm of knowledge but Serena and a few of the others seemed comfortable with the design team's explanation and asked several intellectual and probing questions.

"I realize that my question has nothing to do with computer design but what is the type of propulsion system that will be used?" Eric asked.

One of the computer designers said. "I am also interested in propulsion systems so I asked one of the space engineers and he told me that a recently developed revision of the plasma engine is used. You will need to ask one of the engineers for more information."

The others were more interested in discussing the environmental systems with the biosphere designers. The systems were very straightforward. The water recovery system used a combination of filtration, distillation and radiation. The wastewater treatment consisted of a tertiary system; the pure water would transfer to the water recovery system and the solid material, radiated and compacted would serve as plant nutrients. The hydroponics farm, the "river-pond" system and human-use reservoir all had the circulated water in common. Obviously, all would be closed systems; the major concerns were irreversible contamination. A delicate balance between animal and plant life achieved the oxygen-carbon dioxide balance. A mechanical backup was in place if either of these systems needed support and all systems were computer controlled. The 'farm', vineyards and fruit trees, located on levels A and B, had computer-controlled climates designed for maximum growth and production. A unique system, similar to drip irrigation, supplied the water and nutrients directly to the root zone of the trees and other plants allowing growth without deep soil.

The women asked about their wardrobes. They wanted to know how many changes each of them would have and how many styles they would have.

I jokingly said. "Only one so don't get dirty."

I explained that the brown unisex uniforms were made primarily of lightweight cellulose fibers with five-year wear-ability and they would conform and support each individual's body. The uniforms had a memory designed into them allowing the uniforms to restructure as the body changed and the bodies' heat activated this restructuring. Each of you would be individually fitted with eight uniforms consisting of short pants and a 'designer' tee shirt. Maternity attire consisted of a large circular piece of material with a neck opening in the center and short sleeves positioned out from the neck area. The garment draped over the body to form a loose fitting robe. Reusable baby pads, to serve as covering for the newborn, were made of a moister absorbing 'wick-away' material and attached by using Velcro strips. Each couple would receive uniforms for three children in varying sizes for babies, toddlers, youngsters, preteens, teens and adults. Each of the women gave me a discontented facial expression but did not say anything.

"Alex and I know you will have many other questions, make your lists and they will be addressed all in good time. We will be leaving the estate in the morning. You will have time to return to your previous schools, and pack your possessions for relocation to your respective universities. Tom will make your travel arrangements. If you need to return to your homes, he will make those arrangements also. In addition, let me again remind you to not discuss what you have heard, seen or learned with anyone, especially the press and media."

As we were preparing to leave the estate, our team had the opportunity to visit with Sonya, the head chefs' daughter, and her Mother and Father. Some of the men and women on the team were especially interested in getting some ideas about preparing some of the delicious deserts, which they had prepared. Sonya said good-bye to her Mother and Father and she thanked the hosts for a wonderful two-week visit before returning to her home in Frankfort, Germany, where she would secretly report her observations and overheard conversations to the Frankfort office of the E. A.

CHAPTER 12

We returned to the office building energized and full of hope for the future. The team seemed eager and ready to start the next leg of their journey. The Stanford team was packing and getting ready to leave Geneva at 9:30 tomorrow morning. They would be returning to their respective universities to gather their belongings and then go on to San Francisco. They would then connect with arranged transportation for their transit to a newly renovated sorority house where they would be living during their stay at Stanford. A fast transit terminal was located a few blocks from the house for those commuting to the Medical Center in San Francisco. Although the members of the team were excited and anxious about the adventure, which lay ahead for them, they were fully aware of the secrecy of the mission that each of them would be undertaking.

The California Institute of Technology team were making similar arrangements but were not scheduled to depart until 3:45 tomorrow afternoon. All the team were having feelings of anxiety and were emotional about leaving each other as close-knit bonds had been formed during the last few days. This was evident to Alex and me and these relationships were very rewarding to us as well.

The demanding rigors of their complex studies would occupy their minds and keep them very active.

Alex and I planned, with the blessings of The Committee, to acquire a townhouse in Fresno, California, which was approximately midway between both teams and was a convenient meeting place when the two teams would need to meet collectively. We had convinced The Committee that it would be desirable to be available for the teams for any guidance and advice that they, in all probability, would need. Alex and I had been planning for the possibility of several get-togethers in order to renew their newly formed friendships and the couple's relationships. We were feeling like doting parents, wanting to keep a watch on 'our kids'. With the availability of the high-speed rail system, Fresno seemed to be the most suitable place for us to locate.

We felt that we needed more insight into the interpersonal relationships of the thirteen team members before we could make a final recommendation on the eight. Eric and Mirjam had already convinced us, by their strong leadership roles with the other team members, that they should be a part of the final team. We discreetly told them our plan and asked them to help us by leaving a communicator open in the common areas in both houses, allowing us to gain further insight into the team dynamics. We also asked them to personally communicate with us on a regular basis as time permitted.

Eric looked into Mirjam's room to see what was taking her so long and said. "You have to leave in thirty minutes and we need to have time to say goodbye."

"I have had a most wonderful time the last several days," Mirjam said. "It seems like a lifetime ago since graduation, so much has happened. Everything has been so unbelievable, especially meeting you. I still cannot believe everything which has taken place."

"I came to the Geneva meeting out of curiosity," Eric replied. "I had my future mapped out but seeing you that first night when we all met in my room changed everything. I am very excited about the possibility of spending the rest of our lives together without the worries of where to live; what job to take; or with whom to make friends so the next research project can be financed."

"We need to promise to keep in close contact; I will call you when we are settled at the house," Mirjam reassured Eric. "I will also leave my communicator on vibrate during the flight to San Francisco in case you want to contact me."

Fall of 2057

Mirjam and Rachael were the first to arrive at Casa Toscana, the beautifully renovated sorority house near the Stanford campus. They chose a bedroom suite on the second floor with a view of the open living space below, visible from the hallway in front of their room. The entire house had been tastefully decorated with large, comfortable Italian furniture, wall paintings of the Tuscany countryside, and the small but efficient kitchen was equipped with typical college suite appliances and cooking ware. All the dishes and utensils were in the classic Tuscan country design. All the bedroom suites were equipped with computer access to a data and communication network. As soon as Mirjam settled into her side of the bedroom, she called Eric.

"Where are you?" she asked.

"Fabian and I are stranded here in New York," Eric replied. "We missed the supersonic flight from Frankfort to Los Angeles due to a massive thunderstorm in Geneva just moments before we were to depart. We were able to catch a later flight to Frankfort, then to London and then to New York and we have reservations for a flight to Los Angeles and are scheduled to arrive by 5:30. If it is not too late, I'll call as soon as we get settled."

Everyone had arrived by the next morning and by evening had met with their advisors. Alex and I had leased the townhouse in Fresno near the river. It was very conveniently located near mall shopping. We had fun shopping for our new furniture, appliances and supplies and everything needed to equip our new living quarters. It was ultra-modern and very comfortable and our view of the river and surrounding bluffs were stunning and picturesque and to the

East were fabulous views of the Sierra Nevada Mountain range. We had easy access to the high-speed rail station by using the efficient public transportation system and were able to keep in close contact with both teams physically by rail in case of an emergency and by videoconferencing each week. We were all eager for the next phase of this incredible journey.

The first half of the fall of 2057 went smoothly and fast. Alex and I had many good times together, taking hikes in the Sierras and eating some of the most delicious fresh fruit which grew on the farms surrounding the Fresno metro-area. We were trying to start our family but so far without success, although trying had certainly been tremendous fun. We communicated regularly with the teams by leaving messages. Everyone was much too busy and their schedules were much too hectic for lengthy conversations although we had regularly received communications from each team member and we then passed on progress reports of each student to The Committee.

Spring 2058

We were planning a group meeting with both teams scheduled for late June in anticipation that most of them would be able to schedule the time. I arranged for a self-navigated shuttle to transport us from Fresno to the mountains and made reservations for accommodations at the prestigious, renovated Ahwahnee Hotel in Yosemite. I felt that everyone needed a break and a hike up Yosemite Falls with a good night's rest at the hotel would be just the thing. Spending some time in the mountains always had a way of removing the tensions and stress of school and it would revitalize their bodies and minds. Eric, Mirjam, Rachael, Fabian, Gabriele and Makoto were able to spend three nights in the mountains with us.

The weekend proved to be beneficial to all. Everyone seemed to be more relaxed once we were at the large, comfortable rustic hotel. The mountain air had worked wonders. The next day we hiked up the Yosemite Falls trail and our plans were to hike to the top of Half Dome the following day. We met for a hearty breakfast before our assault on Half Dome. As everyone was finishing breakfast, Alex whispered to me that she was not feeling well.

"The six of you go on without us," I said as we left the dining room. "Alex is not feeling well and I will be staying with her."

It did not take long for the others to head for the continuous hop-on-hop-off shuttle that would take them to the back of the valley and to the trail up Half Dome.

"What seems to be the matter?" I asked Alex as we headed back to our room.

"I'm just a little queasy," Alex replied. "I am going to lie down for a while."

Alex returned moments later very excited and almost child-like with a smile as bright as the sun.

"Grant, we are pregnant!" she exclaimed.

I couldn't believe my ears! This had been our dream for months and finally we were going to be able to start our family. I hugged her closely, held her at arm's length, just to stare at her, and then enfolded her carefully in my arms again, taking extra care not to squeeze her too tightly.

"There are so many plans and preparations to make," I exclaimed excitedly. "When should you see a doctor? I want to make sure you are healthy, strong and have complete care. We will also need to select the very best pediatrician in Fresno. Have you discussed this with your obstetrician-gynecologist? Alex, you are more beautiful at this moment than I have ever seen you; I can't stop smiling, when should we inform The Committee and let the students in on this wonderful news?"

We spent the remainder of the day, relaxing and talking about our amazing future with each other and our baby and about the group of young people in our charge. Alex and I had no doubts about the relationships of Eric and Mirjam or Gabriele and Makoto. On the other hand, Rachael seemed somewhat nonresponsive to Fabian and preoccupied in her thoughts.

"Alex, if there is something bothering Rachael, do you think you should have a conversation with her and inquire if there is anything that needs our assistance?" I asked. "I will talk to Fabian and see if anything in particular is concerning either of them."

Alex agreed that speaking to them separately about any problems would be a good thing to do.

We were out by the shuttle stop as the others arrived from their hike.

"How was the hike?" I asked.

"It was a great hike, and what an amazing view from the top of Half Dome," Fabian replied. "I even liked the last part, climbing up bare rock. I have seen pictures of places in America and we all agreed that we are definitely not disappointed in Yosemite."

"Alex and I have some good news to announce," I reported, without preamble. "We are pregnant!"

"That is great news!" Mirjam said excitedly. "Let me see, this is June so that makes you due in March or early April."

There was a noticeable change in Fabian and Rachael's relationship after the hike and our announcement; she was more responsive to Fabian's attempt to gain her attention. Therefore, Alex and I decided that perhaps our planned talks with them were somewhat premature.

Everyone thanked us individually as each prepared to leave in the self-navigated shuttle for the ride to connect with the high-speed rail which would take them back to their respective universities.

"What a great weekend," Alex said after we said good-bye to the students and prepared to return to our townhouse.

"I am delighted we are finally pregnant," I replied as we snuggled closely, holding hands, and looking out the window on our short travel home.

CHAPTER 13

As the students were travelling back to their campuses, Alex and I monitored their conversations through the use of Eric and Mirjam's open communicators to see how compatible these students were. Their conversations left us somewhat concerned.

"Do you gents feel as re-energized after this week-end as I do?" Fabian asked as he and his two companions sat in the lounge waiting for the rail back to Los Angeles. "For me, it started off a little slowly, Rachael was not very receptive to my affection, but after our climb up Half Dome she seemed to warm up to me, at least, I hope I was reading her correctly, she is definitely the girl for me, and I do not want to do anything to ruin my chances with her. She is so very beautiful and I am beginning to fall for her in a very big way."

"I noticed that Rachael seemed distant to you at first, Fabian, but Mirjam and I spoke about the loving way she was looking at you and responding to you by the end of our visit. You are very right about this being the break we needed for something other than studying all night long," Eric replied. "I needed this break; I have a communication network lab tomorrow morning at 10 AM and I expect the lab to extend well into the night."

"I have a seven o'clock seminar in organic chemistry," Makoto spoke up. "I am going to try to get some sleep while I can, wake me when we get there, please."

After Makoto was sound asleep in the reclining seat across the aisle, Fabian and Eric continued to discuss the wonderful weekend that they had all shared.

"Do you or Mirjam know what could possibly be bothering Rachael?" Fabian asked. "She has stopped accepting my video texts. We were communicating once or twice a week like you and Mirjam do but lately I see her maybe every other week. As I have mentioned, she would not have much to do with me for the first two days of the weekend. It was not until I helped her climb up the last part of Half Dome, after she slipped backward on loose, slippery rocks and I caught her in my arms, that she started paying attention to me. I am falling in love with her and want to spend our lives together, but I am at a loss right now as to how to handle this situation. You would think I, a Frenchman, could put this into words to her, but I find myself tongue tied when I try."

"Since we noticed that she seemed a little distant toward you over the weekend, I will ask Mirjam if she knows anything," Eric said. "Since they are roommates, they probably have discussed lots of things. You should also let Alex know how you feel about Rachael's change in attitude toward you. She may be able to advise you on love relationships."

"Yes, I am sure they have their girl talks," Fabian responded. "I am a bit concerned, and I would appreciate any help you or Mirjam can give."

Eric contacted me and further explained the conversation that he and Fabian had on their ride back to Cal Tech. He expressed his concerns about Fabian's trepidations and hoped that I could offer some advice as a more seasoned man, and in addition, asked how he could help Fabian. He also informed me that he had suggested Alex as someone who could possibly give some romantic counsel.

"Rachael, you seemed to have something on your mind all weekend," Mirjam said, as they rode the rail back to Stanford. "Does it have anything to do with Richard? I have recently become aware that the two of you have been working long hours together for the past two months during your pharmacy research project; and I have wondered what his sudden interest in pharmacy could be. You and Richard have not been commuting home from the Medical Center with Gabriele and me since the two of you started doing some research together."

"Mirjam, I have been worrying about my relationships," Rachael replied. "I respect and am fond of Fabian but I do not know if I want to be with him forever. Richard is very pleasant and we do have a lot in common. I seem to be having mixed emotions since I have had limited experiences with men."

"I cannot help you make that decision," Mirjam replied. "You will have to let your heart direct you. Take your time and weigh each man's best traits, you will make the best decision; you are a very intelligent woman and I have faith that you will make the correct choice, and so should you. Why don't you ask Alex for some advice?"

Upon monitoring this conversation between Rachael and Mirjam Alex and I decided that we would not interfere with the relationship between Rachael and Fabian unless asked. It appeared that Mirjam was being a good friend and was giving her sound advice.

During the summer, the demanding research projects left very little time for any personal life for the students. Alex and I made several visits to each group of students between visits to the obstetrician. Each time we made a trip we were laden with a plethora of the wonderful abundance of fruit grown in the fields and in the orchards in the countryside around Fresno.

We arranged to meet both groups of students in Monterey for the weekend before the resumption of their research projects that fall. On this particular trip, our gifts consisted of peaches, nectarines, grapes of several varieties, along with cantaloupes, and several kinds of melons. The students were always very overjoyed to have these luscious fruits since freshness and flavor were often missing in typical cafeteria food. We had a wonderful two days with them at the Monterey Plaza Hotel, located on the historic Cannery Row, and introduced them to the sights along the Carmel coast, visited the Monterey Aquarium and had a couple of scrumptious seafood dinners on Cannery Row. Alex looked radiant, with a motherly glow; and, I knew that she would be a great mom.

Mirjam and Gabriele, with the assistance of the other women, gave Alex an old-fashioned baby shower while we were in Monterey. We were all invited, men included. Alex was very happy and elated by their thoughtfulness; the small baby gifts included everything petite that one could imagine including one-piece sleepers, tops, diapers, blankets, towels, booties and gadgets. The gadgets were a big hit with everyone, especially the men, which they examined with inexperienced interest. The women had ordered a beautifully decorated cake in varying shades of yellow and teal, which they served on 'Winnie the Pooh' plates, along with fruit punch, a very typical "American" baby shower. As a new expectant mom, Alex could hardly wait until we got back to our home to reexamine the gifts and put everything away.

Alex unfolded and smelled and fondled each gift before putting each item in its proper drawer in the chest. Our baby's nursery had a 'Winnie the Pooh' theme. That explained the question I had gotten from Mirjam about how we were decorating the baby's room!

"We have grown especially fond of our selectees," Alex committed with teary eyes. "The shower was such a wonderful surprise for us, who would have thought that they had had the time for preparing such a grand event. With us and them not having family to carry on these types of traditions, I feel confident that events such as this will carry over into their new lives in a distant place."

CHAPTER 14

Fall of 2058

Richard and Rachael were completing some finishing touches on some research as he gathered up his laptop and headed for the door of the pharmacy research lab.

"Rachael, I am going to catch the next commuter, I will see you at the house," Richard said. "If you are going to be much longer, please give Mirjam a call."

"I am not going to be much longer, but I will call, I want to check some results in the hospital first, then I will catch the 7:34," Rachael replied.

"Do not be too late, Mirjam has done a lot of work," Richard announced as he closed the door to the laboratory.

I will not be long, I thought, just a few more cross checks and then I will be ready. The first thing Monday morning, I will officially log in everything.

I gathered up my backpack and headed for the 7:34, giving Mirjam a call as I left the hospital. *Everyone would be waiting for me.*

It was not often that everyone was off at the same time, just for special occasions, such as my birthday. It was 8:15 as I left the commuter at the Stanford station for the thirty-minute walk to the house. This evening I was somewhat later than usual but there had been several late evenings and some all-night rounds at the hospital. As usual, there were several joggers and some dog walkers along the walk from the station. I thought nothing of the jogger behind me, I slowed down to let him pass but he also slowed, I thought he needed to rest or to tie his shoes. The next thing I realized, a muscular left arm was around my waist, pinning my arms, and before I could scream, he had injected something into my neck. I immediately began to feel light-headed and then everything went black.

When I awoke, I found my arms stretched above my head and my wrists tied with leather straps to a circular metal ring about two meters in diameter. Likewise, I realized that my ankles were tied to the metal ring with leather straps like those that were on my wrists. My legs were in a spread-eagled position and stretched as far as they could stretch. I was completely naked, cold and very uncomfortable, feeling extremely exposed and vulnerable. *I could not fathom myself being in this ungodly dilemma, what could I have done to incite someone to do this to me, how could this be happening to me, nothing good could come from this, how could I escape.* The lack of circulation in my legs and arms was causing my hands and feet to feel numb. I was lying on my back on a filthy, smelly bed in what I estimated to be a three by four-meter room. I felt the dampness of the ugly germ-laden mattress penetrating my entire body. I began to shiver uncontrollably. The room appeared to be a basement of some kind with no windows and only one door. The room smelled musty and moldy and had a single dim light above the door. The ceiling and walls had soundproof material on them. I screamed but all I could hear was a faint echo. I turned my head as far as possible to the right and left and worked at my restraints but could not free my hands or ankles. Everything I was trying to free myself came to no avail and I felt myself getting more and more panicked.

"Don't try fighting your restraints, you might hurt yourself," I heard someone say in a loud and gravelly voice, but no one else was in the room.

"What do you want with me?" I cried. "I am in medical school and am a part of a **very important** international mission. I am associated with some very prominent and influential people. Let me go and I will not tell anyone about what you have done to me. There are people waiting for me to get home."

I noticed a video camera and sound equipment at the foot of the bed.

"What time is it?" I asked. "How long have I been here? How long have you been watching me?"

The door opened and a middle-aged man stalked in. He appeared about two meters tall with a burly physique. He wore a plastic mask over his head that not only distorted his appearance but also distorted his voice. He came over to the bed and stared at me for several minutes. He grabbed me, touching and rubbing my entire body with his hot and sweaty hands. His hands reminded me of a slimy slug, only rougher. He smelled so badly that I began to feel nauseated.

"Please.....do not do that," I pleaded. "Just let me go and I will never tell anyone about what has happened."

"Shut up, Missy," he growled. "Just lie still and keep quiet."

"Do not do that." I screamed and began sobbing, but he continued to move his hands down my side to my groin rubbing me violently and, twisting a section of my pubic hair and lingering there for a long time. "Please stop, let me go."

He remained silent, removed his filthy tee shirt and pants along with his disgusting unwashed and stained underwear, and continued roughly stroking my body with his coarse and calloused hands. I closed my eyes and tried to pull away but my restraints were too tight. I was not certain what was going to happen to me next or what to expect, since I had had very little experience with men, but I had a very vivid and frightening idea. I tried twisting my body away from him but my efforts were to no avail. He moved on top of me and I wished for it to end soon. He was so heavy that I could hardly breathe. He smelled of days of sweat, dirt and oily grimy hair and his breath was hot and smelled of rotting, un-brushed teeth. It hurt immensely. Trying to remove myself from this horrible situation, I removed myself by picturing myself in the beautiful gardens of the estate where we had met with the committee. *I thought of what they would do when they learned about this.* When he was through with me, he dressed hurriedly and left the room without a comment, leaving me all alone. There was no reason to scream, no one was there to hear me. *I wished for Fabian to come and rescue me.* I finally was exhausted, trying to free myself and I fell into a fitful sleep. When I awoke, my raped body was torn, bloody and sore and I was stiff from the dampness and cold. I was very thirsty and felt a wave of nausea come over me. I had had nothing to eat since, what I assumed to be, breakfast the day before. I had no idea whether it was day or night but the sweaty, smelly, hairy and disgusting 'monster' repeated the same ritual as had happened before throughout what I imagined to be the evening of the second day. I was getting weaker by the hour, having had no food or water. *How much longer can this keep happening I asked myself, how much more can I possibly endure and when will this ever end, will I even survive? I told myself that I could not give up trying and had to remain strong and keep my brain active if I were to survive. I started going over the research we had recently been working on as an effort to keep alert and every time I felt myself dozing off, I would jar myself awake by going over data in the research.*

The third time he entered the room he removed the bed and left me suspended in the air, fastened to the frame, attached to ceiling hooks at the corners of the small basement room, trussed up like a pig. He was able to lift me vertically, and from side to side. He did all sorts of horrendous things to me in these different positions. On what I thought was the third day of my capture, after he finished, he dropped me to the damp, cold floor and began to remove the restraints on my feet. I kicked at him as hard as I could but my kicks were ineffective because my strength was gone from lack of food and water. I could not do any serious injury to him. He got on top of me again and when he finished he began to remove the restraints from my hands. I waited until my hands were free and then with all the strength I could summon I kicked and pushed, landing a solid blow to his groin, knocking him off balance and then I ran on needle-prickling feet for the door. I heard a loud pop, it felt like a very hot knife struck me in the back, knocking the wind out of me, I hit the floor, and everything went blank.

CHAPTER 15

Mirjam said. "It is nine o'clock, what could possibly be keeping the birthday girl. It is not like Rachael to be a minute late for anything and she called as she left the hospital on the way to the train. Richard, you did say she planned to catch the 7:34, so she should already be here. I will text her and see when to set the food on the table."

"Yes, Rachael said she would start for home after she finished checking some results in the hospital as I was leaving the pharmacy research lab, you are right, she should have arrived some time ago," Richard replied. "I am beginning to get concerned also."

"This is so unusual!" Mirjam said. "She does not even answer her communicator, or else it has been turned off."

"I will head toward the station and see if I can find her," Richard said nervously.

A short time later Richard came running into the house and reported finding Rachael's backpack by the edge of the walkway two blocks from the house. Everyone agreed that something was terribly wrong. Mirjam made a missing person's report by pushing

911 on her communicator. In fifteen minutes, two campus security officers arrived at their house and entered all the information into their database.

"It will take three days before we can take any action on a missing person's report," one of the officers announced as they got up to leave.

"You do not understand," Mirjam replied. "Rachael is very responsible, something has happened to her. We need to find out what, and do it now!"

The officers did not explain themselves further but excused themselves and left Mirjam standing at the door. Mirjam immediately called Alex and me and then I informed The Committee and I requested that they forward a complete set of documents allowing both Alex and myself medical consent and authority for not only Rachael but also for the rest of the students. In less than an hour, the campus security returned to the house and told Mirjam that they were organizing a thorough campus search but by one o'clock Saturday morning, there was still no sign of Rachael. I also called the Southern California team and informed them of Rachael's disappearance; Fabian caught the next high speed rail to Stanford. We left Fresno and reached the Toscana House a few moments after Fabian had arrived. He had many questions; I had very few answers.

At five a.m. on Monday morning, three days after Rachael's disappearance, the campus security office received a call from a couple of joggers who reported that they had found the nude body of a young woman hidden by some shrubbery alongside the jogging path just west of the campus. The campus security office responded immediately and identified the young woman as Rachael from the photograph that they had been circulating. The campus security officers found her alive but semi-conscious and took her by ambulance to the infirmary where a medical team treated her for hypothermia, dehydration and a gunshot wound. After the medics stabilized Rachael's condition, the school infirmary transferred her to the University Medical Center in San Francisco where further tests determined that there were also evidences of a brutal sexual assault. The UMC medical staff also confirmed that she suffered from dehydration, malnourishment and in addition, that she had experienced extended exposure.

The campus security informed us that some joggers had found Rachael, semi-conscious and injured and that she was now at the UMC, and that their emergency staff was treating her for a small caliber gunshot wound, hypothermia, dehydration, malnutrition and exposure. Alex, Mirjam, Fabian and I immediately caught a commuter to UMC and arrived shortly after nine. The hospital's ICU nurse in charge of Rachael's care informed us that she was still in an IC unit recovering from her surgery and that she was not responsive but that her condition was stable. The gunshot wound had done little major damage; the bullet entered just below the left scapula and lodged behind the clavicle. Later, we would learn from Rachael that she remembered that she had tried to kick the perpetrator several times and that her last kick must have knocked him off balance. Rachael's ICU charge nurse further informed us that if the bullet had not entered at an angle it would have caused major injuries to vital organs and possibly killed her.

The ICU doctor in charge further informed us that Rachael also suffered injuries from repeated, violent raping and assaults perpetrated in very brutal and heinous circumstances. She added that the rape and assault would cause the most lasting scars and that Rachael would be required to seek psychological counseling and would need the support from her family and very close friends.

Fabian came prepared to stay with Rachael until she recovered. The news of Rachael's rape and assault was particularly devastating to him. Fabian's immediate response was one of anger and hostility toward the man that had done this to her. *Had he been stalking her, was it a crime of convenience, a crime of passion, had he somehow had contact with Rachael prior to the abduction?????* He stayed by her bedside, held her hand and tenderly reminded her of all the exciting times which they had had since meeting in Geneva just a few months ago, whispering his devoted love for her. By mid-afternoon, Rachael opened her eyes and smiled at him.

"How long have you been here?" Rachael asked. "I was dreaming about that beautiful garden we walked in at the estate."

Fabian replied. "I came as soon as I got the call and have been here by your bedside since I arrived here this morning."

Rachael had a flashback of her traumatic incident, became subdued, turned her head away from Fabian, and began to sob uncontrollably. Fabian rang for the nurse to attend to Rachael, then reached over and tenderly patted her shoulder, kissed her sweetly on her lips and reluctantly turned to leave the room.

"Rachael, rest now and I will be back very soon," Fabian said.

Mirjam, Alex and I had been in the waiting room until Fabian's return. We all went to the cafeteria for a late lunch and Fabian began to get emotional as we discussed Rachael's ordeal, and he informed us about her waking up from her surgery and the emotional flashback, which she experienced. Mirjam caringly consoled him.

After three days, the doctor informed us that Rachael was healing quickly and normally and that physically she was able to resume her studies. Her doctor also reminded us that she would require a longer healing process emotionally and to be diligent to watch for signs of stress and depression. One of the conditions of her release was that she would schedule psychological counseling, which she did, but insisted that she was fine and that she did not need counseling.

Upon leaving the hospital, Rachael was eager to return to her research project and continue with her program. Fabian returned to Cal. Tech. the day following Rachael's release and pleaded with her to communicate with him at least every other day. She felt very comforted by the fact that Fabian had stayed with her during her time in the hospital. The more she thought about Fabian the more she realized that he cared deeply for her and that she could count on him, this fact made her feel very secure.

As soon as Rachael got back to the house after her release from the hospital, she went straight to her room to put her things away, not wanting to have to answer any questions. She did not want the others feeling sorry for her. She found her backpack lying on the bed and began to cry uncontrollably. Mirjam entered their bedroom and tried to console her.

"Rachael, you are going to be fine. You can easily catch up with your research. 'This' will not affect our mission."

"'It' is not a **'this'**," Rachael replied angrily. "I was raped, abused, shot and left for dead! I am not sure how it will affect our mission and really, I do not care; my capture may change everything. Right now, I am going to take a shower."

She stubbornly stomped into the bathroom, slamming the door!

That evening even though Rachael felt numb from her scalp to her toes she forced herself to eat a little but had to rush to the bathroom a short time later feeling very nauseous. After the lights were out Rachael silently sobbed until she fell asleep. By morning things seemed some brighter and she was able to eat a small breakfast.

"Richard, I would like to get back to work as soon as possible and I may need to stay late for a few days, will you stay with me?" Rachael asked. "I would feel safer if I had a companion to walk with from the station to the house."

"I will be happy to stay with you," Richard replied enthusiastically. "Anything I can do to help."

Richard continued to be very attentive and stayed late with her on several occasions during her first week back to the research lab.

"I was wondering if you would like to go have dinner with me, just the two of us," Richard asked as they walked home on Friday evening.

"You have been very thoughtful and attentive to me and I appreciate you a lot. I think of you as a very true friend but I am not interested in a romantic evening," Rachael replied.

Two weeks after the assault, Rachael and Mirjam were alone in their room after dinner. Rachael was quiet and in deep thought.

Tearfully, she began to tell Mirjam the gruesome details about her attack. Mirjam relayed all the details of the assault to me and I forwarded them to The Committee.

"I have told my counselor all of the details that I can remember but I wanted someone else to know also," said Rachael. "So, Mirjam, I wanted you to know so you can understand my mental state and even my temperamental mood swings and hopefully help me when I become irrational and depressed."

Mirjam monitored Rachael's behavior and habits daily and forwarded a weekly report on her condition to me. Rachael continued to have periods of sleepless nights. On one such night, Mirjam reported to me a very disturbing incident. Rachael fell to sleep only to be jolted awake by a nightmare of her capture, her heart beating so fast that she could not go back to sleep. On many such nights, she would awaken Mirjam and tell her of her nightmares and that she was afraid to tell anyone about her sleepless nights, not even her counselor since she was fearful that The Committee would eliminate her from the program and therefore, The Committee would not allow her to finish her training.

The counselor told her that she needed to forgive herself and that she should not analyze her attack. In addition, she told Rachael that she should stop analyzing what she had done wrong. She directed her council at convincing Rachael that she was not the cause of her abduction and attack. The counselor emphasized that nothing would change the circumstances of what had taken place.

Mirjam was concerned with the fact that Rachael had lost a lot of weight and that she stayed to herself and became absorbed in her research, not entering the conversations with others in the house, especially with Richard. Richard tried unsuccessfully to engage Rachael in conversations about the research that she was conducting at the lab. He and Mirjam also tried to encourage her to attend some campus social activities and lectures held in the library. Nothing they did seemed to have an influence on her state of mind. Rachael had not returned Fabian's calls and he was getting concerned so he finally called Mirjam about his uneasiness. Mirjam approached Rachael a few days later.

"Rachael, we are all getting extremely troubled about how you are feeling," Mirjam said with a keen awareness. "You are not eating, you are losing weight, and you are not returning Fabian's calls, in addition, you seem terribly depressed. Fabian is greatly concerned about you and wants you to let him in; he wants to be a part of your life, we all do. Remember, you asked me to help you out when things started getting you depressed. You should return Fabian's calls; I think that would be especially good for you."

"I will give Fabian a call if you think I should, but I am not sure what to say," Rachael replied.

Rachael returned Fabian's call; they had only a short conversation, in which she agreed to communicate regularly. She decided that she would strive to put the attack behind her as she realized that it was not logical to act the way she had been behaving. She decided to work toward the goal of becoming part of the teams' final selection and that she needed Fabian. That would not be so bad, would it? As the second summer approached, Rachael and Fabian made plans to spend a few days together before finishing their degrees.

><

Spring 2059

March 30th on Easter Sunday morning at 12:30 a.m., Alex jolted me awake.

"I have been having contractions for the past hour," she said excitedly. "The contractions are now about five minutes apart, I think it's time for us to go to the birthing center."

I jumped up wide-awake and called a taxi. Alex had expected to go into labor at any time so she had previously made arrangements and had a bag packed. I, on the other hand had not made any preparations. *What did I need to do? I should probably get dressed.*

"I called a taxi, it should be here in ten minutes," I remarked with a little high-pitched quiver in my voice.

We arrived at the birthing center thirty minutes later and by 1:30, Alex was as comfortable as possible in our room awaiting the doctor. A short time later, Dr. Smokler arrived and I got prepared to assist by holding Alex's hand while the doctor administered the medication. At 3:01, our precious little girl was born and what a perfect little angel she was, with dark red hair and sparkling dark eyes. She had a sweet little round cherub face, chubby, squirmy arms and legs and a voice that let everyone know that she was here. Chloe Alexis Wickham would change both our lives and had already. After Alex and Chloe were both sleeping soundly, I called Tom and asked him to inform The Committee of our good news. I also called both teams and told them that we were the proud parents of a beautiful baby girl. Mirjam asked for all the particulars and I proudly gave them to her.

><

Three months later, Alex and I arranged for both teams to meet for a second time at Monterey before they finished their individual research programs so we could show off our new baby girl. She was grinning, blowing bubbles and making little baby-noises. Mirjam wanted to spend the entire weekend holding and feeding Chloe. Rachael was almost as enthusiastic. They both seemed to be developing a motherly instinct. The men, on the other hand, were content to hold Chloe for a few minutes and then give her back to Mirjam or Rachael. Eric was an exception; he and Mirjam dominated the care of Chloe.

Medical school was going great for Gabriele, Richard and Mirjam. Jabbar and Rachael were both finishing a PhD in pharmacy, with additional work in Biochemistry and microbiology. The members of the engineering team at Cal Tech were putting the final minutiae on their individual projects. The last few months had shown a great deal of improvement in Rachael, she seemed to be adjusting and had become deeply involved in her research. I had been making regular reports to The Committee on the team's progress since Rachael's release from the hospital. Rachael's counselor gave her a clean bill of health to pursue her normal activities. Rachael convinced all of us that she was mentally stable and able to function in a normal manner. After reviewing all of her medical records, The Committee agreed with Alex and me that we should proceed with Rachael as part of the team. "*Fabian will be pleased,*" I thought. "*If Rachael had not been healthy, I was certain Fabian would drop out as well. The integrity of the entire team would have been in jeopardy.*"

CHAPTER 16

Fall 2059

All the students were finished with their research by autumn, submitted their research papers, and each was preparing to 'defend' their theses. Mirjam, Gabriele, and Richard were preparing for their residency by applying to hospitals both locally as well as in Europe. Knowing that the team would be engaged in the life skills training, which they assumed would be at the estate, Mirjam and Gabriele applied at local hospitals in Geneva. Richard decided to accept a residency offered by the San Francisco Medical Center and stayed in California, a decision, which he made after Rachael's announcement that she was not interested in him romantically.

Richard and Susann had become good friends after Rachael's capture, hospitalization and recovery. Rachael's decision that she and Richard should go their separate ways and not become romantically involved had originally crushed Richard. He soon recovered from his disappointment; Susann's beauty, out-going personality and energy quickly won his affections. They discovered that they had a lot in common, especially Richard's dedication to continue medicine and Susann's enthusiasm for human biology. Susann wanted to continue her genetic research and had an offer to teach genetics at the University of California, San Francisco. Therefore, she asked me to contact The Committee to ask if they would excuse her from the life skills training so that she could stay in San Francisco close to Richard. After discussing the possibilities with The Committee, they, Alex, and I agreed that this would not jeopardize the integrity of the team and that she and Richard could serve as a major part of the future colonization efforts, thereby they would fulfill their obligations to The Committee for the education that they had received. This decision freed Susann and allowed her to accept the position offered by UC, San Francisco. Alex and I agreed that sometimes love has to play out on its own terms.

We were very pleased with 'our' team. Tom informed us that The Committee desired that we occupy an apartment at the estate and oversee the training program scheduled to start before the first of the year. We agreed without a second thought and arrived a few days before the team so that we could have time to get Chloe settled into her new surroundings. Our little sweet baby was becoming our inquisitive, adventurous and very precocious little girl. She was constantly exploring her surroundings and therefore, we had to learn to 'baby proof' every inch she could reach or climb to.

Mirjam and Gabriele, eager to begin their residency were the first ones to arrive in Geneva and Tom met them at the airport. Tom informed them that The Committee had arranged for their same accommodations at the château and that meals would be available as posted on a schedule board in the dining hall. Tom also communicated to them that they would have transportation to and from the hospitals in Geneva as needed.

"Mirjam and Gabriele, The Committee recognizes that you need the closeness of the team; otherwise, they would furnish you an apartment in Geneva." Tom added.

"Thank you for meeting us and arranging for our transportation," replied Mirjam. "Gabriele and I would very much like to again be near the team. Have Grant and Alex arrived with Chloe? We are anxious to see that sweet little girl."

"Yes," Tom answered. "They have moved into one of the 'family units'."

"I am certainly going to enjoy having some quality time with Makoto," Gabriele said excitedly. "I am sure that the residency will take most of my time and a lot of my energy but I will still have more time with him than we had while in school. Having a relationship by video leaves a lot to be desired."

"I know how you feel," Mirjam said. "Although Eric and I have had some quality time together during the past year, it has not been nearly enough, we need quantity time also."

Mirjam and Gabriele arranged their rooms, hung clothes and put things away, chatting with excitement by scurrying back and forth between their rooms while they waited for the others to arrive. Both teams had arrived by evening, and everyone was eager to see each other again and to catch up on how everyone was doing. Everybody was very eager to see, examine, hold and play with Chloe, even the men. Now that Chloe was six months old, she was able to maneuver her 'walk-about' and get into anything low enough that a stretch of her little arms could reach. She had two bottom teeth and she was beginning to feed herself finger foods.

Eric and Mirjam were excited to take a stroll in the gardens after Eric settled into his room. They were having trouble keeping their hands to themselves. Fabian and Rachael were doing the same. Alex and I wondered how long each of them could stay at a distance, assuming that they were. We expected that they both might be making an announcement very soon.

We assembled in the dining hall for dinner after everyone had moved into his or her rooms. After dinner, Alex and I asked the team to remain in the dining hall and The Committee addressed everyone by way of a large monitor set up at one end of the hall. The team was still in awe of the size and beauty of the château. I had often wondered if anyone actually lived here.

The Committee congratulated both teams on a job well done.

"All of you will spend the next several months learning the 'how to' for many of the everyday jobs that require attention around a house so," the chairperson began, "if something breaks or a system does not properly function, one of you will need to know how to fix it. A simple repair unattended could jeopardize the mission and possibly even be life threatening. There will be no 'repairperson' to call."

"I have had some experience with heating and cooling systems; therefore, I already know quite a lot about that skill," Fabian spoke up. "I was working for a firm outside of Paris on a summer internship."

"That will prove to be helpful, Fabian," the chairperson replied as he continued. "The supercomputer will monitor all systems, will warn you if a system malfunctions, and recommend a possible solution, but it will be up to one of you to make the repairs. A part of your on-the-job training will be in how to repair and maintain all the systems on the ship. Mock-up systems of the ship are in the barn, the large rock structure just to the north of the château. These systems operate much like a simulator in that they are programmable to represent any foreseeable problem that the design engineers can anticipate. Before this stage of your training, you will need to develop the skills of a variety of repairpersons. Artisans will teach you their skills in a workshop, which is set up next to the barn. Such skills as machine work, carpentry, masonry and various other building trades as well as food preparation."

"What happens if we are unable to master the skills of carpentry or masonry or any of the other skills?" Eric questioned. "There are so many different skills to master."

"I am not mechanically inclined," Jabbar added. "Those artisans will have a difficult task in teaching me some of those skills."

Makoto echoed Jabbar's statement, saying. "I feel inadequate, also, Jabbar."

"That is why we are having skilled craftsmen come here," the chairperson replied. "The artisans will work with you until at least one of you is proficient in each skill. You should not be overly concerned. Each of you will be able to learn these needed skills, after all, we selected and handpicked you because you were all of above average intelligence and your profiles indicated that each of you possess innate abilities, so it follows that you will be quick to learn the skills which we need you to master. Have a good night's rest; we will start the training after breakfast tomorrow. Breakfast is at eight each morning; check the list of other meal times posted by the door."

As everyone left the dining hall, Jabbar waited until he could be alone with Serena.

"May I have a word with you," Jabbar asked.

"Yes, of course," replied Serena. "What is it that you want to ask or say to me?"

Jabbar returned. "I want to tell you that you are very beautiful tonight."

"Are you just saying that because I am the only girl left?" asked Serena.

Serena continued. "Richard and Susann have decided to stay in San Francisco where Richard is to do his residency and Daniel, Robert and Michelle are considering sharing an apartment in San Francisco after we finish our training here. Do not say anything to Grant or Alex because I just overheard them talking after dinner. They were talking about starting an engineering consulting firm. I do not think that their interest in the mission is a high priority for them."

"I was not aware that Daniel, Robert and Michelle were interested in starting their own business," Jabbar answered. "Serena, what you said earlier is not true; I **do** think you are very beautiful, do you not remember my saying earlier that I thought you were the most beautiful woman ever! I am thrilled that you are the girl left for me and that you have not gotten interested in any other man, but that does not change your beauty. I have had my eyes on you from the beginning; I believe I am just self-conscious when it comes to talking to women."

Jabbar is very shy, Serena thought. *Maybe he has liked me for a while.* "I am not sure you really mean what you are saying."

"We have a lot in common," Jabbar continued. "We would be good together. I do not really know how to talk to you. My parents had arranged my life for me before their deaths. They encouraged me to meet, and hoped that I would marry the daughter of my father's business partner. No one from my family knows about my trip to Geneva and I am not planning to tell them. I have been watching you closely every time I have had the opportunity since Alex and Grants' wedding; I just did not know how to approach you."

"Will you go on a walk with me now?" Jabbar asked.

Jabbar and Serena walked for several hours. The night air had a definite chill and Jabbar removed his jacket and put it over the thin sweater that Serena had on.

"This should help in keeping you warmer, Serena," Jabbar said as he allowed his arm to linger around her shoulders.

They decided it was getting very late and that they should head back when they noticed two people to their left. As they got closer, they recognized the other couple as Makoto and Gabriele. The four of them entered the château as quietly as possible and headed straight to their rooms.

The next morning, after breakfast, Eric asked for everyone's attention. "I have an important announcement to make. Mirjam and I have spent most of the night discussing our future. If The Committee chooses us for this history-making voyage, we will make it together as a family. I want to announce that Mirjam is my wife."

Fabian stood with a surprised look on his face.

"Rachael and I have had the same type of conversations and we want to make the same announcement," Fabian said. "We had no idea that the two of you were making the same commitment to each other. We will be together during our entire lives and knowing that we will have a loving partner will definitely make our journey much happier. We have each other and it is a comfort to know that Eric and Mirjam will be a couple also."

"Those are inspiring announcements," Alex commented to me as we and Chloe returned to our apartment. "That makes four down and four to go. I know that Makoto and Gabriele took a midnight walk after dinner last night."

"So did Jabbar and Serena," I replied. "The four of them were very quiet coming into their rooms, but surveillance caught them in the act. It appeared to me that they were developing closeness as romantic couples. Let's see how things develop during the life skills training, I am thinking that the four of them might finish out the exploration team."

After getting Chloe settled for a nap, I notified The Committee that Alex and I had chosen the eight members for the team. The students that we had decided to eliminate were Daniel, Robert and Michelle. The Committee agreed with our selections. The team was now complete!

I called the three remaining students for a meeting and informed them of our decision.

"Alex and I understand that you three have been making plans to establish an engineering firm in San Francisco, and The Committee thanks you for your participation in the process thus far and they wanted us to tell you that they would like to retain your services in the colonization efforts," I informed the students. "You also must continue to honor your secrecy agreement about any portion of this venture. Alex and I also wish you every success and thank you for your participation. Tom will arrange for your travel back to San Francisco tomorrow."

With the help of Tom, Mike and their wives, Alex, Chloe and I had a small farewell celebration in honor of Daniel, Robert and Michelle after dinner that evening. I chose that time to announce the selection of 'the team' and cheers went up from everyone, with hugs, backslaps and handshakes all around. Everyone seemed extremely happy.

"Are you still intent on going on the voyage with the team?" Alex asked, as we were going to bed.

"I would like for us to be included if you still want to go," I answered. "We have to think about Chloe also. Can she safely make the journey?"

Alex replied. "I don't know how a young baby would react to hibernation. We will need to find that out."

"I'll contact Tom to set up a meeting with The Committee tomorrow for us to discuss our desire to continue with the team and I will also ask about infant hibernation," I replied.

'The team' started the life skills training process by first learning the finer skills of plumbing. Other artisans would follow with instructions in their trades during the following months. Alex included each of the women and men in the child care duties of Chloe. Tom's wife shared in the childcare instruction, having raised a boy and girl of her own.

Alex and I met with The Committee at 10 A.M. the following day.

"We would like to accompany our team on the expedition," I began. "We are both in great physical health. We may not have an IQ of 170 or above but we do have above average intelligence and a lot of experience and maturity."

"You and Alex may be in good health but you are not as young as the team and this may present a future problem," the chairperson said. "Now with Chloe, I am not sure how the stress of the inertial boost would affect such a young person; also, the hibernation process may put too much stress on a child under the age of five."

"I too am concerned," Alex replied. "We will have to check with the manufactures and developers to see what the suggested ages are."

We continued presenting our case and The Committee began to see the wisdom in having us go on the voyage. The Committee members contacted the hibernation consultants and were informed that the design of the system would accommodate children five years and above and with careful calibration, the design would not be problematic for younger children. The design engineers gave the same report. The forces during the inertial boost would not be any greater than the takeoff of a supersonic airliner, just longer in duration.

"The Committee will need time to consider your proposal," said the chairperson. "Will you and Alex leave us for a time, please? After we discuss your proposal we will give you our decision."

I called the team members together and said. "Alex, Chloe and I have requested that we continue to be a part of the team. The Committee informed us that they are of the opinion that you, although young, are mature enough to know what to do when faced with difficult decisions. However, they have given us their approval to be a part of the exploration team."

Summer 2060

After several months, every person was comfortable with the training that each one had received. Several of the team members had run into some problems in learning some of the finer skills as quickly as they had wished and this gave them some moments of concern. After some trial and error sessions with the trainers, everyone finally felt comfortable that someone of the group could handle anything, which presented itself. With the analytical help of the on-board-computer system, the team developed confidence that, as a group, they would be able to keep all systems going. We now had well trained engineers, medical doctors, chemists, and physicists as well as skilled plumbers, masons, carpenters, chefs and machinists. The team felt ready and confident to start the next phase.

Tom left a message in our apartment asking us to meet him in the conference room. When we arrived, Tom and Mike met us at the door and introduced us to a very distinguished looking older man.

"My name is Joseph Merrill," the man said as he introduced himself. "I am the chairperson of The Committee. We have spoken many times via the monitor but have not spoken in person. We have had a minor setback at the L5 construction site. It seems that one of the supply ships crashed into the movable containment structure causing moderate damage two months ago. I asked Tom and the security team to look into the cause of the accident. I will now allow Tom to give you the details, which he has discovered."

"I traced the supply ship back to one of our trusted companies which we had contracted to build the ship," began Tom. "The original supply ship crew of three was found dead in the warehouse; and the ship was commandeered, loaded with explosives and flown to the construction site which crashed into the containment structure, killing all but one of the hijackers. We returned the survivor to Earth where he received treatment in a secure and guarded location in a private hospital. When he regained consciousness, I, along with Mike, interrogated him and learned that only a small portion of the charge ignited. If the full charge had ignited, it would have destroyed the containment structure as well as the ship, consequently the ship sustained little to no damage and the repair crews have finished repairs to the containment structure. Construction at L5 is back on schedule. However, before we could question the hijacker further, he suffered a fatal heart failure due to the injuries which he had sustained."

"Who were these hijackers, and why were they trying to destroy the ship?" I asked Tom and Mike.

"After the interrogation, Tom checked into the backgrounds of the hijackers," stated Mr. Merrill. "There was little physical evidence left at the crash site and we could find nothing to connect the survivor to anyone or any cause. I am still convinced; however, that there must be a connection to Environmental Advisors, 'EA', and that they must be responsible for the attack. How they learned of our construction site is still a mystery. The companies we use very carefully screen their employees. Grant and Alex do not tell the team about this incident, not just yet."

The Committee then informed us that we would be relocating to Uglegorsk in Eastern Russia, which was the closest city to the Vostochry Cosmodome where a space transport would take us to the ship's construction site. We would need to pack only a few of our personal belongings; everything that we would need was in the mock-up of the ship's living quarters.

I told the team that Alex, Chloe and I would need a few days to finish with some details here at the estate and that we would be joining them shortly. I informed Eric that he should assume the leadership role until we joined them. It was beginning to seem that we started this process a lifetime ago. Tom and Mike used a large helicopter to transport the team to the Geneva airport where a private jet would take them to Uglegorsk. When they arrived at the mock living site, the first thing they would do, was to learn to fabricate their accommodations from the three-meter panels. The site contained hibernation tanks that would allow all of us to practice before the flight. We would have three months of isolation to familiarize ourselves with the living area and get physical clearance before takeoff. Our plan was to keep the ship free of any unwanted microbes that could cause the project to fail.

CHAPTER 17

Fall 2060

Our team arrived in Uglegorsk as planned. Tom and Mike provided land transportation to the recently modernized and now very new Cosmodome. Each of us team members approached the guard gate with our personal belongings and required papers in a small leather case. Tom spoke to the security guards in Russian and Rachael interpreted for the rest of the team. Before they would allow the team to proceed, the guards ushered Rachael to a private office for further scrutiny because of her ethnic background. After a delay of 15 minutes, Rachael rejoined us and after the guards welcomed the entire team, the guards escorted us to the mock-up quarters located in a newly designed section of the facilities.

The mock-up consisted of a large dome in the form of a structure which resembled a covered athletic field, except much larger. Once the security guards accompanied us team members to our quarters, they left, securing the door behind them.

"That was very comforting," Fabian noted very sarcastically. "It feels as though we are in prison."

"What did those guards want with you, Rachael, what did they ask?" Fabian inquired. "What was that all about, pulling you away from the rest of us? Were they questioning you because you are a Russian descendant? I was afraid for your safety, and that 15 minutes passed very slowly. I was about to come in and rescue you."

"Believe it or not they wanted my autograph," replied Rachael acting very smugly. "I have a feeling that they may have heard some rumors or have figured out that we are involved in something important. I guess this was their way of trying to know someone involved with a significant event."

"I was very worried about what was happening with you; please don't just brush this off as nothing, surely they had other reasons for taking you aside and keeping you like they did," Fabian returned with concern in his voice.

"Fabian, do not be such a worrier, I am a Russian woman and these men were very curious about what is going to be taking place in the Cosmodome," Rachael responded. "I told them as little as possible without raising suspicion and having them curiously asking more. Russian men take every opportunity to question a woman, especially if they think they can find out information, which might be useful, this is a very common event. That is very sweet of you to be concerned about me; I am beginning to think you care quite a lot for my safety and for me."

I said to Rachael, "you should be flattered that Fabian was so concerned for you and your safety, that's one of the greatest gestures a man can show for his partner. Rachael, did the security guards want to know about your Russian Orthodox religious beliefs? Was that all the questioning involved, or did they want to know about anything else?"

"Well, Eric, they did ask several questions about our program." Rachael replied. "I answered as evasively as I could, not wanting to compromise the security agreement which I signed concerning our mission. No, they did not question my religious beliefs."

Mirjam interjected. "Does anyone else feel alone for the first time, truly alone? I believe that we can be confident; however, that the security here is as efficient and complete as it was at the château. Remember, we all concluded that we were being monitored at the dorms and at the estate."

"I do not think that Grant and Alex ever knew that we were aware of the surveillance system, we will probably be monitored here also," Jabbar said. "In some way this gives me a feeling of security, even though it does seem a little invasive at times."

"Being on our own causes me to feel unnerved and somewhat frightened," Serena commented. "Perhaps we will become accustomed to this in time and begin relying on each other for protection."

"From what do we need to be protected?" Gabriele asked. "We are isolated here."

"I feel confident that The Committee has taken measures to insure that our safety and well-being is of the highest priority." I reassured Gabriele and the others. "Jabbar, you are probably correct about us being monitored here, we have grown up with government surveillance all of our lives."

The team found the living quarters to be much smaller than were those at the château but the description that Grant had previously given us was very accurate except that eight separate apartments were already assembled and ready for occupancy and there were living plants everywhere, the place took on the appearance of a Central American rain forest. Fabian and I began to disassemble our apartments and we rearranged the modules to accommodate two people each; Mirjam and Rachael were eagerly helping. Makoto and Jabbar noticed what we were doing and decided to do the same in hopes that Gabriele and Serena would approve. They did! Once everyone had changed into the 'uniforms', as we had been directed to do, and stowed our personal belongings, we began to feel more comfortable. The women still complained about the non-fashionable look of the uniforms. They all agreed that they would have to do something about them as soon as possible.

"Mirjam, I don't see why you are unhappy with the uniform," I commented. "I think it is very attractive on you. It is custom made just for you and it shows off your curves in a very graceful way."

The other men also commented that the women were very attractive in their tight fitting uniforms.

As we finished our apartment updates, the inevitability of things began to settle in on us. Intellectually, we all felt confident but emotionally we had feelings of uncertainty, and were somewhat anxious about our future.

"I suppose that it is up to us to decide what needs to be done next," I said. "Grant is not here to give us any direction and he has temporarily asked me to take on the leadership role until he and his family arrive. Is anyone hungry?"

"I'll look in the galley and see what I can find," replied Mirjam.

"I'm starving and need some nourishment and energy, so I'll help," I added.

Mirjam located nothing prepared so she returned and informed the others that we would need to prepare all of our food. There was only a small amount of flour, oil, salt and other staples in the pantry. She asked Rachael and Fabian if they would gather some fruit and said that she would make some bread.

I said. "Tomorrow Makoto and Gabriele can have the honors of being the chefs. The next day Jabbar and Serena will take their turn at being the chefs followed by Fabian and Rachael then we will start the rotation over. Is this agreeable with everyone?"

"That sounds like a workable plan," Fabian answered. "After we eat, we should explore the mock-up and see what The Committee has arranged for our use. We need to organize our work schedules. Be thinking of what needs to be done."

We feasted on coconuts, papayas, mangos and naan, Indian flat bread, served in the furnished forever-ceramic ware, a lightweight heat resistant material used to cook and bake, as well as to serve.

The women especially, since they had decided that they would direct most of the food preparation, were thankful and excited that the galley came supplied with the latest and most efficient in cookware, appliances, etc. After we enjoyed our first meal in our new home, everyone was eager to begin the exploration of the mock-up. On the level below the living area, Makoto, Jabbar, Fabian and I found wheat and every vegetable imaginable, which were growing in various stages of maturity in hydroponic tanks.

After what seemed to be an hour or two of exploration, everyone reassembled in the common area near the communication center to report on all that we had discovered. There was much excitement about the many varieties of vegetables, fruit and grains, which would supply many possibilities for some wonderful meals.

Makoto said. "I can see you, Gabriele, and the other women creating some luscious dinners. I have always been interested in creating desserts; perhaps you will welcome my help."

"I can whip up some 'mean' pancakes," Jabbar added.

I said to the team, changing the conversation from cooking, "I have no problem understanding what we should do next because of the skills training we have received in farming techniques. We located wheat and every vegetable we could ever desire, growing in our high-tech farm."

"It seems straight forward to me also," replied Makoto. "We must remember to maintain a section of wheat and vegetables maturing at usable intervals."

I said. "Fabian, Makoto, Jabbar and I also located the machine shop and a milling machine for grinding wheat and other grain. All the machinery is 'antique' replicas of modern machinery and all require manual labor to operate."

Everyone assumed this to mean that we would need to develop his or her own technology.

"I have been busy in the rain forest locating and mapping the location of various edible herbs," Rachael said. "I also located several varieties of plants which are suitable for medicinal purposes. This is beginning to become more and more exciting."

"What is the time, my watch has malfunctioned?" Mirjam announced. "I have not noticed any clocks in the common area or in the communication center. I have a feeling that we have been here for over six hours. Do you believe we will need to develop our own time system?"

"I have no idea," I replied. "I will go to the communication center and try to log onto the computer system."

That will not be necessary, said a voice that seemed to be coming from no single location. **I am the system that controls all other systems. I have sensors in all areas of the ship and here in the mock-up except in the private areas of your apartments. When you need me, just say "computer" and I will answer.**

"What time system should be used while here and on the ship?" I asked. "I would like to use our common Earth system of hours and days, at least for now."

You may use Earth time here and on the ship. As you know, the measurement of time on Earth will not be the same as measured on the ship as it increases in velocity. The rotation of Earth and the rotation of the new planet will not be the same; therefore, you may want to consider making adjustments as needed.

Everyone was exhausted and assumed it was midnight so we decided to rest, and to resume the exploration tomorrow. Each set his or her communicators for a wakeup call in six hours. I asked the computer to adjust day and night in keeping with a six o'clock sunrise.

Mirjam headed for the shower as soon as she and I got to our apartment.

"I feel like a shower and I want to wash my hair after a day like this," Mirjam said as she left the room looking back at me. "What should we use for body wash and shampoo?"

"Let's see what is in the storage unit," I replied. We found two small containers labeled 'body wash' and 'shampoo'. The contents had a pleasant ginger aroma.

"This will do for now, we can ask the computer for the ingredients and formula for making it later," Mirjam remarked as she stepped into the shower.

A moment later the shower door opened and I joined her.

"Let me wash your back, Sweetheart," I said.

Finally, the lights were out on our first night in the mock-up, what an exhausting first day!

CHAPTER 18

"Who could that be at 3 a.m.?" Mirjam asked as she awakened from a deep sleep.

"I have no idea," I replied. "Why would any of the team knock rather than use the intercom? We are supposed to be in isolation so how could it be anyone else?"

I sleepily walked to the door of their apartment in the mock-up and was shocked to see a distinguished older man who stood at the threshold. He was dressed in a Brioni suit and wore Testoni loafers. He had white hair, a well-trimmed mustache and a stylish beard.

"This is a secured location. Who are you and how did you get in?" I asked warily.

"Eric, I have some news for you and the team but first let me introduce myself to you in person. My name is Joseph Merrill; I am the chairperson of The Committee. We have talked many times at the estate by way of the monitor. There has been an accident near the estate. Grant and Alex decided to take a short hike after we finished some business yesterday. They had left Chloe with Tom's wife and they were hiking off-trail in the mountains east of the estate. There was a landslide and both of them plummeted down the side of the mountain in an avalanche of rocks. Grant came to rest face down being pinned under a large boulder, which landed in the lumbar area of his back, damaging his spine in L2 and L3 and causing paraplegia. The fall knocked Alex unconscious and when she regained consciousness, she called for emergency assistance. She then called the estate. The rescuers airlifted Grant to a hospital in Geneva. The medical staff evaluated his condition and I had him transferred to the University Hospital in Hamburg, Germany where he is undergoing neurosurgery to correct the nerve damage. The nerves will regenerate in time and with therapy, he should be walking normally in 12 to 15 months. The accident left him partially paralyzed from the waist down."

"You have shown exceptional leadership abilities, Eric," the chairperson continued. "It was not our original intention for Grant and Alex to be a part of the exploration team but they convinced us that they should go. I will leave you in charge, on the approval of the other team members, of course. I can see no reason to postpone the launch date. As soon as all of you are familiar and comfortable with the mock-up here, you can then proceed to the launch platform at the L5 location. You may communicate with The Committee by using the equipment in the communication area. I will give you the specific information later. Now if you will assemble the team I will inform them of the accident and answer any questions any of you may have and, oh yes, in answer to your question, I have access to many secured places."

The team was shocked and bewildered at the news of Grant's accident. Several asked questions about how Alex and Chloe were doing. The team also talked at length about how disappointed the Wickham family must be. They also expressed how saddened that they were that Grant, Alex, and Chloe would not be with them on the mission. The chairperson seemed encouraged that the team readily voted unanimously for me to assume the role of 'captain of the ship', as Mr. Merrill had expected; therefore, his confidence in the team was accurate.

Everyone was exhausted but could not go back to sleep; consequently, we all sat in the common area and conversed at length about Grant's tragic accident and contemplated the ramifications that this incident could possibly create.

Since I was elected as "captain of the ship" I finally said, "It is six o'clock; the 'sun' is up. There is no way that I can go back to sleep. Everyone seems awake so we should eat some breakfast and plan our day. Gabriele, your team is in charge of food preparation for today."

Gabriele and Serena teamed up for the breakfast preparations and decided on English biscuits and asked Jabbar and Makoto to go in search of melons. Serena discovered some dried tea in the pantry and as soon as the men returned with the melons, Gabriele announced breakfast.

After eating, the couples further explored the mock-up and located several different grains that were ready for harvest. Over the next few days, we harvested the grain and milled it into course flour. We picked almonds and pecans and baked the kernels with the grain to form a cereal; we dehydrated fruit and added it to the cereal mix for sweetness. Each couple had enough of this mixture to last the three months before entering the ship. We made milk from puréed, blanched almonds and filtered out the solids. Rachael and Jabbar had located thea sinensis plants and coffee beans and picked the tender shoots and ripe beans. We could now start our day with tea and coffee. By now, things were almost just like home.

After the second week in the mock-up, all of us were feeling comfortable and confident that there were no problems, which might surface, that we could not solve.

"Tomorrow morning we need to acquaint ourselves with the hibernation devices," I announced. "There are two tanks in each hibernation chamber, one tank for each individual. Does anyone have questions on the revisions of the hibernation process that we received? We will coordinate with the computer for a hibernation period of one week."

The first step now consisted of a special shower and a breathing apparatus that replaced the intravenous injections. To control hydration and to help deter the aging process an enzyme and mineral mist replaced the submersion technique.

Each couple used antibacterial scrubbers to help each other cleanse their bodies. Everyone entered the tanks and I asked the computer to revive us in seven days. We placed the breathing masks over our noses and mouths and sealed them securely. The mist now entered each tank and a pleasant smelling vapor filled the masks. Each of us became lost in a dreamless sleep.

As planned, I began to awaken first. I regained full awareness in less than five minutes, reentered the showers, and dried myself with the rotating warm air currents. As I dressed in my uniform, Mirjam began to awaken, as did all the others. The computer announced that we had been in hibernation for seven days. We discussed our experiences and all felt comfortable with the process.

I called everyone into the common area and contacted Grant and Alex to see how Grant was progressing since his surgery.

"Hello to the Wickham's, "I said as my communication to Grant and Alex connected. "Mirjam is excited to ask about Chloe; here she is."

Mirjam asked. "How is our sweet little girl these days? Is she talking, is she climbing out of her crib? I honestly have so many questions; I do not know where to stop. Are we going to see any new videos of her anytime soon?"

Alex happily answered Mirjam's inquiries. "Chloe is laughing, talking in complete sentences, and is even repeating little rhymes and children's songs. She loves to climb; it is getting difficult to keep her contained. Chloe, come here and sing, "Mary had a Little Lamb" to Mirjam, Rachael and the gang. *'Mary had a ittle lamb, ittle lamb,...'* I told you she's a little ham!"

After we had given our best wishes to Grant and Alex and extended our encouraging words to both of them, Alex regaled us with video portraits of Chloe and everyone commented on how cute she was and how much she had grown.

Grant said. "My stem cell regeneration surgery went very well and I will start therapy in two weeks. The doctors tell me that with therapy I should be able to walk in a month or so. My 'boss', Alex, will keep me on my toes and not give me any slack in putting off my exercises. Thanks to all of you for your good wishes throughout my recovery. Alex has completely healed from her injuries; she is a tough girl! The Committee has invited us to stay at the estate while I recuperate, so keep in touch."

"Alex and I have been discussing our disappointment in our not being able to travel with all of you to the new world," said Grant. "We have every confidence that you have been trained and are extremely capable to take on any task or event that may come up in this epic journey. The Committee will keep us informed of your progress as your journey continues and as long as communication is possible."

"Our plans are to be training and instructing Chloe to be instrumental in the future colonization efforts, that is, if this becomes her dream also," added Alex. "Our prayers are with you."

"Thank both of you very much for your encouragement, support and trust," I replied. "It means everything to all the team that you both were our mentors and we have grown to respect and admire you very much. We will be looking forward to having Chloe on board; however, that seems like such a long time in the future. Perhaps, the two of you can 'catch a ride' and come too. We have finished the hibernation exercise and all went as planned. We are ready to go!"

The remainder of the quarantine period proved to be uneventful as far as the project went. No one appeared to have any infectious diseases, not even a cold or the flu. Each team member went to the infirmary weekly where Mirjam and Gabriele administered routine physical examinations.

When we first arrived at the mock-up, all of us couples spent time together while we walked around the lush gardens. We acted as if we were on our honeymoons and enjoyed the uninterrupted time with each other. After a week, everyone agreed that it was time for the 'honeymoons' to be over and that everyone needed to go to work. A person needs only so much free time! There was a lot of talk among the team about the boredom that we were all experiencing. Everyone was anxiously anticipating the time that we could leave the quarantine, board the ship and become involved in something productive.

Rachael interjected. "I have an idea on how our boredom can vanish. We can start a project that will require our daily use of the life-skills training that we received. While we are here, I am interested in running some experiments on the plants that are unfamiliar to me to distinguish what medicinal compounds I can extract. All the plants here on the mock-up will also be on the ship."

"Once on the ship, life should be much like our lives in a research facility here on Earth," Fabian said hopefully. "I will help you with your experiments; we will all help."

The Committee had been monitoring each team members' physical and mental condition during the time we had spent in quarantine. The Committee arranged for a panel of psychologists to give the final approval of each team members' mental state before the final approval to proceed. With the help of Albert (the name we had all agreed was an appropriate name for the computer) all vital information was gathered and sent to the panel of psychologists. ALL WAS A GO.

CHAPTER 19

"We are ready to go, are we not," I said to the team after finishing another video conference with Grant and Alex. "I feel ready, we have received the best training we could possibly get and at no cost to us. We have passed the physical and mental profiles and The Committee has given their permission to proceed. The Committee has delivered everything that they have promised. I have full confidence that the ship will perform as planned. No doubt, there will be some uncertainties in an undertaking such as this; we are going to stretch the limits of present technology. Columbus must have had similar thoughts and feelings when he left the world he knew and sailed into the unknown for his New World. The men and women on the first space flights to the outer planets must have had the same uncertainties. If anyone has any major concerns, now is the time to express them. We leave for the spaceport and our first look at the ship tomorrow morning."

"What more could be accomplished by any farther training?" replied Rachael. "We are all ready."

The others all agreed that each of them felt confident in their abilities to solve any future problems but everyone had a few minor feelings of uncertainty. We spent our last night on Earth in somber thought about our childhoods; we recalled our families and parents and gathered the personal items that we wanted to take as reminders of life on Earth. We sought something tangible to show our future children, something that they might use to connect themselves to their grandparents and family.

Each couple left the common area, some on a walk, others engaged in private conversation. Mirjam and I walked to our apartment; I put my arms around her, held her lovingly, and told her that everything would turn out good, that we would have a fantastic life together. I had the watch that my grandfather had given my father and he in turn had given to me when I entered Yale. I was never very close to either of my parents; they were always too busy, but I kept the watch and planned to pass it down to my son as a legacy. Mirjam had kept the saree that her grandmother wore at her wedding reception. We placed both items in a small leather case along with the memory cards containing each of our families' histories. Everything else that we would need would be on the ship. We had planned to spend our last night in the mockup holding each other, contemplating our future, and thinking about our heritages that we would pass on to our children; however, we both fell asleep after only a few moments. We awoke shortly after we had fallen asleep by the sound of some very beautiful violin music.

"Where is the music coming from?" Mirjam asked, rubbing her sleepy eyes.

"It seems to be coming from the common area," I replied, "let's take a look".

Mirjam and I left our apartment and found the others congregated in the common area with Serena playing excerpts from Mendelssohn's Violin Concerto in E Minor on her Stradivarius.

"Playing has a way of settling my thoughts," Serena remarked as she finished her concerto and we all gathered around her.

"The Tanbur and violin are not made to be played together but I can utilize the electronic keyboard here in the common area and we will be able to make some awesome music together," Jabbar added.

"I am not an accomplished musician like the two of you," Gabriele announced. As she left to retrieve her flute, she further stated, "but I would like to join in if I am allowed. I have been playing the flute for seven years but I never was quite good enough join the philharmonic, or at least no one ever asked me."

We all were astonished at Gabriele's musical talent and she added significantly to our small ensemble. Her playing was as soft and melodious as small children's soft voices during quiet play.

"Jabbar, could you bring out your Tanbur and play some of your folk music for us?" I asked.

Jabbar jumped at the chance to show us his prized Tanbur, handed down in his family for generations. The music he played produced a banjo-like, interesting and somewhat eerie sound. With the three instruments, along with the electronic keyboard, this time played by Makoto, the sound was amazing, and we readily adopted them as 'The Four Voyagers'.

"Jabbar and I have been discussing handing down our musical instruments to our children as a reminder of their heritages," Serena said when 'The Four Voyagers' had finished their performance.

"Everyone remain for a moment longer, please," Fabian announced as he hurriedly left for his and Rachael's apartment and returned with a high-gloss polished wooden box. "Rachael, will you do the honor of showing everyone these wonderful gifts we have decided to pass on to our little girl someday?"

Rachael opened the box and removed some objects, carefully wrapped in her Grandmother's babushka. She began to remove the wrapping from a handmade set of nesting dolls, which her Grandfather had made, and he and her Grandmother had given to her on her seventh birthday. The dolls were colorfully hand-painted in a high-gloss finish.

Fabian said. "The only thing I have to pass on to our children is the amulet which I always wear around my neck. All of you may remember that I have mentioned to you the devastating auto accident that took the lives of my parents and younger sister. I also kept a strand of my sister's hair braided in with the bands of leather, which holds the amulet."

When we had all finished with our 'memory lane show and tell', we decided that we should call it a night and get some much-needed rest and sleep in preparation for tomorrow's journey to L5.

"It is getting late and we leave after breakfast in the morning," I said. "Goodnight everyone, Mirjam and I have already gone to sleep once, we'll see if we can do it again!"

The next morning everyone was too excited to eat; however, each couple had some of the cereal mixture left that we had previously made so we decided to put it all together, and each one of us ate what we wanted.

"None of us have ever been into space before but I feel certain that it will be better if we have something on our stomachs," Eric explained. "We will not want to be concerned with nausea. That would not be enjoyable."

Once we finished eating, we gathered our small 'carry on' containers, headed for the entrance of the mock-up facility, and expected Tom and Mike to greet us. We were surprised when a vehicle resembling a cold storage delivery truck blocked the entrance. The transport had backed up and attached itself to the facility by an airlock. Tom and Mike entered from the rear of the truck dressed in white hazard suits with attached breathing devices.

"We must keep all of you in a sterile environment so that no earth contaminants or pathogens enter the spacecraft," Tom explained.

It was a short ride from the mock-up to the spaceport and the specially prepared space shuttle that awaited us. A crew, all dressed in the white hazard suits, helped us dress in similar gear and attached a breathing apparatus to each of our backs.

When we had backed into an airlock at the spaceport, we exited the transport and a woman suited in similar gear greeted us and escorted us down a long windowless corridor and through another airlock into an assembling area much like any commercial airport. Upon entering the assembling area, we removed the hazard suits and backpacks and made ourselves comfortable in the row of theater seats arranged in a semicircle around a demonstration table.

Our escort gave a lecture, in English, about the physiological effects of exposure to zero gravity. She told us that we possibly would experience various degrees of nausea and disorientation while our bodies tried to adapt to zero gravity. She handed each of us a transdermal anti-nausea patch to apply before we entered the space shuttle.

"The patch will make you drowsy and you may not want to wear it but I would suggest that you keep in on for the duration of the trip to the L5 location," the instructor continued. "You will be having some space suit exercises on the shuttle tomorrow and you do not want to vomit while in the suit. That could be fatal. Now we get to the fun part."

She unveiled a small object, which resembled a commercial aircraft toilet. Each of us took our turn sitting on the device. The seat conformed perfectly to each individual's body shape and then returned to its natural position awaiting its next occupant. The space 'potty' was equipped with a warm water wash and dry cycle. A vacuum would draw all excrement, waste and wash water away from the body.

After the demonstration, we exited the area and then reunited with our carry on containers that we had earlier given to Tom as we entered the transport. Each couple inspected each other to see that our patches were in place. The exit doors opened and we entered a lift that took us to the entrance of the space shuttle. We were all extremely excited but somewhat apprehensive about our first flight into space.

CHAPTER 20

Winter 2060

The shuttle, designed for multiple uses, was the workhorse of the space program. Its primary function was to transport supplies to the outposts that were in orbits around the outer planets or the asteroid belt and then return to Earth with raw materials. They traveled at economic speeds, which made them exceptionally efficient.

Our shuttle, however, contained a compartment much like a commercial supersonic aircraft but could travel much faster. The passenger compartment of our shuttle had eight individual recliner seats, similar to first class sleeping lounges used on commercial transports. However, they were arranged in groups of two separated by a large aisle. There were handgrips located on either side of the aisle, which made it possible to maneuver up and down the aisle more comfortably while at zero gravity.

At the rear of the passenger compartment, a double air lock separated the toilet compartment from the passenger area. This was a safety measure to insure that the passenger compartment remained uncompromised due to our lack of toilet training. In the unlikely event that moisture would escape in the toilet compartment, the vacuum system could remove any unwanted materials.

We found the seats to be very comfortable and buckled ourselves into them, preparing for liftoff. A few minutes after liftoff, Mirjam and I looked out our window and watched, as the Earth became a bright blue ball suspended in the blackness of space. We were weightless, held in our seats only by the restraints. We found ourselves speechless and thoroughly in awe of the moment. After a few moments Mirjam looked over at me and I looked over at her.

"What a beautiful sight," Mirjam sighed, with tears glistening in her eyes. "We are leaving everything we have ever known, Eric. I feel like an insignificant small speck in the enormity and vastness of what is surrounding this shuttle. But, I am thrilled to be entering this venture with you. Darling, my excitement is almost more than I can control."

"You are echoing my thoughts, Sweetheart, It certainly is a magnificent view," I replied. "I wonder if our new home will be as beautiful, from all we have learned, it promises to be."

A few moments later a woman dressed in a blue form-fitting uniform with an aerospace insignia printed on the lapel came floating by.

"Hello, and welcome aboard," she said. "My name is Ann; if you need anything just let me know. Would you like something to eat and some tea?"

The burgers were in vacuumed sealed plastic containers and the tea was chilled and in a cup much like a child's Sippy cup.

"This could be interesting," Mirjam said as she tore open the corner, along the dotted line, and pushed one bite of the burger into her mouth.

Each of us ate a very delicious veggie burger and drank a ginger tea.

"Be careful not to leave any crumbs," I quipped.

Everyone enjoyed our first meal in space and we all laughed at each other chasing down our crumbs. Fabian's burger got away from him and, embarrassed, he called Ann to retrieve it.

The shuttle orbited Earth several times giving us our last look then headed to the L5 location. We all said goodbye to Earth and after the sandwiches and tea, each of us took our turn to acquaint ourselves with the space toilet. It was hilarious when Gabriele lost her handhold on her way to the toilet and began floating up and made several summersaults in the air before the attendant was able to reel her back. One might wonder how we knew up from down! That was easy, down was the direction your feet were pointing. Once we settled in and buckled into our recliners the attendant checked to see that we were all doing well, and said that she would see us in the morning, which meant after eight hours of sleep. The lights went out and I reached over and held Mirjam's hand as we allowed the effects of our medicated patch to lull us to sleep.

Day 2 started with a wakeup call over the intercom and Ann's voice asked if we wanted coffee or tea. We ate a mixture of nuts, grain and dried fruit, drank our coffee, tea and orange juice and prepared for the activities of the day.

Then Ann led us to a large area in front of the passenger compartment where we saw nine space suits neatly arranged on hooks and suspended from the wall. We followed her with the aid of the handrail attached to either side of the room. Mirjam let go of the rail to get a better look at the suits and began floating away. I reached out and grabbed her with one hand while holding to the rail tightly with my other hand. Ann demonstrated the proper way to put on the suit. She attached a lifeline to the rail and with her left hand on the left side of the suit; she swung herself around so that she was in front of the suit and facing out. She worked her feet into the opening, slid them into the shoes, and pulled the lower part of the suit up over her lower body. She then worked her arms into the sleeves, attached the clips, and secured the seals on the suit.

Each of us put on an extra space sickness patch since it would be very undesirable if any one of us became sick enough to throw up while in the enclosure or in the space suit. Then each of us tried to repeat Ann's movements. Makoto was the first to suit up, followed by Serena. They each accomplished the suiting up on the first try. The rest of us had more difficulty but after two or three attempts, we all managed to get suited up. The suits were similar to the design used on the first space missions. The major differences were that they now combined the upper and lower parts into a single unit that opened from the neck to the crotch and had a built-in cooling and ventilation system. Oh, I must mention that space diapers were still a part of our wardrobe!

Ann inspected each of our suits and demonstrated how to move from one side of the room to the other without turning upside down in the process. We spent the next two hours (Earth time) becoming acquainted with how to maneuver in the suits.

At one time, we all found ourselves on the ceiling based on the orientation of the room. Makoto and Serena had been the first to suit up and they were the first to master the space swim. Gabriele and Makoto were having a good time walking on the ceiling. Even though we were all adults, there were a lot of giggles and laughter. Everyone had a good time. By the end of the two hours, we were all becoming experts at space walking and our muscles burned with exhaustion.

"You will probably never need to go outside the ship yourselves," Ann said after we all finally got into an upright position with our feet back on the floor. "After we put on our gloves and helmets I will remove all the air from the compartment to simulate a true space environment. After that, I will demonstrate the robotic glove that you will use when operating the robots, which will make all the out-of-the-ship repairs. Your suits on the ship are specifically made to your individual body measurements."

We 'played' in the space suits for a few more minutes and continued to check out each of our intercom systems. Everyone had gotten tired; maneuvering in zero gravity was a lot of work. After the compartment was again pressurized, we reversed our suit-up procedure in order to remove our space suits.

Fabian and I especially were interested in the robotic glove activity. It was substantially more than just a glove. Arms, hands and most of the upper body fit into the apparatus. We sat on chairs at one end of the room and a duplicate of a robot, like the ones on the ship, was at the other end. Monitors were in front of us so that we could not see the robots. We each took turns with the robots and directed them to do simple tasks. They unscrewed a nut off a bolt, tightened a screw, removed and replaced a bottle cap, along with several other tasks.

"In space you must remember to anchor yourself and have the robot anchored when doing any work in zero gravity," Ann reminded us. "Remember Newton's Laws of Motion."

Our second day in space was very action-packed. We were all dead tired and had not stopped for lunch. That evening we had a hearty vegetable soup and a very good tasting bean casserole, bread and tea. We all had seen and studied the ship's design and read and studied the dimensions. Fabian and I discussed what we imagined the ship to look like. We all fell asleep before the lights were out; we would near L5 in ten hours and would have our first glimpse of our home for the next thirty years. I had no idea of what to expect tomorrow!

We awoke to the music form the Final Frontier and Ann served us coffee and tea. We were excited, and eagerly awaited the first glimpse of our future home. The thought that we would finally see the ship energized all of us to the point that we lost our appetites and our desire to eat breakfast. Therefore, we all took a measured package of dried fruit and granola and returned to our seats after the morning trip to the lavatory. We then gathered in the observation area at the front of the shuttle and strained to see the ship. The Sun seemed extremely bright but nothing was yet in sight. After 45 minutes, we were able to see some small silvery objects in the distance, which gradually grew larger. The first thing, which became distinguishable, was the large rotating living quarters for the workers. Shortly, the ship, surrounded in part by the construction containment, came into view. It was hard to describe what I saw next because I had never seen an object this large!

Protruding out of one side of the construction containment were the biospheres consisting of a series of two very large torus shaped structures. Each looked to be almost 1000 meters in diameter when compared to the space construction robots, which maneuvered in and out of the containment. The two torus shaped structures rotated in opposite directions around the central hub of the ship and a stationary disk separated them. The rotating structures were so large that it was difficult to judge their true size but I recalled from our study of the ship's specifications that they were several hundred meters in radius. The hub extended the length of the ship and I recalled that it contained the linear accelerator and nuclear reactor. A smaller structure located at the front of the ship contained the command center and shuttle bays. The moveable containment structure was presently located near the center of the ship, and I estimated this structure to be well over one kilometer wide and it completely encircled the top and sides of the ship. Several extremely large circular tanks rounded at either end surrounded the central hub and extended behind the containment structure. Everyone was awestruck at the sight of this massive structure created from a grey metallic-composite material.

"We will be docking in 30 minutes," Ann informed us. "Please return to your seats and apply your restraints for the docking procedure. I will direct you to the conference room when we dock."

We would all be eager and pleased to walk around again. We circled the donut shaped structure that served as the workers' living quarters twice so that we could get into position for docking. After disembarking, Ann directed us to the conference room where we were to meet with the engineers and designers.

A panel of the engineers and designers went over the ship part by part and answered all of our questions. We learned that the command center, the smaller circular structure in front of the rotating biospheres, would be our home until after the engine burn. The command center contained eight living quarters that were much like those occupied by the commander on an aircraft carrier. Each time we accelerated, decelerated or the ship refigured itself we were to go to the command center. During those maneuvers, 'Albert', our computer, would give us directions.

"At the initial blast off, you will secure yourselves in your seats in the command center for the duration of the inertia boost engine burn which will produce over 3g,'s of force on you," the lead engineer told us. "After jettisoning the boost engines, the main engines will produce an acceleration of approximately 10 m/s/s and you will be free to move about the center. When the ship reaches the cruising velocity, the computer will then direct you to enter the biosphere. The transportation system on board consists of two small capsules containing four seats each and they each contain a small cargo area. They travel along a tube connecting all parts of the ship. Anytime you use the system other than going from the command center to the living area or the farm area you will need to be suited up. Everything is clearly marked on the control panel so you should not have any trouble finding your way. You will need to return to the command center when the ship begins the deceleration at the end of your journey. The computer has full knowledge of the ship's design and function and will interface with you should you need to clarify anything."

"Thank you for your assistance and information," Eric said. "When do we enter the ship?"

"Tomorrow morning," replied the lead engineer. "Ann will show you to your accommodations for tonight. We all wish you a safe and very successful journey. Tomorrow will go down in history as a giant leap for human kind. Again, be safe."

Ann showed us to our quarters, which were almost as plush as were those at the château, and told us to make ourselves comfortable. She gave us a map of the facilities, which contained a gym, lounge, library and cafeteria.

Ann told us. "After this mission, the proprietors plan to renovate these living quarters and add two major hotels with expanded recreation amenities and several fine dining establishments. They plan to explore the possibilities of using this facility as a base for sightseeing tours of the solar system. I am hoping to be placed in the position of the manager of the operation."

We explored for a while but we were so tired that we soon returned to our quarters for a good night's sleep before the beginning of our journey tomorrow morning.

CHAPTER 21

We were all up by 6:00 o'clock Earth time. I had not slept more than four hours; most everyone else reported that he or she also had had problems sleeping; the excitement was building. Jabbar was the only one that had slept through the night. We assembled in the cafeteria for a breakfast and sat at the table with several of the workers.

"You have to be the team that is going to use the ship that we are building," said one of the workers, as we began eating our breakfast. "My name is Josh Pryor."

"Good morning, my name is Eric," I said and I introduced the rest of the team.

Josh, who was sitting at the table across from me said. "Everything is repaired and back to its original perfect condition. There was no significant damage done to the ship, most of the damage occurred on the containment structure."

I could hardly take in what I was hearing. What damage was Josh referencing? We had never heard about any damage. It was hard to process what we were hearing; we were all looking around at one another with stunned expressions.

Rachael said. "What are you speaking of, Mr. Pryor, what damage and when did this damage occur?"

All of the team was asking similar questions. There was an abundance of voices occurring at the same moment, everyone was asking his or her questions with bewilderment and concern showing in their body language.

"About three months ago," Bill, one of the other workers, replied, "I was in charge of the repair detail. It was my opinion that you would have been told of the crash and resulting explosion. A supply ship accidentally crashed into the structure as several of us were finishing with the fuel assembly. Unfortunately, two of the ship's crewmembers lost their lives due to the explosion that followed; only three of the workers received minor injuries including myself."

"This is somewhat disconcerting," I responded after regaining my composure. "It is comforting to know that all is well with the ship now. What was the damage and how long did it take to analyze the damaged area and to determine how to make the repairs? It is so unfortunate however, that lives were lost and some of you workers sustained injuries."

A man in a lab coat, sitting at the end of our table, spoke up and said. "I was responsible for conducting the final inspection of the biospheres and I can guarantee that everything is functioning properly and has been now for six months. After the accident I headed up a crew that rechecked the biospheres, there was no damage to them, they are functioning properly now."

"This news is reassuring," I said. "We are going to have to have a while to digest this development and decide if we feel comfortable in proceeding with tomorrow's launch."

In speaking with the team about this most unfortunate event, several members had very specific concerns.

Serena spoke up. "I want to be able to communicate with the on-board computer. It does not have emotions like ours; however, it can interface with us and it would analyze and determine if there were any malfunctions."

"Couldn't the computer manufacturers program it to indicate that everything is working properly?" Fabian asked. "I don't want us to be circling around in outer space with no knowledge of how to handle an accident or something disastrous on the horizon. We have to keep in mind the history we have of the first space program and some of the problems that seem to us that they should have been able to detect before blastoff."

"Remember, Fabian, this is not your typical computer; it is not programmed in the traditional sense; it is designed to detect and analyze malfunctions in all systems," Serena answered.

"I feel that I need to be reassured that mechanically the ship is completely trustworthy in its ability to sustain all the pressures that outer space will throw at it," Makoto said. "Just how thoroughly have these checks and balances been discussed with the engineers, and how many potential problems have been ignored, just to stay on schedule?"

Fabian said. "I would like to make a visual inspection of the ship."

"That's a great idea, Fabian." I replied. "I will feel more comfortable if we can get a closer look of the damaged area. In addition, I will contact the engineers here and set up a time that we can have that visual inspection. Postponing launch for a day for us to get some questions answered hopefully will not be a problem."

After discussing this alarming news with the team, I decided that communication with Grant and then The Committee was in order.

"Grant, how are you, Alex and Chloe?" I began. "We have just been informed by some of the construction workers this morning about the explosion on the L5 platform a few months ago. Did The Committee inform you about this? If so, why didn't you tell us?"

"Yes, Eric, I was informed but was admonished not to mention the explosion to you because it was being taken care of and they did not want you bothered with this information because it was a trivial matter."

"We are not feeling that it is a trivial matter, Grant, so I asked the engineers for a visual inspection of the ship so they took Makoto, Fabian, Serena and me on a tour of the damaged area and explained thoroughly what had happened," I replied. "I plan to contact Mr. Merrill also. In your opinion, does the ship meet all the checks and balances for an immediate launch?"

"Yes, I have been convinced that there was only slight damage in the form of some scarring to one of the ship's fuel tanks," Grant explained.

Immediately following Grant's communication, I contacted The Committee.

"Mr. Merrill, we were having breakfast with some construction workers and they mentioned to us that an accidental explosion occurred on the L5 platform around 3 months ago," I announced when he appeared on the communicator screen. I have just now spoken to Grant and he explained the damage, now, can **you** assure us that the ship is repaired and sound and ready to go?"

Joseph Merrill answered. "I can assure you that the ship sustained only superficial damage and all is repaired and ready for your trip, Eric. We did not inform you at the time because we did not want to add undue worry and stress to your busy and hectic schedules since the workers restored the ship to its original state. The damage was due to flying debris scaring one of the fuel tanks. We were also saddened about the lives of the two supply ship crew members and the injuries sustained by the three L5 construction workers."

I responded to Mr. Merrill. "You should have informed us about the explosion when it happened, I am having some reservations about going ahead with the mission and I am having to try to calm some nerves of the other team members. We all need to feel that every possible measure of precaution has been done to insure that the ship is as sound as ever. I would personally feel more confident if the chief engineers and the repair personnel could convenience us that every effort has been made to rectify any problems and that this is not just a cover-up. Our engineering team members met with the chief engineer and toured the damaged areas. In all outward appearances all seems to be properly repaired. Can we be confidant that no other such attempts to disrupt the mission will occur?"

"I have to confess to you, Eric, that The Committee, Grant and I are under the impression that this could have been a covert operation to destroy the mission. We commissioned our security team to conduct a very systematic search of the ship, consequently, they could find nothing to hinder proceeding with the mission," stated Mr. Merrill.

After hearing from Grant, Mr. Merrill and the engineers I relayed all of the information to our team. After a lengthy discussion of the pros and cons, we were persuaded that everything possible had been done to insure our safety and success. We now had confidence that The Committee was on top of everything.

"Now, are the rest of you team members satisfied that all is a go?" I asked. "We are still within the launch window, so are we ready?"

"This entire endeavor is a project of faith," Makoto answered.

Every member responded with a 'thumbs up' and a resounding. "Let's go."

We boarded the shuttle that had transported us from Earth to the construction site. We had just settled into our seats and fastened our restraints when Ann welcomed us onboard.

"I will be escorting you to the ship this evening," she said. I will help you settle into the command center and will keep in voice contact with you as long as possible. I want to tell each of you that I have the utmost respect and admiration for you. This is a most courageous endeavor that you are undertaking."

"Thank you for those kind sentiments," I said. "And for all of the assistance you have provided us. There will be many other expeditions in the future. By then, I anticipate that you will be managing this facility and can wish future colonists the same success."

The others agreed and thanked Ann for her gracious attention to our needs. The shuttle support team secured and sealed the shuttle door and we prepared for the short ride over to the construction site and for docking with the containment structure.

"Look!" Rachael said as she drew our attention to the monitor in front of the cabin. "This is incredibly fascinating. This ship is now our destiny."

Mirjam responded. "That is a perfect name for the ship – Destiny."

A round of applause followed, and I said. "O.K., Destiny it is."

We saw the construction containment slowly moving forward by jets of gas. It came to rest and completely covered the command center. As soon as all movement ceased we docked with the structure. Then, as the airlock was sealed, we disembarked the shuttle into a tube just large enough for us to 'stand', if standing were the proper term to use. In a weightless environment up and down must be clearly marked. There were handrails attached to either side of the tube and we used them to propel ourselves along as we followed Ann. She directed us to a lift located at the end of the tube that would take us to the top of the structure, which now covered the command center. As we exited the lift, a transport awaited to take us to the center of the upper portion of the structure and then through another air lock that led down into the command center. The orientation of the command center seemed odd at first. The seats were located on the 'side' of the circular structure, which served as the command center. We entered, remembering that orientation was relative since we were in zero gravity. When the ship accelerated, an artificial gravity would force us to the wall containing the seats. Using this as a reference for down, we now had an orientation for 'the floor'. As we looked across the seating area, we noted there were doors that lead to the eight living quarters that we would call home for the next several weeks.

"Will we be suiting up for the take off?" Gabriele asked, remembering Makoto and her walk on the ceiling during our first encounter with the space suit.

"No, that will not be necessary," Ann replied. "All living areas are pressurized and after the g-forces of take-off, which will only last a few minutes, you will be in an artificial gravity much like Earth's gravity."

The command center consisted of two rows of four seats each, identical to the ones we had on the shuttle. Ann informed us that take-off would force our bodies into the foam-cushioned seats allowing them to conform to our individual body structures. I took the seat on the first row and to the far left; Mirjam sat next to me, followed by Rachael and Fabian. Behind me was Makoto and next to him was Gabriele, followed by Serena then Jabbar. Each of us fastened our seat restraints and Ann verified that our restraints were secure. She again told us that she would stay in contact with us through the initial phase of our blast off. She informed us that the shuttle would return her to the control center.

"Even though you engineers had your visual inspection and conversations with the chief engineer, I continue to have some apprehensions since we heard the workers' conservations yesterday morning about the crash and explosion," Mirjam nervously stated.

"Remember, Mirjam, the inspectors reassured us that the biospheres have been functioning properly three months before the crash and now for three months afterward," Rachael said, comforting her. "I take this as a good omen."

"But, the supply ship crashed into the structure while it was at the back of our ship, any damage would have occurred there, and not at the front of the ship where the biospheres are located," Mirjam stated, still being nervous and not totally convinced.

"Mirjam, I understand your concerns and think that we all have been shaken by this news," I said. "Josh Pryor told us that everything is back to its original perfect condition, and the ship was not damaged in the crash and explosion, just the structure. If everything were not in order, The Committee would not allow us to proceed. The Committee has been planning this enterprise for years and I feel that we must trust in their decisions. Remember Grant and Mr. Merrill informed us that their reasons for not informing us of this incident, was so it would not overly concern us. Are you still nervous enough for us to scrub the mission?"

"No, we cannot scrub the mission, too much has been invested and we do have the assurance from Grant and The Committee that all is ready," replied Mirjam. "I feel that we must remind ourselves daily, however, to be very diligent with our inspections of all the ship's systems. I suppose that I am just being overly protective of our physical and mental well-being, could it be I am being a worrywart!"

I stated. "You have brought to our attention that being cautious has to be a top priority and I thank you for that reminder, Mirjam. How do the rest of you feel about continuing our journey? We all have some reservations since we are stepping out into the unknown. If any system is in need of repair or attention, I am certain that Fabian, Makoto, Serena and I or any of the rest of you will be able to diagnose and repair the problem. Remember the simulators, we have all had specialized instructions in all of the systems, and our computer will give us assistance when needed."

Everyone responded again with a cautious 'thumbs up'.

When the airlock sealed, I looked over and saw Mirjam's eyes grow wider as Ann began the countdown, 10 – 9 – 8 –7 – 6 ----------.

CHAPTER 22

Spring 2061

The force of the inertial boost engines during the first few minutes of flight disfigured our faces forming unusual shapes. Mirjam attempted to smile at me and stick out her tongue. However, the face I saw was a mouth that seemed to stretch from ear to ear. Some light-hearted fun was definitely in order since our ordeal earlier that day! Our bodies formed perfect permanent impressions of us in the foam seats due to the increased force. Talk about a form fit! Ann told us that the fitted seat cushions would be useful during future ship maneuvers. The force of the inertial boost moved us out of the L5 location and on our way. We would use the sun as a slingshot and, with Albert's navigational skills, continue on the course to rendezvous with our new home in 30 odd years. The Sun's photosphere came into view and the image continued to expand on our monitor as we approached. Boiling clouds of super-hot gasses began to fill the area on the monitor. I knew that our course would take us around the Sun at a safe distance and that our shields would protect us. Nevertheless, inwardly, we knew that the shields had never undergone tests outside the laboratory, and this knowledge concerned us, especially Makoto, Fabian and me. The jets of gas coming from the Sun seemed to leap out and engulf the ship, adding to our feelings of alarm. In a few moments, our entire monitor filled with a vision of a bright-yellow glow. I crossed my fingers and so did Fabian and Makoto. I also uttered a prayer I had learned as a child, but had not been keeping in touch with God as much as I grew older.

With the pull of the Sun's gravity, along with our main engines, the ship would accelerate until we reached 10 meters per second squared. This acceleration would continue until we reached our maximum cruising velocity at which time the engines would close down and the biospheres would begin rotating, creating an artificial gravity. When the biospheres began their rotation, creating Earth's gravity, we could then move into our home, where we would live until we had reached our destination.

You may remove your restraints now and move around freely in the command center.

"Computer, may we address you as Albert?" I asked.

Yes, that will be nice. I am flattered.

"Albert, do you play chess?" Jabbar inquired. "It is going to become very boring here in the command center over the next several weeks."

Do I play chess? Jabbar, of course I do. I am always ready for a challenge!

While Jabbar engaged Albert in a friendly game of hologram chess at a table in the common area, the rest of us were eager to look at our quarters. Mirjam and I headed to the first door on the right and were shocked at how small the room was. As we entered, we saw a bunk bed, which looked to be about one meter wide, just large enough for one person. The bunk bed was located to our left, as we entered, and had enough storage space beneath it to stow our personal items. On the other side of the meter-wide aisle was a desk, approximately one meter long and equipped with a monitor, keyboard and a chair. To address Albert we used verbal commands; the key board's function was primarily for data processing. In the center of the wall at the head of the bunk was a sliding door that led into the latrine.

"I guess we are spoiled; this is extremely different from the living quarters at the construction site," Mirjam commented to me disappointedly. "Those arrangements were so beautiful and plush, just like the ones at the château. How are we going to manage this sparseness and these cramped conditions? That bunk is seriously too small for the two of us. In addition, where is the shower? The latrine is only equipped with a toilet and a sink."

"The bed is big enough if we lay on top of one another," I replied jokingly. "Let's go to the next room and look at it and then we can locate the showers."

Unfortunately, the next room was the duplication of the room we had just seen, but just in reverse.

"Somehow we can make this work," I said with a little concern in my voice, but trying to encourage Mirjam. "You take this room and I will go to the one next door. We will give this some thought and surely your engineering husband can figure a way to make some adjustments."

Our personal Items, which we had placed in the small carry-on containers, our changes of clothing and sandals were in strange lockers located near the entrance into the command center.

"Let's get our carry-on containers from the storage lockers and think about how this arrangement will work." I said. "Then, we can locate the showers."

"I am *not* going to be pleased at not having a shower in my room," Mirjam announced. "How long are we going to be in here? I have a feeling that all is not going to be as perfect as I hoped. Maybe I am whining, but with all the money this mission cost, you would think things in here could have been better planned!"

We left our quarters, still puzzled about the location of the showers and the compactness of the rooms, and saw Fabian and Rachael walking across the center on their way to the storage lockers.

"The quarters are going to be a tight fit," Fabian commented when he saw us.

"I agree," was my reply. "Mirjam and I were discussing how we were going to manage the sleeping arrangements. We could remove the mattress from the bunk in one of the rooms and place it in the aisle between the bunk and desk in the other room or lay on our sides very close to each other."

"I am still wondering about the showers!" Mirjam expressed again, with frustration.

"There are two showers located to the left of the galley," Rachael answered. "Each one has a separate entry."

"Ah, this is going to be a lot of fun," Mirjam uttered under her breath.

We retrieved our belongings from the storage lockers and returned to our quarters. Mirjam and I had already decided to use both quarters and stowed our belongings in the rooms. I went next-door and found Mirjam sitting on her bunk bed looking around the small room.

"No one mentioned this living arrangement," she said irritably. "I suppose we can manage for a few weeks. Again, how long will we be in an acceleration mode?"

"Albert will inform us when it is time to enter the biosphere," I replied, trying to change the subject.

We met the others in the common area and together we explored the galley and pantry. We also looked over the showers and decided that they would be quite adequate. All of us were greatly less than enthusiastic about our sleeping arrangements. With some creative planning, we could figure out a way to be together at night!

"At least we will not have to gather our food while we are in the command center, Gabriele said. "Makoto and I found three to four month's supply of everything that we might need stored in the pantry. All we will need to do is to prepare it."

When Jabbar finished his chess game with Albert, in which Jabbar lost, Serena was a little irritated with him since she had had to examine their living quarters alone.

"Jabbar, you are no longer a child, playing games instead of helping me locate our living quarters," Serena stated rather hotly. "Do not assume that I am going to manage all the household chores alone?"

Jabbar apologized to Serena and immediately assumed the task of helping her check out the preparation and cooking utensils. The cook top consisted of a line of induction-operated surfaces. They reported that we would have an adequate supply of everything we would need, exact duplicates as were on the mock-up. The dining ware and eating utensils were also the same.

"That will be a plus," commented Makoto. "We have explored the pantry and found it to be as well supplied as a small fishing boat. We will manage the food situation, now let us figure out how to manage our living quarters, it seems to me we are all having major problems in this area."

The couples were eager to hear if anyone of us had any brilliant solution to the sleeping arrangements. It became quite evident that that situation was consuming most of our energies.

Mirjam and I decided that we would sleep in our individual quarters and visit one another regularly. After dinner, when everyone had returned to his or her quarters, I was at the desk in the process of entering our first day's events into the ship's log, when I heard a soft knock on my door.

I was happy to see that my wife had become content to accept the sparse living conditions of our temporary quarters. It was my intent to make her life as pleasurable and uncomplicated as possible, after all, she had put her complete trust in me to lead this journey, and her contentment was of paramount importance to me.

"Come in, Sweetheart, I have been sitting here in hopeful anticipation that you would come for a visit.

CHAPTER 23

I awoke the next morning on my left side and curled around Mirjam's beautiful petite body. When she awakened, she looked at me with her large twinkling black eyes. I felt like putty in her hands.

"Good morning," she said and gave me a kiss. "I should go and try out the shower."

The night before, I had asked Albert to put the ship on a twelve-hour day light schedule with two hours of gradual brightening in the 'morning' and two hours of gradual darkening in the 'evening'. The exception to this schedule was in the sleeping quarters in the command center and later in the biosphere. In those areas, the individuals would control their individual lights.

Mirjam reached for the door and realized that she had nothing on, grumbling as she pulled the sheet off the bed and wrapping it around her she said. "Our wardrobe designers did not provide us with nighttime attire. It seems they have given us some latitude of figuring out some things on our own! However, this arrangement is very inconvenient."

"Sweetheart, I know how your brain works, you are probably already figuring a way to make some night gowns for yourself; however, I think our sleeping attire is just perfect," I said as I pulled on my uniform pants and headed for the showers with her.

"After we shower and dress we need to start preparing breakfast. Today is our day to cook," Mirjam said. "We need to hurry this along; some will most likely be getting hungry. We need to keep the troops happy and well fed."

I accompanied Mirjam to the showers, as she struggled to hold the sheet around her. The showers were just a few steps from our doors and we were in the showers before anyone else was up. Gabriele and Makoto were waiting outside the shower rooms when we were finished.

Mirjam prepared cooked grains with dried fruit while I located the almond milk, sweetener, and bowls. Breakfast was nothing elaborate but it was nourishing and it would be our staple breakfast for the next several weeks. I proceeded to make coffee, my style, which is strong, and received a few complaints, but oh, well; the cook has the discretion to decide things like that, maybe these 'adolescents' will grow up!

"You cannot believe what Rachael and I found last evening," Fabian said, as we were finishing breakfast. "As you know, the rooms are in pairs sharing a common wall. The space on the wall beside the desk has a framed-in doorway. Rachael and I used a serrated knife from the galley and cut an opening in the acoustical fiberboard. It is not a finished job but we now have a doorway between our rooms."

Makoto and Jabbar immediately found knives in the galley and began their room modification. I did the same as soon as Mirjam and I had finished cleaning the galley.

Later, Mirjam checked the storage locker to get a sheet replacement. She discovered an ample supply of linens. She took a sheet to replace the one she had used this morning getting to the showers.

"I am going to take this sheet and our soiled clothing to the laundry room," Mirjam said. "Eric, honey, will you retrieve them in 30 minutes, please."

Our laundry room consisted of an all-in-one unit that washed and dried in one operation; it even added the correct amount of cleaning and softening solutions. All one had to do was to push the correct button. It was located at the back wall of the pantry, reached from a door opening from the common area.

Mirjam took another sheet, which she folded in half from end to end and cut a half circle in the middle of the fold. She cut the bottom portion of the sheet into even strips that would work perfectly to make a sash. This made a covering to wear when the uniforms were not wanted. The women liked Mirjam's fashion statement and proceeded to copy her design. We now had day and nighttime attire. I overheard the women talking about the amazing material used to make the sheets and other linens. They commented that the material was extremely strong and did not fray when cut and appeared to be the same material used in the making of our uniforms. My thought was, no sewing required here!

After I retrieved the laundry, I returned to our apartment, put it away, went to our desk and checked the monitor about our progress.

"Albert, will you give me a progress report on our journey around the Sun?" I asked. "This is the first time for this maneuver and Fabian and I am curious about the calculations, we certainly do not want to be drawn into or to form an orbit around the Sun."

I know that the calculations are correct. I am in control of the ship and can maneuver it whenever necessary and make adjustments to maintain the desired orbit.

The World Space Program had placed several probes into orbit around the Sun but no one had ever used the Sun as a slingshot into interstellar space, because no one had ever gone into interstellar space before, we were the first. We were on schedule to approach our closest encounter with the Sun in a few hours. Albert indicated that everything was as planned but I was moderately apprehensive.

Fabian walked into our apartment and was standing behind me, listening, and he shared my uneasiness. Everyone was aware that the first leg of our journey would take us around the Sun but Fabian was concerned and so was I; however, we had not made our concerns known to the others. We had temporarily lost communication with Earth but we should soon be able to resume contact; the reality was - we had our doubts.

Makoto walked by, heard our conversation, and asked. "Is our path around the Sun nearing the time schedule and is it advancing as planned? I have been having some troubling thoughts and trying to confirm our path."

"Come on in and join us, Makoto," I said. "We can always use another brilliant engineer to help us determine if everything is proceeding correctly; Albert has just informed us that everything is as it should be."

When communication resumed and I was able to continue my daily log of our activities, Albert forwarded the message to Earth.

"Albert, will you please establish a video-com connection with Grant," I requested.

A short time later, the desk monitor blinked on and Grant appeared.

Grant greeted me with a "Hello, Eric and hello to you too, Fabian and Makoto, how is everyone doing up there, is it getting hot and how are the accommodations; how may help you men?"

"You know, since we talked to you about the incident that happened at the construction site, that there were some real concerns about our safety," I responded. "It unnerved us, especially Mirjam, and there was even some discussion about the mission being scrubbed. Please don't leave us in the dark when something of this magnitude happens; we need to be informed."

Grant replied, by giving a more complete explanation of the incident, which reassured us even further, that the ship had escaped without damage.

"I have some other information that I learned about yesterday and need to dispatch it to the team," Grant continued. The communication is rather lengthy so rather that verbally relay the information, I will send it as a text. We will talk again soon."

Grant's text was somewhat alarming. It began:

Tom received this message on the video-com in his office. *"Inform Joseph Merrill that I know about The Committee. I am responsible for the ship's accident at the construction site. Too bad the charge did not destroy your efforts at contaminating the galaxy. Your companies have already destroyed the Earth and the other planets of the solar system. Your project is squandering the remaining resources of the Earth while poor people are still starving. By the way, we are experts on avalanches."*

The Environmental Advisors

Eric, "When Tom advised Mr. Merrill of the message, he asked the chairperson what he wanted him to do about this. Mr. Merrill replied that he wanted Tom to find out how the E.A. acquired the information about the construction site and the possibility of any sabotage to the ship. Mr. Merrill informed Tom to contact him, Alex and me as soon as he had any informative answers. He also wanted your team to be informed."

I immediately relayed the information in the text message from Grant to the team and they were all relieved by his clarification that the ship had escaped damage; however, the new information involving E.A. had deeply concerned everybody involved in our mission.

We were several million kilometers from Earth by now and were leaving the solar system, never to return when we received the next text from Grant.

The monitor signaled:

"Hello to Eric and the team, Tom has been working diligently on the investigation detail that Mr. Merrill assigned him. Do you remember Sonya, the daughter that visited her parents at the château and assisted with the serving of the dinner, when you were there meeting with the designers of the ship. Anton Harloff, the former European director of the E.A., had recruited her and assigned her the task of acquiring information about Mr. Merrill's association with large corporations. The E.A. had decided earlier to investigate

20 of the wealthiest citizens in the world. The E.A. agent assigned to investigate Akalina Vasin, an original member of The Committee, found her vulnerably to be her young teenage daughter. The E.A. kidnapped her daughter, Elaina, and contacted Akalina Vasin with a ransom note demanding that she divulge her knowledge of the Saturn Aerospace Corporation, who was developing a new space engine. The kidnappers tortured Elaina until Akalina divulged her knowledge of the space engine and consequently the construction at L5. Eventually, after a couple of weeks, the kidnappers released Elaina; Ms. Vasin quickly resigned from her corporate position; and she, and her daughter went into seclusion."

"You further need to know that Sonya introduced Richard and Susann to Mr. Harloff, but at this time we are not certain whether or not they divulged any information that they know about The Committee and your mission."

"Additionally, Tom was unable to determine whether the E.A. ever sabotaged the ship. The Committee strongly recommends that you search the ship thoroughly for explosives. Also would recommend that you very diligently scrutinize all systems on a regular basis."

"Wishing you a successful mission," The Wickham Family

We immediately set up a schedule of checks and balances for the systems of the ship. We began a thorough search of the interior of the command center and conferred with Albert about using his robotic eyes and senses for the detection of any explosive devices on the exterior of the ship. The revelations which Grant had texted us were overwhelming. However, I kept my anxiety to myself, not wanting to arouse unnecessarily the concerns in the others but wanting to keep a calm and positive attitude. Fabian and I became sounding boards to one another even more after these troubling reports.

On the third day after passing the Sun, I turned on the large monitor, located above the seating area, and asked Albert to fix on Earth. We watched, mesmerized, as the majestic blue ball, we had known as home, shrank to a dot and finally disappeared from view, giving all of us an emotional feeling of nostalgia. The Sun had the appearance of a large, brilliant, glowing, yellow street globe, which was becoming just a large star surrounded by countless other stars.

Days became weeks. There was not much to do until we could finally move into the biosphere, which really was not a sphere but a giant wheel approximately ninety meters wide. Jabbar was getting better at chess, at times, he even occasionally won, much to Albert's dismay. We soon grew tired of Sudoku and Ken-Ken, but we had each other and that made the nights very pleasant.

Mirjam and I discussed when we should start our family. We were still old- fashioned enough to hope that our first child would be a boy.

"Eric, I believe that a girl would want her husband to be older than she, Mirjam commented.

"That may be true but the first children born will be only months apart," Eric replied. "We cannot assume that our children will have the same ideals as those established on Earth, a few months apart or a few years apart in age cannot make a huge difference."

"If we had access to the labs we could control the X-chromosome," Mirjam said. "Gabriele has perfected this technique."

"We will be moving into the living area very soon," I replied. "Maybe we should wait on starting our family until we move. I will check with Albert as to when we will move into the biosphere."

Shortly after I had finished my conversation with Mirjam, Albert announced that we would be moving in six hours. (Is Albert reading our minds?) The ship was still on a twenty-four hour Earth schedule.

The main engines will stop; when they do, you will again be in a weightless environment so remember to use the handrails. Make way to the transporters located near the airlock and push the button marked level A. There are two transporters located on either side of the airlock; each will accommodate four persons. When you have arrived at level A remain in the transporter until you regain gravity. This maneuver will take approximately thirty minutes.

Summer 2061

We removed our personal items from under our bed bunks and our lockers and then gathered near the air lock. Mirjam and I, along with Makoto and Gabriele, chose transporter number one, located to the right of the air lock. The others used transporter number two located to the left. As soon as we became weightless, we pressed the level A button and the transporters moved through the tube making several turns, causing a slight pressure on us. What must have been no more than five minutes, we came to a stop at the docking area of level A. We remained in the transporters until we felt the force of gravity on our bodies. Everyone was *exceedingly* eager to exit the transporters and explore our new living area.

CHAPTER 24

Fabian was the first one out of the transporter, but not by much. We were all out before his feet hit the (?), what I supposed we would call, ground. The transporter dock opened onto the common area. We discovered the area to be very inviting and comfortable, there was a slight breeze blowing with the temperature somewhere between 22 to 24 degrees. It felt as though we had arrived on a South Pacific island.

We gathered in the common area and were amazed at the size. The width of the living space looked to be at least the length of an average soccer field, maybe a little less. In front, as well as behind us, lay the living area, the enormous expanse of the curvature of the torus. Looking up, the ceiling appeared not to have a surface but had the appearance of depth and was uniformly illuminated. This was an awesome and beautiful area; we, especially Mirjam, would have no difficulty in becoming accustomed to this splendid amount of space after our cramped arrangements in the command center.

The designers had arranged the apartments much like the ones in the mock-up. Each apartment was a self-contained unit, which consisted of a bedroom, bath (including a shower), galley and private lounge area. Each lounge area had a monitor and access to the data banks. We could address Albert by calling his name and if we were not doing things to suit him, he would let us know about it! It was like having a parent looking over our shoulders, 'big brother'! It would appear as though privacy would be outdated, except in our private apartments.

Mirjam and I chose our apartment, the one nearest to the transport dock and to the right of the common area.

"Look what I found," Mirjam said as we were putting our personal items in the apartment's storage area. "These must be the maternity clothes Grant told us about. They look a lot like the ponchos which I made out of the sheets when we were in the command center."

"It looks like your wardrobe has more than doubled," I teasingly replied. "I have discovered the instructions on how to expand the apartment when we have children. Perhaps we can now get busy with this 'project'. At least, I'm ready, are you?"

"We will need to discuss this at a less busy time," Mirjam replied. "Keep the thought, sounds interesting to me."

"Gabriele and I want to check the medical facilities as soon as we get settled," Mirjam said. "If you don't need me any longer, we will be in the medical unit."

Gabriele and Mirjam used the transporter to go to level B and spent the next several hours in the medical facility exploring each cabinet and storage component. They found the facilities to be ultra-modern with robotic assist units capable of performing very delicate operations as well as the latest in diagnostic equipment; however, they were amazed at the lack of medications.

Rachael and Jabbar were in the chemistry laboratory next to the medical facilities. They were also astonished at all the sophisticated equipment that they now had at their fingertips.

"We will need to spend several days just to discover everything that we have available here," Jabbar said. This molecular analysis and synthesizer is much more sophisticated than what I am accustomed too."

"I have never seen so much equipment in a single laboratory," Rachael said, not believing her eyes. "Our labs back at the medical center were not this well supplied. This must have cost an enormous fortune. Take for instance this 3-D electron microscope and analyzer. We can be very thankful that The Committee seemingly had unlimited resources to equip things so beautifully, I remember their promise that we would be able to do everything here as we were doing at home. It seems to me that their promise has been fulfilled."

"We should be able to analyze the protein makeup of any plant and be able to extract and concentrate any wanted substance," Jabbar answered in amazement. "I am excited to get started."

"I plan to return tomorrow and start inventorying all of the equipment and supplies," Rachael said.

Because they could control the lights in the laboratory and medical center, they turned them off and stepped into the corridor that led to the transporter where they met Mirjam and Gabriele leaving the medical facility. The light in the corridor was gradually dimming as they approached the transporter.

"The ship's lights are beginning to dim which means that our first day at 'home' must be coming to an end," Gabriele said. "I have been so enthralled in our discoveries that I have forgotten lunch. I am glad that we managed to gather some of the supplies from the command center when we left. I promise to do better the next time it is Makoto's and my turn to prepare the meals."

When they arrived at the common area, Makoto had commandeered Serena's help and they had managed to make a vegetable stew from the supplies, which we brought from the command center. They were all enjoying a steaming hot bowl of stew when Fabian and I joined them. Mirjam was very excited telling me about the medical facilities and all of the sophisticated diagnostic equipment.

"We, Gabriele and I, will be able to diagnose just about anything we might need diagnosed," Mirjam said with a glint in her eye.

"While you and Gabriele were off playing doctor, Fabian and I were exploring the environment of our new home as well as double checking all the ship's systems and searching for explosives." I said. "This is quite an interesting place. We walked for three hours and arrived back here at the common area. There is a lot more exploration to be done; keeping a close eye on everything has become a much larger task now than when we were in the command center."

"That is very nice but Gabriele and I were *not* playing doctor I have you to know!" Mirjam answered emphatically. "Quit being such a smart aleck."

"I'm sorry," I replied. "I didn't mean to imply that what you are doing is not of the utmost importance in any way."

We all finished our stew with the satisfaction that all was well with our new home, we found no explosives and all the systems were functioning within their parameters. Serena, Jabbar and Gabriele entertained us with a new overture that Serena had composed during our confinement in the command center. The sound was brisk and made us feel like springtime and the beginning of everything new.

"How about dancing with me," Mirjam said as I yawned and stood to leave for our apartment.

"I guess I'm turning into an old man," I replied as I turned to her and took her hand and led her to the middle of the common area where we began dancing. "This is much better than I ever thought it would be, our accommodations are wonderful and spacious compared to our living area the last three months. Look, the others are beginning to join us and Albert is now playing the music, it seems obvious that Albert has all kinds of talents."

As I sat at the desk in our apartment, I started to record the log of our first day of living in our 'new home' on the ship. This was to become my nightly ritual for the next thirty years. It would certainly be more advantageous to converse with Earth without a cumbersome communication lag. I reminded myself to speak to Fabian about working out a solution to the communication problem tomorrow.

As I began daydreaming, my thoughts started going to all the 'firsts' that we eight had had together. I expected many more 'firsts'.

The texts that we had recently received had not completely dampened my enthusiasm about our mission. The text messages were somewhat worrisome; therefore, I would remind everyone to keep all systems checked and rechecked. I would post a schedule of system check assignments. Each couple would be responsible to monitor their assigned systems and log in the results on a regular basis and I would organize a search for explosive devices throughout the living area, and ask Albert to expand his search throughout all other areas of the ship.

CHAPTER 25

Before we started on our planned day of exploration, I called Fabian over and asked for his help in working on an update of our communication system.

"We need to speed up our communication to Earth by discovering a way to circumvent the very bothersome lag time," I said. "Do you think that Makoto, you and I can work on this and come up with a plausible solution? Are you acquainted with superluminal-communication?"

Fabian answered. "Yes, I have read about it but have done no extensive research on the subject. Perhaps Serena will have more input and may have even done research while working on her doctorate. I seem to remember her speaking about this while we were in the command center."

Fabian and I motioned over Serena and Makoto as we were discussing the communications project.

"Serena and Makoto, Fabian and I have been discussing a problem and we would like your input," I said.

"What kind of problem have you two gotten yourselves into now?" Serena asked.

"Fabian and I were discussing high-speed communication systems." I returned. "I asked Fabian if he were familiar with superluminal-communication and he told me that he was not but remembered you speaking about it in the command center."

"Yes," Serena replied. "I had been working on the mathematical model of a superluminal-communication during our down time, but I am not completely satisfied with my formulation as yet."

"Fabian and I would like to work with you on this project; if you and I can work out the mathematics, Fabian and Makoto can get it operational."

We spent the next day exploring the ecosystem of level A. Mirjam and Gabriele were eager to spend more time in the medical center but decided that locating various plants to help supplement the meager supply of medications that they had found yesterday would be more beneficial. Rachael and Jabbar said, with confidence, that whatever compounds the doctors might need, they could extract, isolate and purify them by using the elaborate equipment in the lab. Rachael and Jabbar located many plants, with which they were familiar and several that none of us had ever seen before. Rachael and Jabbar also collected samples and marked the location of as many of the unknown plants as they could carry.

"I will come back for the known samples," Rachael said. Jabbar and I plan to spend the next several days running tests to see what useful compounds we can isolate and extract from the plant collection. Everyone seems to be in very good health so I mostly will be looking for compounds that we can use in making antiseptics just in case some pathogens slipped through the quarantine."

It took all of us most of the day exploring the approximate three thousand meters around the perimeter of level A. I was thankful for Serena's wisdom in picking some mangos and papayas as we traveled along the stream that meandered throughout the living area.

Especially, since we had not thought to fix a lunch before we left the common area.

Mirjam said. "I am getting hungry. Why not stop and have a picnic on the grassy area by the small lake up ahead."

"I agree with you, I am getting hungry too," Serena agreed. "We should be about half way around by now.

"Not quite," I replied. "Yesterday when Fabian and I walked the entire circumference, if I remember correctly, this lake is about one thousand meters from the common area so we have approximately two thousand meters to go before making the complete circle."

"We are going to need to restrict our children from coming here unsupervised," Mirjam said.

"Mirjam, are you telling us something?" Rachael asked.

"No," Mirjam replied. "But, I am sure this will be in all of our futures very soon."

After lunch, we continued through orchards and nut trees intermixed with tropical vegetation. The undergrowth was getting more and more dense each step we took and we were becoming so engrossed in our exploration that we had forgotten about the time until the "sun" began to grow dimmer.

"We should move faster before it gets dark," I commented. "It might be difficult to find our way through the dense undergrowth in the dark; we only have about an hour and a half remaining before the darkness overtakes us."

An hour after I had made that comment, the light was almost gone and there was no sign of the common area; it was quickly becoming very dark.

"Albert, can you make a moon and stars for us?" I asked

I certainly can. How many moons do you want and what part of the heavens do you want the stars to represent? Do you want them depicting the Earth's sky or the sky of the new world?

"You know what the new world will look like?" I asked.

Certainly, just tell me what you want.

"We would like the sky to represent the new world," I replied.

"Look," cried Serena. "There are two moons glowing brightly, one is large and the other one is smaller. In addition, the stars are magnificent, and so many, but they are not located in anyway similar to the ones we always saw from Earth. What a strange feeling, we have another area to explore and learn to recognize so we can teach our children."

Gabrielle exhaled a long-held breath and said, "I am so amazed at the sight of our beautiful sky, it is wonderful and romantic beyond belief, we are so privileged to be having this experience."

Soon we were back to the common area and home. Fabian and Rachael prepared a delicious meal from the lentils, which had been set on a timer to begin simmering over low heat until done. They also prepared a large fresh salad with a dressing made of lime juice and avocado oil; the pita bread, leftover from the command center, rounded out the meal. We sat and admired the sky of our new home. The most notable part was the two moons. It was beautiful but astonishingly different from what we were familiar to seeing on Earth, so many areas to take in and wrap our minds around, we will probably become so accustomed to the beauty of our new sky that we will forget our old way of viewing a sky.

"Jabbar and I want to do some further mapping of strategic plant locations tomorrow," Rachael said as she and Jabbar began organizing the collection that they had acquired before it became dark. "We want to start our analysis of the new species as soon as possible."

"Do you need any help?" Serena asked. "I could bring a data book, input the data and map the locations as you discover wanted specimens."

"That will be great," Rachael replied.

"Makoto, Fabian and I will explore level B and see what is growing in the farm and determine what we will need to plant," I stated. "While we are there, we will take the opportunity to begin our search for any explosive devices which may have been left by any E.A. sympathizers."

"We are going to have to replenish our pantry soon," I continued. "Mirjam, you and Gabriele will probably want to spend time in the med center tomorrow. So, do you have any ideas as to what we need to look for since the two of you have agreed to be responsible for most of the evening meals?"

"You're right, Eric," Mirjam replied. "Gabriele and I do need to spend some time in the med center familiarizing ourselves with what equipment and supplies are there and where they are located. In answer to your question, look for rice, beans of all types, corn and tomatoes. In addition, I hope there is some wheat that is ready for harvesting; we are about out of flour; and, as always, look for some luscious fruit and melons."

Serena mentioned. "While I am out collecting data with Jabbar and Rachael I could also try my luck fishing since I saw several fish swimming near the lake."

"Serena, fish would be a very nice addition to tomorrow night's meal, thank you. Gabriele and I will plan a special meal, with Eric and Makoto's help of course," Mirjam excitedly said.

When Mirjam and I returned to our apartment, I sent the daily log back to Earth; we had not yet received any additional communication from The Committee or Grant, concerning the possibility of sabotage by the E.A. Tomorrow Makoto, Fabian and I would begin a thorough search for explosive devices.

CHAPTER 26

The next morning Mirjam and I took the first transporter and Fabian, Makoto and Gabriele took the second one. At the medical center, Makoto and I kissed our wives good-bye and told them to have a good day and that we would be back by dinnertime. We left the transporter corridor that contained the labs and medical center and headed counter clockwise around the farm ring. It was an awesome sight; it looked like a gigantic hot house, like those we were familiar with in northern Europe. As far as the eye could see, there were fields of every imaginable vegetable and herb.

We had no problem finding all of the items that Mirjam had asked us to locate. There were handcarts, small baskets and gardening equipment in the supply shed next to the door into the transporter corridor, and we took one of the carts and four of the baskets and began filling them with items from Mirjam's list. We collected fresh corn and tomatoes along with okra and several varieties of beans and filled the baskets to overflowing. A thought came to my mind again, a big 'thank you' for the thoroughness of the planners and designers that The Committee had commissioned. Makoto mentioned feeling the same thankfulness to The Committee.

"We are just a few hundred meters from the transporter corridor," I said. "One of us should take the produce back to the galley. I don't want to have to carry everything around all day, while we are exploring the farm, also the vegetables need refrigeration.

"There is not a lot of room in the transporter," Fabian said, "One of us should stay here. Makoto and I will deliver the produce, gather a melon or two and pick some oranges and then we can continue our tour of the farm."

We transferred the baskets of produce to the transporters, and as soon as Fabian, and Makoto left for the galley I headed for the medical center.

><

"I believe I am getting accustomed to this robot," Mirjam said to Gabriele as she manipulated the robot's arm to remove the appendix in the life-sized and anatomically correct human replica. I cannot comprehend how easy and with such accuracy, this robot responds to my commands. It is a much-improved model than the one we used in Geneva. I hope we never have to use the surgical robots but I am pleased to know that they work with such precision, I could not do better by myself."

"When you finish, put him back together," Gabriele said mischievously. "I would like to replace a heart valve. I did not have an opportunity to practice with the robots when we were doing our residency training in Geneva. Perhaps you can assist with my surgical undertaking. I will be performing this, using a minimally invasive procedure. Didn't you say that the robots are capable of also doing stand-alone surgery?"

"Yes." Mirjam replied. "And, I'll be happy to be your assistant. While in Geneva, I observed several stand-alone surgeries. Markers, implanted in the patient, provided a guide for the computer-driven robot; and a cradle, specifically made for the patient, kept him or her in the correct position. The robot has sensors that give it the sensitivity of human hands and eyes. Actually, the results of robotic surgeries are just as successful as traditional surgeries, or often superior."

I found Mirjam as she was finishing her surgical procedure using the surgical robots; she was surprised and startled to see me.

"I was thinking over our conversation, which we had the other evening about the possibility of artificially determining the sex of our first child and the fact that you would prefer a boy because he would be older, or at least the same age, as his future wife," I whispered to her.

"You could obtain a sample and I will ask Gabriele to work her magic," Mirjam replied.

We discussed the pros and cons for a few more minutes, and then I gave her a quick squeeze, patted her backside, and left the medical center to meet Fabian and Makoto. My evenings were going to start being much more pleasant!

><

Fabian and Makoto returned shortly and I met them at the transporters. We retraced our steps and after walking a short distance the vegetation changed from row crops to tanks of wheat in various stages of maturity, followed by oats, rice and a small field of flax, all grown in hydroponic tanks.

"I am not sure that I would have recognized the flax," Makoto said. "I am glad that each field is labeled and includes harvesting and replanting instructions, everything we find has been painstakingly developed and well-designed."

"I have used flax grain in cooking," Fabian said. "Isn't it also used to make linen fabric?"

"I believe that's true" I replied. "All that I know about making fabric is what we learned during our life skills training, so we should ask our 'resident expert', Albert."

"First, we will need to make a thread out of the fiber and then we will need a loom," Fabian said. "I will check the inventory list for a loom when we get back."

"If we are going into the fabric business we should also look for cotton," Makoto said with a little skepticism in his voice.

"I have no doubt that we can figure out how to make cloth, with Albert's stored information," I said with confidence.

We had gone approximately one hundred meters further, when a small area of cotton appeared, followed by an open area covered with a mesh-like fiber. This area backed up against the algae basin which was used to help supplement the oxygen supply. Beyond the algae basin was a blank wall.

"This wall must be the back side of the laboratories, and isn't that a door located between the algae basins?" I questioned. "We can check out where that leads later."

"By my calculations we are just shy of three thousand meters." Fabian replied.

"At least we know that we can grow cotton," I said. "I am going to look for cotton seeds when we return to the supply shed. There is enough open area to expand the cotton field, that is, if we can make or find a spinning wheel and loom and if we can learn how to make fabric, which I am confident that we can."

><

Rachael, Serena and Jabbar spent the morning locating and mapping the location of plants that they expected would be useful in preparing medications. By lunch, they arrived at the lake and after feasting on the fresh fruit and leftover breakfast bread, Serena began her fishing expedition using the small seine, which she had located in the supply shed. After a few minutes, she was very excited that she had enough fish for everyone.

With a reluctance to leave Jabbar, Serena said. "I will take the fish back to the galley and clean them for Mirjam and Gabriele to prepare for dinner if the two of you will not need me to stay. The fish will not keep until evening."

"We can manage," Jabbar said reassuringly and gave her a quick kiss. "We will be finished here in a few hours. What we don't complete today can be finished tomorrow. We have collected enough specimens already to fill several days of lab work. Why not contact Eric when you are finished with the fish and tell him that you will come to help them search for explosive devices, your expertise may be needed."

Everyone was back in the common area before the sun began to dim. Mirjam and Gabriele closed the medical center by the middle of the afternoon, returned to the galley and began dinner preparations. We ate the fish prepared with fresh coconut sauce; spiced okra; potatoes with spiced spinach; and accompanied with the last of our rice. What a meal! Quickly, the spicy Indian cuisine was becoming a very appetizing favorite. The final addition to this luscious meal was a mango sorbet served with coffee made from freshly roasted coffee beans. The odors permeating the common area were nothing short of spectacular. This certainly diminished our trepidation of having to live on a bland diet.

"We are going to have to go grocery shopping," Mirjam said lightheartedly. We need flour, oil, sweetener and rice. We will need to begin the harvesting of the crops soon. The fresh corn, tomatoes and beans, along with the melons will make a good meal for tomorrow."

"I need to look over the workshop and electronics lab," I said with some frustration in my voice. "There are several projects that Fabian and I have not been able to work on or even to itemize the equipment; we are getting anxious to get things moving. Fabian and I have given a cursory look and we recognized a computer controlled shaper lathe, a precision milling machine and a 3-D duplicator-copier. I would like to continue my fuel cell research as soon as possible. Serena suggested to Fabian and me that we design and build a 'sniffer' device, which can detect explosive devices, patterned after Albert's robotic nose. She even suggested that we could borrow a sensor from his 'nose' for this purpose. This has to take top priority before we can continue with any of our other projects. It seems to take an extraordinary amount of time to finish our daily chores. Of course, we will still have to allow time to gather and prepare our meals."

"Gabriele and I will not need to be in the medical center all of the time," Mirjam replied. "We can help harvest the wheat and rice; you men will not have to be full-time farmers, Eric."

"Everyone will need to be involved during harvest," I said. We should start after breakfast tomorrow; perhaps we can get an early start and speed things up a bit."

The hydroponic tanks were two by three meters and came equipped with a set of cutting shears attached to guide-wheels, which rolled along the top of the three-meter side. By adjusting the cutting speed and blade movement, we were able to remove the top of the mature stalks and catch the heads in a tray that moved behind the cutters. It was not difficult to lift the cutting apparatus and move it to the next tank. Fabian and I operated the cutting tool while Mirjam and Rachael gathered the cut grain. Makoto and Gabriele managed to separate the grain from the chaff while Jabbar and Serena checked the drying process in the drying ovens, located near the tanks. By the end of the day, we were almost finished with the wheat and rice harvest. None of us was accustomed to this much physical labor. All of us voiced a new appreciation for farmers and agricultural workers.

Serena's 'sniffer' was operational by the second day of harvest and on the third day, the 'sniffer' detected an anomaly under the back corner of one of the flax tanks located against the outside of the torus. She summoned all of us to assist her in locating the anomaly. Fabian lay on his back and worked his way under the tank. It was a very tight fit, so he used his heels to push himself forward until he could find what the 'sniffer' had discovered. A moment later, he scurried out, looking as though the blood had drained from his face.

"What is wrong, what happened to frighten you so?" Rachael inquired.

"There's a large charge of plastic explosives set on a timer and the timer is at '0'," Fabian said breathlessly.

"This is going to require a very delicate and tricky maneuver," I said. The charge should have already blown a very large hole through the torus wall. Serena, will you check the device and give us your recommendation on how to handle this problem?"

"There must have been a malfunction in the timer switch," Serena said after she crawled under the tank to make her assessment of the device. The charge could detonate at any time. Time is at a premium, we must attempt to disarm it a.s.a.p."

"Does anyone know anything about disarming explosives?" I asked.

No one answered my question, so I consulted Albert after relaying a video gram of the device to him. Using Albert's input, Serena concluded that the device, set to detonate when the timer activated a primary charge, would in turn ignite the secondary charge.

"If we can remove the primary charge along with the timer we may be able to prevent the secondary charge form igniting," Serena stated. "Needless to say, this is a very delicate situation and we must handle it with the utmost care because the slightest jarring could activate the timing device."

Serena was able to disconnect the primary charge and timer unit and gently she removed them from under the tank. Makoto stepped forward and carefully took the primary charge and timer unit from Serena. A small blast occurred and caused a reverberating sound, which echoed throughout the torus. When we recovered from the loud blast, we found Makoto lying on the floor holding his damaged right hand. Gabriele screamed at seeing Makoto's injury and hurried to his side. His thumb and index finger separated from the remainder of his hand. Ligaments and badly broken bones held his hand together.

"We must rush him to the medical center," Gabriele cried. "He is beginning to lose consciousness and will need to be given some antibiotics and antiseptics soon."

"I will rush into the pharmacy laboratory and get the needed medications," Rachael hurriedly said, as she started to run to the laboratory.

I called to Rachael saying. "There is a door at the back of the flax area that Fabian and I are certain leads to the medical center, come this way."

Fabian hurriedly removed his shirt and wrapped Makoto's hand tightly to stop the blood flow. Gabriele stepped closer to Makoto and held his hand while applying pressure to his injured hand while Fabian and I rushed him to the door at the back of the algae basins with the expectation that it would lead into the medical center.

CHAPTER 27

I was the first to get to the door and was bewildered as I opened and saw nothing but darkness.

"What is this?" Fabian cried out as he followed me into the darkness.

We lay Makoto down outside the door and I searched on either side of the door for a light sensor but had no luck. As our eyes adjusted to the darkness, I could see that the room contained conduits, junction boxes and cables tied in bundles. We ventured farther into the room, feeling our way forward. I could make out the outline of a door on the opposite wall and prayed that it led to the medical center.

Mirjam was directly behind us as we reached the medical center. Gabrielle was running along beside me applying pressure to Makoto's wounded hand. I was supporting Makoto's shoulders and Fabian was carrying him by his ankles. He was still semi-conscious. Albert, somehow, knew about Makoto's accident and had the robotic medical facility prepped for us as we entered. Fabian and

I laid Makoto on the examining table while Mirjam and Gabrielle scrubbed for Makoto's surgery.

"Mirjam, I want you to assist me with the surgery," Gabriele said with urgency however, with the practiced calmness of a surgeon.

"We will use the robot to perform the micro-surgery of rejoining the nerve fibers and capillaries," Mirjam responded. We'll be able to rebuild his right hand by a reverse duplication of his left. Gabriele, please let me take the lead on this and you can assist me. You will be able to attend to all the support equipment we will be using."

Gabrielle began with administering the anesthesia and monitoring Makoto's vitals. Fortunately, the medical facility came equipped with a small supply of anesthetics and other medications. Mirjam used a 3-D fluoroscope to survey the damage and to scope his left hand to use as a reference for the rebuilding of the skeletal structure of his right hand. His hand had sustained severe damage by breaking the index metacarpal and damaging the trapezium and the trapezoid. She discovered severe muscle and nerve damage as well. Mirjam pinned the metacarpal, trapezium and trapezoid bones. She then ran an electromyogram to trace the electrical activity in the nerve grafts that she had just transplanted. With the aid of the surgical robot, she and Gabriele were finished with this most intensive surgery procedure in 90 minutes. Since Makoto had lost a moderate amount of blood, Rachael had started typing everyone's blood so a supply was ready if needed. My blood was a type A+, the same as Makoto's blood type, so I became his donor. Gabrielle began a direct transfusion as soon as the surgery was completed.

Gabrielle was exhausted and still very worried about the success of the surgery. Makoto had always been her 'rock' and she did not know how she was going to handle things if he did not recover. She had every confidence in Mirjam and her surgical abilities but this was her most dearly loved partner lying on the recover gurney, and she was a woman and needed to stay by his side.

Makoto regained consciousness in the early afternoon following his surgery. He was thirsty and wanted to know what had happened and whether his hand was going to be usable. Gabrielle reassured him that if the surgery were successful and with physical therapy, he should be good as new in a month. She started explaining the procedures Mirjam, the surgical robot and she had performed, but she noticed Makoto was nodding off to sleep again. Gabrielle was thankful that the anesthesia was still working its magic for Makoto so he could sleep and not be in so much pain. She stayed with him through the night after his surgery; I doubt if we, or even a Yale man, could have pried her away with a ten-foot pole. The next morning I had planned to help Gabrielle bring Makoto back to their apartment but when I looked up after entering the common area, Gabriele had Makoto cozy and convalescing in the seating area.

After the accident to Makoto, we were even more vigilant in searching everywhere for other explosives using Serena's 'sniffer nose'. We did not leave an inch unsearched: over, under and between every area in the farm and living rings. Albert's eyes and nose helped in our search of the outside areas. If the timer had detonated as the perpetrators had planned, we would all be floating around in space by now!

Three days later, we, minus two people, finished the harvest. Our progress was somewhat slower; however, we were all very relieved that Makoto, it seemed, was going to regain the use of his hand. All the mature rice and wheat were in the drying ovens and after dinner, we were in the common area listening to another beautiful arrangement of one of Serena's concertos.

I was sitting caressing Mirjam's shoulder as she leaned her head on my shoulder and whispered softly as she snuggled closer. "We are pregnant."

"Wow, that is wonderful news," I said with a knot in my throat, which I could not swallow. "You will be a wonderful Mom and I will try to be a good Dad, and together we will create a great family."

"Listen up everyone, Mirjam has just told me that I am going to be a Dad!" I announced.

All the couples congratulated us and suggested a toast of P.O.G., a combination of pineapple, orange and guava juices, for a successful pregnancy, a healthy delivery and a strong, beautiful baby.

Mirjam had an easy first three months of her pregnancy. She was gaining more weight than we had anticipated but we decided it was probably because she was not having morning sickness and nausea and her appetite was very healthy.

Mirjam's pregnancy seemed to be contagious. At breakfast, a few weeks after our announcement of being pregnant, Jabbar and Serena announced that they were expecting a baby also. I started the toasting for the new parents-to-be and their pregnancy; we would need to renew our supply of P.O.G. if this trend continued.

"I will help with meal preparation while Mirjam is pregnant, Gabriele," I announced. "I am a self-proclaimed chef you know!"

"I will still be able to do most everything, after all pregnancy does not mean that one is impaired, but thank you for the offer," Mirjam said with jest. "None of us has had any experience becoming or being a mother. Alex taught me a lot during her pregnancy and the birth of Chloe and I have helped in several deliveries. Gabriele is the expert when it comes to delivering babies."

"While growing up I assisted my mother with several deliveries in rural China," Serena explained. "But, I am concerned that I will not know what to do during my own delivery and then during the important first three months."

"We will need to ask Albert to help answer any of our questions about child rearing." Mirjam said. "I think the rest of the process will come naturally."

"Rachael, what are you waiting for?" Serena lightheartedly quizzed.

"We are trying!" replied Rachael, thinking that everyone should mind his or her own business.

The baby conversation continued for most of rest of the morning. Fabian and I took advantage of the moment to spend a few minutes in the laboratory. Neither of us had yet had any opportunity to inventory the equipment. I immediately located a 3-D interactive micro processing apparatus, the same as I had previously used at the university while doing subminiature microbial fuel cell research. Fabian also discovered equipment that he needed to continue his research on subcompact power supplies. In addition, we were busily attempting to complete the development of the superluminal-communication system. Serena's latest design looked very promising.

"Eric, I am happy for you and Mirjam," Fabian told me. "You will make great parents. I understand that you may be having twin boys, that will be very exciting,"

"When are you and Rachael going to start your family?" I asked. "It is my understanding that Gabriele is also pregnant. She and Serena are both having girls. My boys are going to need some more male buddies."

"That would be excellent," replied Fabian. "It is my hope that we will be able to start our family soon, I want children, and we have been commissioned to 'replenish our new home'."

"I have some exciting news from Earth," I announced as we gathered in the common area for dinner. "When Fabian and I returned from the laboratory this afternoon I had a communication waiting on my in-room monitor."

I put the message from Grant on the large monitor in the common area and we sat listening to Grant's communication and watched the holograph of Chloe as she played and jabbered excitedly. It gave us a feeling of contentment knowing that Earth was monitoring our progress. Everyone's excitement grew as we listened and watched ---

Earth to Destiny:

Alex, Chloe and I are doing fabulously developing the plans for the colonization. Although Chloe is only two, I am sure that she will lead the first colonists to the new world. Alex and I are still very disappointed that circumstances were such that we were unable to be on the voyage with all of you. Eric, I am keeping all of your logs in a data bank for Chloe. I made a full recovery from the sabotaged avalanche. Richard, Robert, Daniel, Sue and Michelle each are working either directly or indirectly with The Committee to insure that the colonization plans become a reality. We are happy to hear that your numbers are increasing, congratulations! In your next log report, please send an update on each member. How are you, Rachael? I am pleased to inform you that the police apprehended and identified the perpetrator who abducted you. Fred Kinland, a high-functioning psychotic, had captured several other young women in the past. His last victim managed to escape with non-life threatening injuries and she led detectives to his residence where they located the squalid basement where he had held you and the others captive. She selected him in a lineup with no hesitation, since she had been able to grab his mask off at one point. His trial climaxed last week with a guilty verdict and he will never see another day of freedom, he received three life sentences! I hope that this information will offer you some peace. We like the ship's name - it is very appropriate.

More from us later,

The Grant Wickham family

"It was nice hearing from Grant and Alex," Fabian said. "Doesn't it seem strange that it took all this time to receive another communication?" "I am glad to see that the remaining members of the team are still involved even though Richard and I did have our differences. I was almost ready to duel him for Rachael's affection!"

"I am not sure that the lack of communication really means anything," I replied. "They have been busy organizing the colonization efforts. Let's not try to read anything into the message that is not there."

"We have our own problems to solve," I continued. With four babies on the way, our lives are not going to be the same. We may need to suspend most of our work in the laboratories and concentrate on our families and their needs."

I developed a schedule that would allow the new mothers to spend the first three months being a mother. The expectant mothers designed a schedule where one would oversee the nursery, either allowing the others to continue their work in the laboratory or to help with the everyday needs.

We continued with our jobs since our time now allowed more freedom than it would after the babies were born. Jabbar was working in the organic laboratory extracting and isolating a compound that he believed would be useful as a local anesthetic while Rachael was using their map to locate the plants that contained compounds useful for muscle relaxation. Now that Makoto had regained much of the function of his hand, he and I had farming detail, although his hand continued to bother him with overuse. Mirjam and Gabriele were working in the medical center; Serena and Fabian were working on a small solid-state laser to serve as a backup in case one of the existing lasers malfunctioned.

"Why are you staring at me that way, Fabian?" Serena curiously asked. "You are making me feel very uncomfortable, please stop. And you are standing much too close to me."

"I am sorry; I did not mean to make you feel uncomfortable," Fabian replied as he continued to stand very close to her, pulled her into his chest, and tried to kiss her. "You are very beautiful and I admire you very much."

Serena pushed Fabian away fiercely and told him never to make advances toward her again.

"Rachael is very attractive; you should want to love her and honor her above everything, not looking at me or especially thinking about me in a romantic way, my heart belongs only to Jabbar," Serena returned. "I do not want you thinking that I, in any way, would be unfaithful or disloyal to Jabbar, _ever_. Have I ever given you any reason to think that I am interested in having a relationship with you? This could be a very unsettling situation if you were to continue having any thoughts about me that you should not have. We are all living in very close proximity and a situation such as this could completely destroy our social stability and make things most unbearable to continue living in harmony. You must stop acting this way, whatever got into you?"

"During the life skills training, Rachael was tender and loving but for the last several months she is either too tired or too preoccupied, she is not interested in me touching her or anything else," explained Fabian. "We have not been together in almost a year and I am getting very frustrated, I am a man with needs like all the other men here. To answer your question, no you have never done anything to suggest to me that you are interested in me in any sensual way, this is not your fault, you just happened to be the one near."

"Fabian, I am very sorry," Serena said with compassion. "Rachael said that she was trying to get pregnant. You are a handsome man but I respect and honor Jabbar and I am pregnant with his little girl. Fidelity is very important to him, and to me. We are such a small community; you just cannot have these thoughts. Above everything else, we must honor and respect the sanctity of the family unit, or jealousy and resentment will grow and that will destroy our relationships and the community we are building. It would probably be a very good idea if you would consult with our doctors, they may be able to help you and I promise you that this incident will not be spoken of ever again."

"You are absolutely right, I will seek Mirjam's advice," Fabian replied. "She was a great help to Rachael and me through her recovery after her abduction. Again, Serena, I am very sorry that I acted inappropriately and I promise this will never happen again. I let a weak moment guide my actions, I have never acted in this way before and I assure you that I will never approach you again; I am so very embarrassed and sorry. Thank you for being very understanding."

Fabian confided to me that he would like to consult Mirjam about his and Rachael's relationship. Mirjam had given him encouragement to talk to Rachael about her feelings and his feelings. Fabian told me that they had begun to have long conversations and that he was being very patient with her, letting her tell him about how the text from Grant that had mentioned the capture of her rapist had brought so many bad memories back to her. She was so enveloped with her thoughts and consumed with the feelings that she had tried so hard to suppress. After about a month of nightly conversations Rachael had come to him wanting to be intimate and her strongest desire was to be a loving wife to him and to have his children.

CHAPTER 28

Last week Serena and Jabbar became the proud parents of Dorri, an adorable little girl with long tendrils of thick black hair cascading down the back of her neck. Mirjam was now in the clinic with Gabriele and Makoto preparing to deliver their baby girl. They had decided on the name Miko. I was babysitting our two-month-old twin boys, Robert and Ravi. It was difficult to imagine that our small group had almost doubled in number. Life onboard was certainly changing, we now had four babies and a fifth on the way, Rachael and Fabian were now in their fourth month of pregnancy. Fabian's attitude and outlook on life had greatly improved over the past four months. No one had time to do any research in the laboratories these days, it took all of our time caring for the children and learning how to be parents. It was a fun and exciting time, however, and none of us had any complaints about parenthood, with the exception of less sleep time.

In addition, gathering fruit and harvesting the farm, just to have enough to eat, left little time for anything else. I was experiencing frustration with keeping everyone on task. It was somewhat more time consuming than I'd imagined. We had previously stocked prepared dinners in the cold storage. Fabian, Makoto and I had been working late at night revamping several of the ship's robots by converting them into workers to help operate the farm. The conversion was not straightforward but now we were able to use the robots to harvest the various grain crops mechanically, which allowed us to have more quality time to hone our skills at being dads.

We were almost settling into family routines. Mirjam, Gabriele and Serena took turns with the nursery duties during the day while the rest of us managed the farm and somehow found a small amount time to spend in the laboratories. That is, all but Rachael. Gabriele had confined her to bed rest during her fourth month of pregnancy. Albert was in charge of the farm robots, which had saved an immense amount of time and the robots could accomplish the job almost as well as we could; we should have thought of this idea weeks ago!

><

"Fabian!" Rachael cried out during the night. "Something is wrong, I am having terrible cramps and I am bleeding, hurry, go get Gabriele."

Next, Fabian called me to help. It was three o'clock in the morning when Fabian and I carried Rachael to the transporter. We met Gabriele at the transporter entrance and carefully put Rachael in the back seat with Fabian cradling her in his arms, trying to comfort her and ease her pain. Gabriele and I were in the front of the transporter for the two-minute ride to the medical center. There was a wheel chair waiting for us when we exited the transporter. Albert, with the aid of his 'Army of Robots', had opened the center and had an examination room ready for Gabriele when we arrived. It was certainly comforting to know Albert interacted with us by foreseeing our needs in a way that seemed unreal. After I helped Fabian carry Rachael from the wheelchair to the examination table, I returned home to help Mirjam with our twin sons.

Gabriele gave Rachael a mild sedative and began her examination. After a short time, she explained to Fabian that Rachael had had a miscarriage but that she was resting comfortably.

"It appears that Rachael has a lot of scaring as a result of her traumatic attack and rape; so the embryo was not attached properly," Gabriele told Fabian. "I am going to stay with her for the rest of the night and I will perform a minor uterine surgery tomorrow morning. That should correct any problems. As you recall, Rachael and Jabbar have discovered several medications. I will administer one of them, and it will speed her healing process and along with the present surgical techniques, she will be healed and ready to try for another pregnancy in three to four weeks. Fabian, she is calling for you now; I will look in on her after the two of you have a few moments together."

"I'm so sorry we lost our baby boy, will anything ever turn out good for us again!" Rachael cried with frustration, and with tears streaming down her face, as Fabian entered the room.

"I am sorry that you had to go through all of the emotional strain caused by your abduction and trauma alone," Fabian replied, kissing Rachael gently, and laying his head over on her chest. "I wish that you had talked to me sooner, I could have been of more comfort to you, please, never try to solve all of your worries by yourself, I will be here for you and I love you deeply and I want to share everything with you. I am also sorry that we lost the baby, but when you get to feeling better, we will try again."

"Gabriele told me that I should be healed in a few weeks and after that it should not hurt when we have sex," Rachael said optimistically. "I realize now that I should have talked to you about what was troubling me and that making love was painful. Women in my culture would never have spoken so boldly about such things, even with their husbands but I will learn to be open and share my feelings with you. Gabriele thinks that it would be wise if we had an in vitro procedure. What do you think?"

"I think that that would be fine," Fabian replied. However, I would like to try the old-fashioned way; making love has been a distressing experience for you and I could not figure out the cause but I am so happy you are on the way to recovering from some of your past trauma you had been experiencing and you should recover from your surgery in a short time, I am very ecstatic to have you healthy again."

><

Gabriele called Mirjam to inform us about Rachael's miscarriage. When Gabriele called, it was almost the time that we had scheduled to start our day. Everyone was curious as to what had happened in the early morning. We were becoming such a close-knit community that there were very few secrets. The early morning activities had awakened Makoto, Jabbar, and therefore the two moms and the two baby girls as well as our two baby boys. There was no more sleep for any of us! I held a town meeting and informed every one of Rachael and Fabians' disappointment. We were all heartbroken for the Granville's loss. I realized that we were a very focused and motivated group and that our mission was our primary concern; however, we had realized that living so closely we should constantly keep aware of the every-day needs and responsibilities of each family unit. Our group had become 'a real family'.

Several months after Fabian and Rachael's miscarriage, I stopped by the nursery when it was Mirjam's time to work with the children. She didn't realize that I was there. I was so impressed with her easy, confident way with the children. She had the four children sitting in little jump chairs arranged in a semi-circle, which were attached to a low table top, and she was passing around a toy kitten which I had made out of soft corn fibers, that looked remarkably like cat fur.

Mirjam had the children's rapt attention. "This is a kitten, it says meow, isn't it soft, it is white and has blue eyes. Can you point to its eyes?"

That night as Mirjam and I were lying in bed not able to go to sleep easily, because of the excitement of the day, I put my arms around her.

"You were amazing with the little ones today," I said.

"Mirjam, there is something that I have wanted to ask you," I said softly with a little hesitation in my voice. "Our boys are going to be a year old very soon. I grew up celebrating Christmas and birthdays and I would like to continue that tradition with our family. What do you think?"

"It is O.K. with me, in India we did not have such a traditional religious holiday, as your Christmas, but when I was a small child my family did exchange gifts near the end of the year. We have so many different backgrounds represented in our community. I don't know how the others will accept a traditional Christmas, but I do not think celebrating birthdays will be a problem with anyone. If it is important to you, then I will not object. Someday I would like to learn more about your traditions and celebrations."

During a conversation with Fabian and Rachael the next morning, Mirjam and I mentioned that we were going to be celebrating the birthdays of our twins next week. Especially now that they are were expecting at any time, Fabian and Rachael had also been discussing the idea of celebrating birthdays and Christmas but had not mentioned it to any of us.

"Rachael and I are excited about celebrating our children's birthdays and have discussed wanting to celebrate a traditional Christmas with our family," Fabian said. "Rachael is orthodox and grew up celebrating Christmas, in a similar way as I. We have discussed that our desire is that all of the families will want to celebrate holidays together."

Fabian and I took a lot of pleasure in making toys for the children. We made the toys the old-fashioned way, out of wood that we gathered from the trees near the common area. The toys depicted items known to Earth children, such as blocks, cars, trains, planes and of course, a space ship. We made tea sets and dolls, in a similar manner that I utilized in fashioning the toy kitten. We wanted our children to know and be associated with the things that Earth children grow up knowing. After all, by the time they became adults we would have established an earth-like colony. On the monitor in the common area, the children learned of life on Earth by pictures and dialog. The moms were doing a great job of early childhood training.

Year 2065, Fourth Year of voyage--

As a community, we decided that a formal education should begin when the children were four years old. By then, each mom and dad would have had time to nurture and bond with the child. Mirjam and I could hardly wait for our boys' first birthday and our first Christmas as a family. Mirjam suggested that we invite everyone for a special feast to celebrate the end of the year. She named the feast 'winter festival' since we were all accustomed to having four seasons with the end-of-the year season being winter. What a strange feeling.

The idea of celebrating a festival was a pleasant surprise for each couple and each parent was excited to make toys and special gifts for their own children, as well as presents to exchange with everyone. Preparations for our 'winter festival' soon began and took up our evening hours after our children were put to bed for the night. Since we had such an eclectic group, everyone contributed decorations, which they hand-made, depicting their original backgrounds. With the decorations and the gift making, our festival was beginning to take on a colorful array of fascinating trinkets and our expectation of adding to our own celebration began to take on a 'family' tradition of its own. This would be the beginning of our traditional festivities, which we would hand down to our children, and they, in turn, could add ideas of their own and pass on to their children.

The twins' birthday party was very exciting for Robert and Ravi, as well as everyone else. Two months after their party, we celebrated Dorri's birthday and shortly after, we celebrated Miko's birthday. Our 'winter festival' followed and our own traditions had become wonderful and thrilling events for us all to anticipate each year.

Serena and I made what we anticipated to be the final calculations on the superluminal communication system. Fabian had completed the construction of a power system capable of operating the unit. According to our calculations, the next log to Earth should take only 4.3 hours.

Our message contained the basic premise behind our new communication system with the expectation that physicists and mathematicians on Earth had been working on a similar system and that they were successful.

The Grant Wickham Family

Log 2065-5

Rachael and Fabian are expecting very soon. The older children are now one. We are communicating by way of a new system that Fabian, Serena and I have developed.

When received, please verify receipt.

Destiny

CHAPTER 29

Year 2069, Eighth Year of Voyage--

It was Mirjam's scheduled time to teach. Gabriele was managing the medical center. She and Mirjam shared the staffing duties and they decided that one of them should always be in the medical center during the day. Our twin boys and the two little girls were five years old and behaving as typical-five-year olds. Fabian and Rachael's son, André was advancing rapidly; having his older playmates as examples. Their attention spans were increasing sufficiently for a full four hours of instruction. They were grasping the rudiments of mathematics and their vocabulary contained several thousand words. Today Mirjam had asked Rachael to assist her in a lesson on botany using several eatable plants as a show and tell. At the end of the lesson, Mirjam dismissed the children and told them to play in the common area while she put away the supplies used in day's lesson. Robert had an adventurous temperament and usually assumed the leadership role during playtime. He and Ravi easily convinced Miko and Dorri to venture away from the common area.

"What will we do with André?" Ravi asked. "He is too small to play with us."

"We cannot leave him alone," Miko said.

"All right," Robert replied reluctantly. "Let's go but he had better keep up."

Mirjam lost sight of the children after putting away the supplies; she looked around the common area but did not see any of the children. She was not immediately concerned because they were accustomed to playing, keeping the common area in sight. She did not panic but made a second search around the area. Then she made a third search, by now, moving faster and calling their names, and becoming more and more concerned. She still could not see any of them. She became very frightened and the loud cries of Mirjam attracted Rachael, who had not yet left for the laboratory. They both frantically searched the common area; then began to widen their search.

"They couldn't have gone far," Mirjam said with a panic-stricken voice.

"They can't be lost," replied Rachael as she continued calling out the children's names. "We are in a rather confined space, there is nowhere for them to go."

"I am concerned that they may get hurt," Mirjam returned anxiously. "It is not like them to wander off like this, call Fabian while I call Eric."

When I arrived, Mirjam and I continued the search in the direction of the lake. We had not gone more than one hundred meters when we saw Ravi crying and running around animatedly, heading in the direction of the common area!

"Ravi, what is wrong?" Mirjam called. "Where is your brother? Where are the others? Why have you children gone so far away from the common area, you know you are not to wander away from your play site?"

Shortly after having questioned Ravi, Mirjam calmed herself and then quietly asked him again what had happened.

"We were exploring some of the plants from the lesson today, Robert is asleep, and we cannot wake him up," answered Ravi, still sobbing.

Mirjam and I could see the other children stooping over Robert, shaking him, as he lay on the ground, not far from the path, not moving. Instinctively, Mirjam rushed over to him, calling his name as she took in the surroundings, looking for some plant which he may have touched or tasted, might have caused Robert's problem.

"Quickly, show me where you were playing and exploring," I said to the other children.

They all pointed to an assortment of plants, which were growing near the water's edge about five meters from the path. Some of the plants had small red berries and other plants had dull-blue berries. Mirjam recognized the plants and remembered that Rachael had used each of the plants to extract compounds for making medications.

"Did Robert eat some of these berries?" Mirjam asked, still in a panic, pointing to the Daphne and Atropa.

"He only tasted one of the berries, I think," Miko said. "He was saying something like sweet but I could not really understand what he was saying."

Mirjam called Gabriele at the medical center, and said. "Set up for pumping Robert's stomach, I believe he may have eaten or at least tasted a belladonna berry."

Mirjam further examined Robert by taking his pulse rate, and noticed his swollen lips and dilated pupils.

With my heart pounding, I immediately picked up Robert, who was limp but slowly attempting to move his lips and hands. I ran for the transporter with Mirjam running along beside me tickling Robert's throat attempting to cause him to vomit.

"We will be at the medical center in a few minutes," I said trying to reassure Mirjam as well as myself.

Fortunately, Albert was a step ahead of us *again* and had a room already prepared with the aid of his robotic helpers. When we arrived at the medical center, Gabriele took Robert's vitals and found a slight pulse and an irregular heart rate. Mirjam was apprehensive and very anxious; she blamed herself for not watching the children more carefully and began to sob uncontrollably. I tried to soothe her but I was not much help.

Mirjam cried. "I should have been watching the children more closely; I should never have let them out of my sight, if Robert dies, I'll never get over this."

"Calm down, Sweetheart, Gabriele is taking good care of Robert, you should not blame yourself, he is just an adventurous and headstrong child, he'll be alright," I said, trying to reassure her, as my insides were still shaking and my heart pounding out of my chest.

After pumping Robert's stomach, Gabriele cleansed the intestinal and urinary track and administered a saline drip with frequent small doses of apomorphine. Robert lay semiconscious for three frightful days; Mirjam was so intensely worried and not able to leave his side and we could say nothing to persuade her that he would recover. I was in and out of the center, with my time divided looking after Ravi and trying to comfort him that his brother would be fine.

"In times like these I wish I were religious," Mirjam kept repeating as we sat by Robert's bedside.

"I want to pray but I don't know how to pray or to whom I should pray," She continued. "Eric, are you religious enough to know how to pray? Can you pray for Robert? What are we going to do? I do not know if I can manage if we lose Robert. What is going to happen to us?"

I was unable to comfort her successfully, although I desperately tried. I could not answer all of her questions and I doubted an answer would have convinced her anyway. While in a semiconscious state, Gabriele began very small doses of Jaborandi and Calabar bean extracts. By the end of the third day, Robert began to have an almost normal pulse and began to open his eyes. In another two days, he was out of bed and wanting something to eat. By the sixth day, he was up running around and playing as though nothing had happened-- kids are so resilient! Robert must have had an allergic reaction to the belladonna or to his injection, causing his recovery to be so lengthy. Mirjam was almost back to normal but was hesitant to be in charge of childcare. Rachael persuaded her that what had happened was not at all her fault so Mirjam reluctantly resumed her turn at teaching and caring for the children, keeping even a keener eye peeled for problems. Rachael and Fabian were a great help comforting Mirjam and me, having gone through the loss of their first infant due to their miscarriage.

I don't know what I would have done without their help. I was so worried about Robert and very anxious about Mirjam. I am thankful that she is recovering and able to assume her duties in the medical center. I internalized most of my emotions trying to remain 'the leader' but during the touch-and-go moments with Robert during the first days, I was not the leader I needed to be. Thanks to Fabian, every problem found a solution. I frequently continue to have emotional setbacks. What a responsibility I have! I have to constantly remind myself we are all just human, but I have trouble convincing myself to understand this personally. We need a plan to isolate harmful plants so that what happened to Robert doesn't happen again.

I continued to send logs periodically, although I realized that Earth might not be receiving our communications in a timely manner. We had not received a reply back from the log 2065-5. Fabian, Serena and I were continuing to work on improving the superluminal-communication system. As we finished what we expected to be our final adjustment, my monitor indicated an incoming message.

Earth to Destiny--Earth year 2070

Received your log 2065-5

We have returned the conformation of receipt using
equipment we built from your design.

Our engineers have discovered a 'bug' in your design. Enclosed
is a redesigned system.

We should be able to eradicate the flaws in our system and send
the first FTL message before our first hibernation.

Year 2071, Tenth Year of Voyage --

We began preparing for our first hibernation period when Fabian
and Rachael's son turned five. The designers of the hibernation unit
assured us that the system would accommodate younger children
but our original information recommended that children should
be five or older. We did not want to take any unnecessary chances.
All of the adults were prepared for what would happen during the
hibernation but the children were apprehensive and more than a
little on edge, especially André. Mirjam explained to Robert and
Ravi that they would be going on a new adventure, which they
had studied about in science. Both of Miko's and Dorri's parents
explained the hibernation process, reassuring the girls and answering
each of their questions, even though the children each understood
the 'fundamentals' of the process that they had studied during their
science classes. Fabian took special care to reassure André who had
told him that the hibernation chambers looked big and scary and he
appeared more frightened than the older children did.

"You will be taking a long rest, not in your own bed but in a new
type of bed next to Mom and Dad," Rachael said in a comforting
voice. "Dad and I will be right here in the same room with you and we
will be taking a long rest with you, then we will all wake up together."

Each family entered their own hibernation chamber and after
their showers to remove keratinocytes and hair, the mothers placed
the special breathing apparatus on their child, in our case, children,
and Albert began the enzyme and nutrient mist. We parents waited
until each of the children were asleep then we entered our own
tanks. I instructed Albert to awaken me in two years, followed by
Mirjam and the other parents. Our plans were for the adults to be
fully awake, dressed and alert before Albert awakened the children.

CHAPTER 30

Year 2073, Twelfth year of voyage --

A shrill sound in my ear awakened me out of an unconscious sleep. It frightened me, I could not figure out what was happening, I had trouble recognizing my environment, I was very confused and my eyes would not focus. Was this a dream? Where was I? I looked around trying to identify my surroundings. I finally realized that I was lying horizontally in a small tube filled with a sweet-smelling mist. My memory shortly began to return and I recalled putting on my mask and lying down in the hibernation chamber and closing the cylindrical cover and then everything going blank; but this was not how we were supposed to awaken from hibernation. Then, I recognized Albert's voice, sounding as though he were in my head.

Eric, do not be frightened. I have prematurely awakened you by only one day. A situation has arisen that needs your attention. I detected a problem in the second stage of the accelerator. My sensors indicate a loose cable and this has a potential to cause an immediate system overload if it were to short-circuit. The problem

needs your attention. My sensors cannot get visual confirmations of the problem. I have awakened Fabian also. Meet him in the suit-up room and the two of you should have ample time to make a visual identification and repair the problem before it is time to awaken the others.

"Albert, awaken Mirjam and Rachael also," I strongly requested. "They will be frightened; especially for the children if we have not returned from the repair of the problem and they are awakened without seeing us. In fact, go ahead and awaken everyone now, one day early is not going to affect the mission and if the children see their dads are missing, this could greatly upset them; they were apprehensive about the hibernation tanks to begin with. The moms will be able to calm the children's fears and this will also keep their minds occupied."

I met Fabian at the transporter and we discussed how to best identify the problem in the number two accelerator. Our decision was to use one of the robots, attached to one of the monorails, which ran along the side of the plasma engine to make a visual inspection of the accelerator. Fabian was more agile than I so he manipulated the robot as I looked on. Fabian suited up in the robotic harness and tested the response of the robot by moving his fingers, hands and shoulders. The robot responded accurately and Fabian directed the robot to travel to the number two accelerator. Each of the acceleration units had an access panel fore and aft. Fabian manipulated the robot's fingers and hands and on the third try managed to unlatch the front panel and swing it open. The robot's cameras displayed a network of cables but we could not detect the loose cable on the two dimensional monitor.

"It is unfortunate that with all of this expensive and sophisticated equipment someone forgot to include a holographic 3-D monitor," I complained to Fabian. "It is time for me to take a look."

Fabian returned the robot to its docking position, near the airlock, as I began to suit up to make a visual check. I trusted that with Fabian's help in manipulating the robot I would soon locate the problem. When we make our approach to 'Kairos' the malfunction of accelerator number two would affect the deceleration and would cause our approach velocity to be too great to obtain orbit. It was paramount that we repaired this malfunction. It puzzled me why Albert awakened us from hibernation a day early. It would be several years before we would need to decelerate, why was there a rush to fix the accelerator now? Why did the problem appear now? Our acceleration phase went as planned. My presumption was that a vibration somehow had loosened the cable connection. I thought that Albert perhaps wanted to test our reaction time and our ability to think after hibernation, sort of like a fire drill. I was leery to ask Albert why he awakened us a day early, however, suspecting that I may not want to accept his answer.

This was the first time since the flight to the space dock that any of us had the occasion to think about our space suits. With Albert's guidance, I managed to maneuver into the suit by carefully recalling the steps that were required to suit up properly. I finally managed the steps of sealing myself into the suit. I was preparing to exit the ship for my first official spacewalk when Mirjam, Rachael and the others appeared.

"Why are you suited up for a spacewalk?" Robert asked with uncertainty. "You just now awakened us; I thought we were all going to wake up at the same time. What is going on? How long have you been awake, and when did you wake up? Ravi and I do not want to be kept in the dark when things are happening; we are now old enough to know what is taking place."

"A problem needs to be fixed with a part of the engine," Mirjam said in a consoling voice. "Dad and Fabian were awakened by Albert and alerted that a problem exists in the engine. Dad wanted all of us to come out of hibernation early because he knew that this would cause anxiety, especially for the two of you, if you saw that your dad was not in the hibernation unit when we awoke. So, Dad compelled Albert to awaken all of us a day early."

"I am confident that it is only a small problem," I stated as I readied myself to enter the airlock. "The robot monitor is not three-dimensional and it can't determine which of the power cables is loose. So I am going to take a look."

"Eric, please be careful," pleaded Mirjam. "I remember that Ann reassured us that this type of situation probably would not happen; that we would not need to suit up and leave the spaceship. You have no experience working in space; you have had very little training."

As I began to leave the suit-up room, I turned, winked at Mirjam, blew her and the boys a kiss and gave her a 'thumbs up'.

I exited the suit-up room through the airlocks and attached my tether to the robot waiting just outside the airlock. Fabian manipulated the robot to accelerator number two and I clipped my tether to the eyelet on the unit.

"Fabian, no wonder we could not find the loose cable," I reported a few minutes later. "It is too obscured to reach from this side. Go ahead and direct the robot to close this panel and I will attempt to open the one on the other side."

I maneuvered my lifeline to the other side of number two and attempted to unlatch the panel by hand but the suit restricted my movements, not allowing enough torque to open the latch. I selected a wrench from my utility belt, anchored my feet securely into the footholds, and applied all my strength to the wrench handle trying to open the latch, which suddenly came loose, and I fell forward with my chest hitting the housing, knocking the breath out of me. All I heard were the screams of Mirjam in my ears, or was it my own screams that I heard? After a momentary period of disorientation, I regained my breath and found myself at the end of my lifeline tether dangling freely between accelerators number two and three. Mirjam's words of caution echoed in my mind. She was correct; I had not had any experience with working in space. My fear was not for myself only, but for my family and the rest of the team back in Destiny. I became frightened, feeling all alone outside the ship and in the vastness of space. I fatigued quickly, and I could not fathom the extreme amount of effort I had to exert to accomplish such a simple task. I could see the robot, controlled by Fabian, pulling on my lifeline reeling me in like a big fish. I began pulling hand over hand and soon I was back to the acceleration unit with my feet firmly in the footholds and searching for the loose cable. I located the troubling cable, which was in a spider web of different colored cables and wires. I could not readily determine how to reach it so I immediately consulted Serena, our electrical expert. As I moved cables around, she viewed the jumble of cables through the monitor, referred to the ship's schematic and confirmed my diagnosis. I followed her advice by disconnecting several wires to reach the loose cable, and tightened its connection, securing it. I then replaced the ones which I had disconnected and secured the panel in less than 30 minutes and I was finally on my way back inside.

On my way back to the suit-up room, my thoughts were on why Albert had not detected this loose connection earlier, instead of now. Fabian, Serena and I needed to determine how the cable could come loose. Was this another sabotage attempt, vibration or what???

Mirjam was waiting for me when I exited the suit-up room jumping into my arms and enveloping me with hugs and kisses. Robert and Ravi were impatiently waiting for their turn to give me their great big bear hugs. I walked them all back to the common area where the others were waiting. What a wonderful feeling to have a family who loves you this way!

"This is not the type of wakeup that I was expecting," Mirjam said, laughing nervously as we were arriving back to the common area.

"You don't look two years older," I replied with a smile. "Robert and Ravi may look a little older but not by much, maybe a year. You are as beautiful as the day I met you in Geneva. Prepare yourself, Sweetheart, for lots of romantic catch up time. I feel as though I have been dreaming about you and our love making during the entire 2-year hibernation. We will spend some time with the boys for a while, visit with the other families and then begin fulfilling my plans, O.K.? All the other couples are probably planning the same type of evening."

Mirjam gave me a sideways glance and the sweetest smile I had ever seen. "Of course, silly, you think only guys have been making plans! Make sure our socializing time with the others does not take too long, I am also pretty confident that everyone else has similar plans."

Everyone looked the same as when we went into the hibernation phase. Each parent examined his or her own child being very curious as to what affects hibernation may have had. There were no major physical changes except in height and overall bone plate growth as Mirjam and Gabriele explained to the rest of us. There were, however, some significant objections now from the children since they were older and wanted more privacy. Each of the older children appeared to be about eight years of age and André about six. Mirjam and Gabriele, with Albert's help, organized a mental evaluation for each of the children with plans to administer the tests the next morning. In addition, each adult would conduct self-examinations of his or her mental awareness as quickly as possible, and Albert, our unbiased source, would evaluate the results.

The women all were anxious to assess their living quarters to determine if everything were still organized and in working order. The children were very anxious to talk with each other about their hibernation experiences and my spacewalk adventure. After several invigorating games of 'beach' volleyball, they, especially the girls, were ready to head to the showers and a normal night's sleep. Some time for their own preparations for a lovely night of re-acquaintance with their spouses was also a major plan of the grownups.

Before we retired to our apartments, Fabian and I discussed with Serena the possibilities that may have occurred if the loose cable had remained undetected. We concluded that we could not manage the voyage without the help of Albert and his invasive sensors.

"Fabian, if the cable had come loose, the second accelerator would not have functioned properly, this would have affected the flow of plasma, and this would have altered our deceleration," I said with relief. "If the problem had encompassed a short, we could be experiencing all sorts of problems, now or in the future."

"There would have been a very good possibility that the ship would not go into the proper orbit or, the worst-case scenario, we would bounce off into space, never to reach the planet we want to call home, as for a short, who knows, it could have blown out our power supply," Fabian added. "That must have been why Albert awakened us early and called it to our immediate attention."

"The cable must have loosened after the original acceleration due to a vibration when the biosphere began rotating," I said. "When I repaired the cable I noticed that the connection did not have a lock nut, so I installed one."

"The lock nut may have purposely been omitted," Serena conjectured.

"I do not think so because the E.A. expected the explosion to end our mission," Fabian replied. "So why would they need to sabotage the accelerator also?"

We kept our worries and questions of a possible sabotage to ourselves, even though we still were not sure that E.A. was not responsible.

CHAPTER 31

Year 2074, Thirteenth Year of Voyage--

We had located no other explosive devices and if there were any, we should have found them by now. My expectation was that no others existed because our searching had been very diligent during the years following the explosion at the farm. The incident was still haunting to me, however. We were very thankful that Makoto had made a full recovery and had almost normal use of his hand.

All was well with our individual families and the entire team. We had grown accustomed to our style of living and working for the good of everyone. I was aware that there had not been any major discontent, well, at least none that was lasting, among the team members or between the couples and that was amazing to me. Nevertheless, we realized that we must continue to strive to live in harmony without jealousy or quibbling if we were to remain sane and focused on our mission goal. The Committee must have had indisputable insight in the selection of the psychological team that administered our evaluation tests. The psychologists that were involved in the selection of our team had concentrated on choosing people that demonstrated strong personality traits with an emphasis on being compatible with others, and without thoughts of selfishness or trying to 'one up' others. It seemed to me that they had succeeded in those areas.

After our 'long winters nap', everyone felt as though they had two years of catching up to do. Fabian and Rachael announced that they were having a second child. I would not be surprised if the community were to continue to increase. There was very little house cleaning to be done even though everything lay dormant for two years. Albert kept the farm producing while we were in hibernation with the help of the robotic farmers. They accomplished the harvest of all the grain crops, dried, and stored them. They also dried and stored many of the fruits and vegetables; they made compost from the abundance of all the other food crops and excess plant debris. Before hibernation, we preserved a supply of food to sustain us until we could harvest a new crop.

All of the adults were enthusiastic about returning to their research laboratories now that the older children were of a dependable age to manage their own education with the assistance of Albert. Everyone had expressed their desire to resume the unfinished projects in which they were involved before our hibernation. Now that our childcare demands were at a lull, at least for now, we were eager to get back into a routine again.

Mirjam and I announced yesterday after our common dinner that she was pregnant, hopefully with a girl, although we had decided this time to let nature dictate the sex of the child. Now that our families were growing again, each family prepared most of their own meals although we still scheduled a common meal once or twice a week with each family taking a turn, this arrangement proved to be something that we looked forward to weekly.

The twins were only ten but often Robert and Ravi conducted themselves more as if they were sixteen. Robert's persuasive abilities continued to develop; he was able to convince the others, including André, to engage in activities that they may not otherwise have engaged in. Mirjam and I had spoken to him about how his persuasiveness could be an asset when used wisely. Actually, it could be one of his greatest assets. We had also warned him of misusing his gift. We reminded him how he influenced the others to follow him on the plant exploration excursion and how his adventurous nature almost cost him his life. Mirjam and I were not sure he fully recognized the significance or gravity of our talk, time would tell.

After breakfast a few days later, Fabian and I were in the laboratory working on a solar energy supply for the laser weapons to supplement our automatic hunting rifles we could possibly need when we arrived on Kairos. Serena and Makoto were developing a small portable chemical/gas laser capable of cutting thorough titanium. Mirjam and Rachael were busy with the organization of the children's educational program for the day and then they planned to spend the completion of the day doing research. Mirjam was working with Jabbar and Rachael developing a drug that would aid muscle regeneration. Gabriele was in the medical center actively involved with some new processes of laser bandaging. She was a consummate reader of all things in the medical field and found the data bank to be her daily companion.

The children were finished with a lesson in mathematical concepts and were eager to start the anatomy lesson, which included an experiment dissecting a virtual image of a cat. Ravi pulled up an image of a human torso and motioned for Robert to look.

"This looks almost life-like," Robert said. "See if you can find an image of a girl."

After several failed attempts, Ravi finally obtained the image he was looking for but quickly closed the screen when Miko and Dorri came over to see what he and Robert were doing. Something seemed to be interesting, the girls did not want anything special hidden from their eyes and ears, since they were as curious to learn about anatomy as the boys were. It was then that Albert intervened.

This image is not a part of your lesson for today.

"What did Albert mean 'this image is not a part of the lesson'?" Dorri inquired. "What have you and Robert found that is so interesting?"

"We are just looking at some anatomy images." Robert replied smugly. "We need to finish the dissection experiment now and after lunch we should spend some time on the history assignment that we have been neglecting. Dad is going to be disappointed if we do not become history enthusiasts."

"We should take a walk to the lake during lunchtime then after lunch we could do the history assignment," Ravi suggested. "We could stop by the galley, get some of the breakfast bread and pick some papayas and mangos and have a picnic."

Dorri and Miko agreed with the idea of a picnic, André also agreed that a picnic would be a fun outing. They took their time hiking to the lake eating the bread and fruit on the way and discussing the biology and anatomy lessons that they had just finished. They were eager to learn more, however, the dissection images of the cat was disturbing at first. The study of human anatomy was going to be much more entertaining and interesting to the boys, as well as the girls. Our children were growing up!

After the picnic, they lay on the grassy area around the lake and daydreamed of being on some tropical beach that they had seen images of during their history assignments about Earth. The children were always dreaming of places on 'Earth'. They sometimes complained that they were never going to be able to visit such an exciting and interesting place, a place of their ancestors. The girls were now practicing applying small amounts of makeup such as their moms made from plant, fruit and vegetable dyes and oils. They also had regular hair styling 'parties' with each other and the moms. Dorri and Miko especially dreamed of wearing the sort of clothing depicted in the images on tropical beaches, in ballrooms and theatre productions and pretended to model for the boys.

"Let's go swimming," Robert suggested.

"What about swim suits?" Dorri asked. "People wear swim suits at the beach back on Earth. I suppose we could go into the water with our clothes on."

Miko said. "How will we explain our wet clothes? I do not think that going swimming in the lake would meet the approval by our parents."

"OK, let's take off our clothes," Robert said as he was taking off his shirt.

"The water is fine," Robert said as Ravi joined him in the lake. "Dorri, Miko, come on in and join us."

"Turn your heads and do not look!" Miko said, giggling with excitement and a little embarrassment, as she and Dorri quickly took off their clothes and joined the twins.

"You shouldn't be self-conscious, Ravi said. "You look just like the pictures of girls we saw while we were in the anatomy class."

"André, aren't you going to swim?" Miko asked.

"No, I do not want to," replied André feeling a little awkward and left out. "I do not have a girl to swim with."

Fabian had mentioned to me on several occasions that André thought of himself as the 'outsider' since he was younger and had no one really to call his special friend. This birth order of our families was beginning to create some confusion and feelings of isolation on André's part.

"Come on in," urged Robert.

"*No,*" insisted André. "Leave me alone, I am going back to the study area."

"You had better not tell any of the parents that we went swimming," Robert said with an intimidating note in his voice. "Or, you will be sorry."

A short time after André left the lake the other four began playing 'king on the mountain' with the girls riding on the boy's shoulders. After a short time of minor 'hands on anatomy', they decided that it was time they should go back to the study area and at least pretend to finish the history assignment. The children had gotten a little more embarrassed and uneasy at their 'play'. They hoped to be back before their parents arrived from working in the laboratories and began questioning André about where they were. They all agreed that the parents should *never* know about the swimming party.

As they continued walking to the study area, Robert said to the group. "Someday we will probably marry one another."

Dorri answered. "Yes, after all, we seem to be the only choices, but we are all pretty and handsome people."

"We will be able to continue our lives together and raise our babies together just like we have been here on the journey," added Miko. "Our parent's lives together began in very similar circumstances and they all seem very happy."

"Whoa, slow down a little, we are a long way to being old enough for marriage and especially having babies, give us time just to be teenagers, I do not want to think about anything so involved," injected Ravi.

The sensors that monitored the delicate water system indicated a disturbance in the lakebed and Rachael had noticed the abnormality. She, in turn, had notified me and we were suspicious that the children had gone swimming but were waiting for them to admit it.

Several days later while Rachael and André were studying plants near the lake she asked André if he had ever gone swimming. He told her that he had never gone swimming and that he had never wanted to. He reluctantly admitted to her that the older children went swimming a few days before, but that he did not go in the water. He told her that they had removed their clothes and jumped into the lake. He said that they had asked him to join them but since he had no girl to swim with, he went back to the study area.

Rachael informed Gabriele, Makoto, Serena, Jabbar, Mirjam and me of what André had told her. Each of us parents spoke with our own children. Mirjam and I spoke with the twins at length about swimming nude with the girls. Mirjam told me that she was not really surprised at the boy's curiosity, after all, they were growing up and it was only natural that they would want to see first-hand what the difference really was between boys and girls.

"Yes," I said. "We need to put a stop to these excursions, but also we need to not let the boys feel that they did something that was not normal, just that it was not appropriate for their age, and that there will be time for learning about the opposite sex when they are older."

No sooner than I had said this to Mirjam, Serena knocked on our door.

"I am very disappointed in our children's escapade which took place a few days ago," Serena said with concern and directness in her voice. "I am especially unhappy that your twins, mostly Robert, have the ability to persuade the girls with such ease. Are **you not** teaching morals to your sons! We really need to address these issues soon, before more serious happenings occur. The children are growing up in very close proximity and are constantly together, please help us take care of this now. Gabriele and I have talked about this and she feels the same."

Mirjam and I looked at one another with surprise and concern.

Mirjam said. "Serena, I, and I'm sure Eric, are very disappointed in all the children's behaviors. We cannot let the girls off completely however since they willingly took off their clothes and swam with the boys. We have spoken with Robert and Ravi very directly about never acting this way again, and **yes**, we do instruct our sons about morals, but now, it seems, we have to be more direct. Please do not let this build into a bigger problem than it already is, kids are naturally inquisitive, boys and girls. Please accept our apologies."

After Serena left, I decided that I should call a town meeting and have each of our children apologize to the parents of Miko and Dorri and to each of the girls. I opened the meeting explaining to the four children that we were aware of the swimming incident. Having to apologize in a public setting would take no small amount of courage on the children's parts. We all hoped that they would learn their lesson from this embarrassing situation.

"It is natural to be curious about the body of the opposite sex but exploring one another's body needs to stop **now**," I explained. "There will be a time in the future for you to investigate the opposite sex but now the behavior is wrong. We are a very small community and we must learn to respect each other's privacy. It is all right to admire one another but you must keep clothed at all times in the public areas. For the present, none of you is to venture outside the common area without adult supervision! Robert and Ravi, please apologize to Miko and Dorri. You are also *not* to blame André for telling his mom about the swimming incident since she had a reason to question him."

"Miko, I am sorry I convinced you to take your clothes off and go swimming," Robert said in a low embarrassed voice. "Dorri, I am also sorry I convinced you to go swimming without your clothes. Mr. and Mrs. Saito, I promise not to be a bad influence on Miko. Mr. and Mrs. Bishana, I also promise not to be a bad influence on Dorri."

Each of the other three children repeated a similar statement and we agreed that we would not discuss that issue again.

I had informed Fabian and Rachael of the nature of the meeting and had asked them to attend, even though André was innocent in this incident. We further discussed and decided that while we were such a small community we would not involve ourselves in activities that would compete with each other. Once the colony was established and the community grew larger, we could engage in competitive activities. We also discussed the issues of jealousy and fidelity. We collectively decided that we must avoid both of these issues at all costs because either could and would destroy our mission.

After the serious nature of our meeting, we told the children to go and play a game of beach volleyball. When all the 'kids' had gone we parents finally relaxed, resolved our feelings of anger and disappointment and had a good laugh about the inquisitive nature of our children and therefore decided that although they were very bright, they were still normal in almost every way.

CHAPTER 32

Fabian and Rachael were the proud parents of a beautiful baby girl. They chose the name Faina. Mirjam thought that she looked just like her mother. I admitted that you could easily mistake her for a picture of Rachael when she was a baby, especially her eyes and mouth. She had a lot of dark fuzz on her head with a little twist of hair down the back of her neck. Mirjam and I were expecting our baby girl any day and I was sure that she would be as beautiful as her mother was as a child. Gabriele and Serena were both in their seventh months. Makoto and Gabriele were having a boy; Jabbar and Serena were having fraternal twins, a boy and a girl. We would have a thriving city by the time we established the colony of Kairos!

The older children were rapidly advancing in knowledge thanks to the brilliant tutelage of Albert. We parents were each making plans to involve ourselves in the instructional process by beginning instruction in our individual disciplines. Presently, we continued our laboratory work during the morning while Albert completed the elementary education of the older children. Robert, Ravi, Miko and Dorri were almost teen-agers, they would begin their advanced education in a few months; André was only slightly behind them and thought that he was just as mature as they were. In the afternoons, we were starting life skills training with the older children, including André.

Now that we had five new babies added to our number, the mothers were spending the mornings being mothers while Robert, Ravi, Miko and Dorri were taking turns helping manage the nursery in the afternoons as a part of their life skills training. With advanced education, life skills training, and babysitting duties, they had very little time left for getting into mischief, so we, as parents, had lifted the adult supervision requirement. Miko was like a second mother to Aaron, her baby brother; Dorri assumed the same role with the twins; Lei, her baby sister, and Kian, her baby brother. Our twins were also a great help with Susanne and Faina.

Year 2077, Sixteenth Year of Voyage--

Two years had passed very rapidly, now that the new members of our community were in the toddler stage, the moms returned to their normal routines. One day, shortly after Rachael returned to her laboratory, she came to me with some troubling and potentially dangerous information.

"I have been studying the water conditions ever since the children's swimming incident," Rachael informed me. "Although over the past several months I haven't been as diligent as I should have been but now that I am back in the laboratory every day I have monitored the water flow and there has been a noticeable slowing in the flow ever since the children went swimming."

"What's your opinion of the cause?" I asked. "I trust that we are not losing volume, the system is closed so the sensors should indicate any loss in the volume."

"You are absolutely right, the sensors should indicate a loss if the problem is due to volume loss, but small losses due to evaporation or a very small gradual leak in the system may not be detectable," She replied. "Any loss in volume that would affect any noticeable change in the rate of flow should be detectable by the sensors."

"Fabian and I will go see if we can locate the cause of the water flow problem," I said, trying not to sound alarmed.

That evening I called a meeting to inform the others of the potential problem with the water system.

"Rachael has noticed a change in the water flow in the river," I began. "Has anyone else noticed any differences?"

"If a problem exists, why has Albert not notified us?" Serena asked.

I am aware of the variation in the rivers' water flow. It is normal due to the farm needs. This is normal! You were not aware of this variation until you began monitoring the flow after the children went swimming in the lake. The filtration system needs routine maintenance so before the next hibernation period select a crew to make a manual inspection and removal of any foreign matter. The sensor on the coupling connecting the living area and the farm indicates a slight restriction but the sensors do not yet indicate a problem; however, you should also correct this before the next hibernation. I would have notified you of these concerns before the hibernation period.

"Thank you Albert," I said. "Fabian and I will do the inspection tomorrow."

"I can help with the inspection," Serena said. I am interested in seeing firsthand how the computerized system works anyway."

"You and Fabian inspect the filtration system and let me know if you need any assistance," I replied.

The water filtration system was located beneath the 'ground' of level A and served to filter the water circulated through the river system, including the lake, before returning it to the main water system. 'Mount Everest', the mound of artificial rocks just beyond the lake, housed the entrance to all of the water filters. Water from this filtration system furnished our drinking water and our other daily water requirements as well as that of the lake and river after purification. The filtered water passed through a tertiary process and a radiation process before returning the water to the main water system. The system was a very extensive network of conduits and access ports, which allowed for the physical inspection of the hydroponic system on deck A as well as in the farm on deck B.

Once inside the filter housing a set of stairs extended down to the lower level where the filters were located. The water for the river and lake, separated from the main water system, had its own filtration system, which removed the plant nutrients. Fabian and Serena had no trouble cleaning the removable filters. Once they temporarily stopped the water circulation in the river, they rolled out the two by three meter filters on rails with the aid of electric motors, and then they were able to remove several mango seeds and other plant debris, which they placed in the compost recycling. When Fabian and Serena replaced the cleaned filters, Albert was able to verify that the system was now functioning properly.

I asked, "Fabian, where are you and Serena located at this moment?"

"We are completing the positioning of the filters," Serena replied. "You would not guess what we removed."

"I have no idea, what did you find," was my response.

"Five mango seeds and a small amount of other plant material which should not have been enough to restrict the water flow," said Fabian.

"Albert just notified me that the restriction in the coupling located in the hub between deck A and deck B is now indicating a problem that needs repairing. Pressure is building because of the restriction and now needs our attention," I continued. "Jabbar and I will close the valve on deck B if the two of you will do the same on deck A. Once we pump the water out of the coupling compartment one of you will need to enter from that end and one of us will enter from this end. Remember, this will not be a straightforward task because of having to work in zero gravity, although, we will have a sufficient supply of air. Happy hunting and we will meet you in the middle."

The couplings consisted of a two-meter metal box located at the hub of both decks. A large conduit delivered the water to a valve located on the side of the box. A hatch was located on the top of the coupling. Two rotating unions connected deck A and deck B couplings to a conduit, which connected the two systems. Deck A and deck B had independent circulation systems and the couplings served to equalize the two systems.

Jabbar was just enough smaller than I, so he entered the coupling compartment through the hatch on deck B and Serena entered though the hatch on deck A. They found that a part of the housing, which covered the movable portion of the coupling on deck A, had become unattached and was restricting the water flow through the equalizer.

"I'll go to the storage area and get a tube of epoxy to temporarily hold the housing in place while one of you welds it with a laser torch," I said. "The blowers should have the surfaces dry enough to apply the epoxy by the time I return."

I located the epoxy in the deck B storage, and returned to the hub as Jabbar and Serena were finishing the drying process. Jabbar and Serena reattached the housing and they both were preparing to exit onto deck A. I had just secured the hatch to the coupling compartment on deck B as Jabbar and Serena were approaching the hatch on deck A when a shrill sound filled the area. The sound was similar to the one I heard that awakened me from hibernation. At the same time that we heard the sound, the hatch to the coupling compartment on deck A closed and sealed before Jabbar and Serena were able to exit. Fabian tried to open the hatch but the locking mechanism prevented it from opening. I was getting ready to ask Albert what was happening when he announced:

The valve in deck A has malfunctioned and is releasing water into the coupling compartment. The pumps are attempting to remove all the water so that you may reopen the hatches.

I immediately entered the transport and pressed 'deck A hub'.

In a few minutes, I arrived alongside Fabian and asked with alarm. "Serena, what is the condition in there?"

Fabian said. "I have pressed the 'close' switch on the valve repeatedly but the switch will not close completely."

"The water level is entering at about one milliliter every minute because the hub is in zero gravity so the incoming water is forming small droplets," replied Jabbar in a concerned voice. We are beginning to have difficulty breathing."

"Don't worry," I said, trying to be reassuring as I watched through the display of my communicator. "Serena, do you know where the schematic for the electric valve is located?"

"I believe it is in the top left desk drawer in our apartment," she answered. Send me an image of the contents and I will tell you which one is correct."

Jabbar and Serena floated in what seemed like a swamp. They covered their noses with cloths, which they had used while making the repair of the coupling housing. The epoxy vapors on the cloths were making them dizzy and they were gradually depleting their air supply. They were holding on to each other closely.

"They will find the schematic and locate the problem," Jabbar said, trying to show reassurance in his voice. "We have a few hours of oxygen left and it will not take Eric or Fabian long to figure out what is wrong with the valve. We should stop breathing through the cloths containing the epoxy vapors. Let's remove our shirts, wring them out, and breathe through them; they should trap much of the moisture."

"What is going to happen to our babies if we cannot get out?" Serena sobbed with great anguish showing in her voice and becoming a nervous wreck.

"We will be out of here in just a few more minutes," Jabbar said, trying to comfort her while hiding his concerns and fears from her.

"But, what will happen to Dorri, Lei and Kian," Serena said again and began to cry with huge tears flowing down her cheeks and adding even more moisture to our breathing difficulties.

Jabbar gathered her closely, kissed her, and said. "Sweetheart, I love you, but you need to hush crying now, you need to conserve our oxygen and your strength. We have more than enough moisture to breathe through!"

Serena began to lose consciousness and Jabbar was beginning to reach that state also.

CHAPTER 33

Albert notified the remainder of the crew about the valve problem on deck A and that the coupling compartment held Jabbar and Serena trapped inside. Everyone immediately came to help. After two hurriedly but unsuccessful attempts, we vigorously shook out our hands trying to calm our nerves and then, using the schematics which we had located in Serena's desk, we were able to reset the valve. Once we were able to reset the switch properly, it closed correctly and we were able to reopen the hatch. We looked inside but did not hear any sound nor did we see any movement from either Jabbar or Serena. They appeared to be lifeless, we saw that they were holding each other lovingly in their arms. Our hearts felt as though they had dropped to our feet, fearing the worst. We soon determined that they were unconscious.

Mirjam hurried in through the opening with some medical supplies and oxygen and when she reached Jabbar and Serena, she examined them and found that they each had only a very faint pulse due to their limited oxygen.

"Makoto, come quickly and help me," Mirjam said with urgency. "I need some help moving them to the opening, they are both unresponsive."

I reached for Serena as Mirjam and Makoto pushed her head through the opening. I laid her on one of the gurneys and covered her topless body. Fabian and I carried Jabbar to the other gurney. Gabriele and Mirjam then rushed the two of them to the transporter for a quick ride to the medical center where Albert's robots had arranged for two beds and had an IV waiting.

After about twenty minutes on the IV and oxygen, Jabbar began to regain consciousness.

Being greatly disoriented, he asked. "Where am I? I have a terrible headache. What happened? I remember Serena crying, becoming lifeless in my arms and then everything went black, where is she, is she OK?"

Seeing Serena, lying motionless, Jabbar asked fearfully as he started to get up to go to her. "Oh, no, what is happening, is she O.K., why is Serena still unresponsive?"

"Don't worry, Jabbar, lie back down, she is still unconscious but stable," Mirjam replied. "You need to lie still to regain your strength; Serena should recover in a few hours. Get some rest and I will look in on both of you in a short while."

By the end of the day, Jabbar had improved enough to sit up and begin walking around so Gabriele informed Dorri that she could bring Lei and Kian in so that they could see their Dad. After they shared relieved hugs and kisses with their Dad they began to tearfully ask why they could not see their Mom. Gabriele informed them that their Mom was still not feeling too well and needed longer to rest. Dorri helped get Jabbar home to their apartment and returned to the medical center to be with her Mom.

Log 2077-10

The Committee and the Wickham family,

We found a problem with the water equalization system.

Jabbar and Serena entered the coupling and made the repairs.

The deck A valve malfunctioned, closing the hatch
trapping them inside.

Both are recovering. We had a very frightening experience
but working from

Serena's schematic we were finally able to get
the valve unstuck.

I think that I am becoming paranoid; but we cannot imagine

any reason that the valve malfunctioned, unless someone
tampered with it.

Destiny

> <

"We have never finished our discussion of religion," Mirjam said one night a few days after Jabbar and Serena's incident.

As we were lying in bed, Mirjam turned toward me and continued with her comments. I tried to put my suspicions about the valve incident out of my mind and to concentrate on what Mirjam was saying.

"Our little Susanne is almost the same age as Robert was when we almost lost him. That episode, along with the scare we all had when Serena and Jabbar nearly drowned, demonstrates to me just how uncertain life is. When we started this mission, I had a feeling of invincibility, that nothing could happen to us, but now I see that I was mistaken. I have been thinking that we need to have some kind of belief structure to introduce to our children; the boys are still young enough and need something or someone to trust in. They are very outstanding and charming boys and we have done a very good job so far but they need something more, don't you think?"

I answered. "Before my brother died my parents took us to church every Sunday but after his death they stopped going and I have not been to a church in many years. We could use the data bank to answer any question that we might have about religion, it contains all of the earth's history including sociology and philosophy. I do remember the Bible stories that I learned as a child and I remember that it was a good time in my life. I have previously depended on science to reveal all the answers but the more I learn about physics, the more I realize that humankind does not have all of the answers. We do a fair job of explaining the universe and then someone discovers a new theory or develops a new technology. We are in a constant growth and revision process and each revision presumably improves our lives. It is because of these new technologies that we are where we are today. You are right, we should put together a belief structure, some moral standard for us to live by and instill in our children."

"Although my family and extended families were Hindu we seldom observed any religious festivals but after my mother's death, our family fell apart; therefore, religion ceased to be of any importance," Mirjam continued. "We were never very religious although Hinduism was the accepted family belief. I would like to learn about your Bible stories."

"We should use early religious writings as a basis of our belief structure," I replied. "During our family time I could begin by telling some Bible stories I learned as a child."

I will be thinking about these things you have mentioned and feel as though I can be open-minded enough to learn your religion and your beliefs; I think we need to stand unified in the way we teach our children. We can talk more about these topics tomorrow," Mirjam said softly in my ear as she snuggled closer to me."

The next morning after breakfast, Mirjam and I continued our discussion on the moral standard that we wanted to live by and that we wanted to pass on to our children. For the next week, we studied ancient Christian manuscripts. We decided on a moral code that we should not do anything that could cause envy or resentment between our family members and those of the community. Not allowing umbrage to develop seemed to us to be of paramount importance. We should hold all life sacred and abstain from causing another person mental, emotional or physical injury. We should love and respect each family member as well as other members of the community. If we killed, it must be for food or protection of self or family. Mirjam said that this was somewhat like 'ahimsa'. We also believed in the significance of practicing tolerance and understanding between family members and among members of the community. We further believed in the idea of cause and effect, that is, our actions could influence the thoughts and actions of others. We believed that we should live a virtuous life of good conduct, thinking of others before ourselves.

Greetings from Earth

I received your log 2077-10. Alex and I are happy that Jabbar and Serena made a full recovery.

What an improvement in communications!

I explained your feelings of paranoia to Joseph Merrill and The Committee.

After discussing the valve problem with the engineers, they do not believe

that the Environmental Advisors were involved. The authorities arrested Joseph McFarland.

The World Court tried and convicted him on charges of conspiring to commit bodily harm in

reference to our accident while hiking near the Estate. The E.A. has gone underground

but I suspect that they are still active.

It is rumored that someone from Germany has taken over running the organization.

All of you may be interested to learn that work is now underway to make the L5 location

a launch site for the tour shuttles leaving for Mars and beyond.

The old manufacturing facility will house the site for the
construction of the shuttles.

In addition, the worker's unit will become a five star resort.

Grant Wickham

I called a town meeting and shared Grant's latest communication omitting the paranoia concern. I discussed, with the others, the need to establish a community code of ethics or standard of morality. I shared with them the moral code that Mirjam and I had adopted as our family code and asked them to consider those ideas as a model for their individual family codes. After discussing the ideas, the others decided to think about them and after breakfast the next morning each family shared that they had adopted a similar family code of conduct based on the principles of the 'Deville Code'. Realizing that as time went on and the new colonists arrived, increasing our population, there would be a need to establish a Kairos code of conduct.

Fabian spoke up and said. "I will put together a sample code of conduct for Kairos, the ones we have for our families will be a fine pattern to follow."

"I will be happy to help you with drawing up this code, Fabian," said Makoto.

The older children were beginning their advanced studies. André, as usual, was also beginning even though he was two years younger; he had already managed to complete elementary education. Robert was interested in engineering and would be learning from Fabian and myself. Ravi and Miko would be studying medicine with Gabriele and Mirjam. Dorri was interested in pursuing chemistry, and was very interested in writing about what she saw, and what achievements were completed as we colonized Kairos. André was interested in sociology and human behavior and he would be spending many hours with Albert learning the principles of psychology. He was of the opinion that perhaps we, as well as the future colonists, could need assistance in adjusting to life on Kairos.

Makoto had finished a chemistry lecture, assigned a laboratory exercise for the afternoon, and had given the young people a break with time for lunch. Robert and Dorri agreed to meet in the common area for lunch before taking their turn to manage the nursery. The young children were between three and four years of age and would not need constant supervision although Dorri remembered when she and Robert were about the same age how terrified she had been when they ventured away from the common area and Robert ate the poisonous berries.

"Robert and Dorri," Serena said. "You will not need to manage the nursery this afternoon. I have a special lesson planned for the children, thank you however."

"I suppose we could see if the laboratory in available for us to start the exercise," Dorri said, not sounding very enthusiastic.

"Yes, I suppose we could, but I would rather take a walk," Robert replied.

"I would like that," Dorri said with a lot more enthusiasm.

"What do you suppose we would be doing if we were back on Earth?" Robert asked as they walked toward the lake. "I will be greatly relieved to be off this space trap."

"I agree with you," Dorri replied. "I do not know what I would be doing. Anything would be better than nothing!"

"We have a lot to do here, there is nursery duty, there is studying, there is learning how to be a farmer!" Robert answered with a sarcastic tone.

They arrived at the lake and sat down on the grass looking at the small fish as they swam by.

"Look at those fish, they seem happy here," Dorri said. "They do not know another life exists."

"I know, but we do." Robert said. "We know only because Albert and our parents informed us. We are going to need to make the best of what we have. It will be a great deal better when we can have *real* ground below our feet."

"Do you remember the first picnic we had here by the lake?" Robert asked as he moved over closer to Dorri and put his arm around her shoulders.

"Yes I do," Dorri admitted. "We got into a lot of trouble because we went swimming."

"I think that the 'skinny dipping' was most of the problem," Robert replied.

Playfully, he added. "Someday I would like to again go swimming with you in the same way."

With a blush, Dorri said. "Someday I would like that ---- but not now."

They sat by the lake holding hands and Robert kissed Dorri's cheek. Turning toward him, she returned his kiss, and they decided that they had better go back to the common area.

"Miko, I am looking for Robert," Ravi said. "I have been looking since the chemistry lecture. He and Dorri should be in the nursery but Serena closed the nursery for the day."

"They are probably together somewhere," Miko said. "I think that they like each other a lot. Ravi, would you like to be with me? How old should we be before we become a couple? Our parents were twenty-four when they started the voyage. I think that we should become a couple when we awake form the next hibernation, scheduled to begin in just over a year. What do you think?"

"Miko, we must be patient," Ravi answered as he smiled shyly, and took her hand as they walked toward the lake. "I am very happy to hear you say that you want us to be a couple, I have the same feelings for you Miko, let's hurry and get this next 'sleep' over with."

CHAPTER 34

"Jabbar, what's wrong!" I asked as Jabbar ran toward me from their hibernation chamber.

"Serena did not wake up," Jabbar replied. I awoke as planned and looked over at Serena, but she was not moving. The children are still asleep but will be waking up soon. I need Mirjam to check her over."

There is no need for alarm. I have injected additional drugs into her chamber. She will be awake shortly.

"Albert, why didn't you notify me that a problem existed?" I asked as Mirjam and I rushed to Jabbar and Serena's hibernation chamber.

I am not aware that there is a problem. Serena is still within the tolerance given by the manufactures of the hibernation unit.

This was not like Albert. Were we overloading his 'whatever it was that replaced the standard computer memory? Serena was the only one that understood Albert's internal drives. Did Albert know that Serena was the only one that understood how he worked? It was hard not to think of Albert as not being human. Was it just a coincidence that she had been the one involved in both malfunctions? I needed to keep those thoughts to myself for now. Could this be more of my paranoia?

"Gabriele, will you look after Susanne?" I shouted as I hurriedly explained our situation to her.

When Mirjam entered the chamber, she noticed that one of Serena's hands was covering the nozzle that injected the enzyme mist into the hibernation unit.

"This should not have happened but somehow Serena must have moved as she was going into the sleep state," Mirjam conjectured.

"There must be some other explanation," I speculated. "If her hand accidently covered the nozzle, how did she go into hibernation to begin with?"

Serena was not responding to Albert's second injection of the drugs designed to bring her out of hibernation. We opened Serena's chamber and Mirjam examined her and found that her heartbeat was slow and irregular. Mirjam gave her an injection of several stimulants including epinephrine, and after a few minutes, Serena regained a steady, regular heart rhythm and began to breathe normally; her eyelids began to flutter open. Once Serena recovered and everything seemed to be fine, I inspected her chamber. In doing so I found that the clamp, designed to hold the tube, which connected to the nozzle, was missing, and that the tube had formed a loop, trapping the mist and causing it to liquefy and clog the tube. Albert must not have detected the restricted flow, which must have occurred near the end of the hibernation cycle and a vibration was probably the cause. I searched the compartment under the hibernation chamber and found the clamp lying at the bottom of the compartment. I also discovered that the pump used to supply the mist had a vibration in the barring, which was the probable cause of the malfunction.

When Serena had recovered, her greatest concern was that the lack of the proper amount of enzyme mist had caused her to age more than the rest of us. She and Jabbar hurriedly went to their apartment so she could examine herself in front of a mirror, no matter what, women are always aware of their appearance!

"Serena, please know that you are still the most beautiful woman on the ship, actually the entire world," Jabbar said with a deep reassuring voice. "I cannot tell that you look any older than I and you still have a very shapely body after giving birth to three children and also you still have a very beautiful face. You look young and healthy and I am sure that you can also play the violin as magnificently as ever. I am just as attracted to you now as I was when I realized, as I gazed at you at Grant and Alex's wedding, that at that moment I knew in my heart that you were the woman for me, and nothing has changed, only gotten much, much better!"

With the help of Robert, Ravi, Dorri and Miko, it did not take long to survey the entire ship. They were no longer children and assumed their duties as adults; they were almost twenty years old, 'real age', although they looked more like eighteen years of age after our three years of hibernation.

The first evening out of our hibernation phase Robert and Dorri announced their engagement, as did Ravi and Miko. Mirjam and I did not try to discourage them; after all, they were now almost our age when we began the voyage. All four of them were working with us in our research projects and were willing to learn all that we could teach them. Albert was helping through his vast data storage with facts, which were beyond our expertise. Robert had developed an interest in geophysical engineering and was now becoming an expert on Kairos. He was very anxious to begin surveying the planet as soon as we could establish the colony. We were now only a few light years away.

Several days after our hibernation as Serena and Gabriele were preparing a double wedding for Dorri and Miko; Mirjam asked if she could be of any help. It was still hard to believe that our twin boys were about to be married. It was also difficult to realize that they had not experienced life beyond this 'doughnut', which we were living in. It had been our life for so long it was hard for me to realize that we once lived on Earth.

While Serena and Gabriele were discussing the need of prettier napkins, Gabriele noticed Serena acting as if she were not feeling well and called Mirjam over to make an observation also.

"What kind of dresses should our girls wear?" asked Gabriele.

"I don't know," Serena replied angrily as she folded, unfolded and refolded a napkin and then threw them down.

"Are you alright?" Gabriele asked. You seem to have a shortness of breath; have you been sleeping well?"

"Sleeping well, what do you mean?" Serena snapped in a disturbed voice as she picked up the napkins and folded, unfolded and refolded another napkin. "I am tired; I am going to my room. You do whatever you and boss lady want."

"Mirjam, what do you think?" Gabriele asked. "She has been through a traumatic experience, have you noticed any odd behavior in anyone else? I'll ask Jabbar if he has noticed Serena acting strangely. I will also consult with André since he has become our 'expert' on human behavior."

"I haven't noticed any abnormal behavior except what we just witnessed; let's see what, if anything, Jabbar has noticed." Mirjam said. "This might be a reaction to prolonged hibernation and Serena is the first to show any symptoms. The manufacturers did not find any side effects in any of their trial studies. We should run some tests on everyone and compare with his or her base line."

"Jabbar, how are you feeling?" Gabriele asked him as he got off the transporter on his way to his apartment. "Have you noticed any changes in Serena's behavior lately?"

"I am feeling fine," Jabbar returned. "Since you asked, I have awakened the last two nights to find Serena sitting outside our room gazing out at the forest. Last night I approached her but she did not acknowledge my presence even though I continued to speak to her. It was not until I gently shook her that she blinked wildly at me and finally asked what I was doing. I walked her back inside and lay down beside her and she began to sob quietly but would not tell me what was wrong. I was getting worried and planned to have her see one of you this afternoon."

Mirjam and I met at the medical center and she filled me in on Serena's unusual behavior. The two of us decided to watch her for the next two days and see what we could observe. The wedding plans would have to be on hold for the next few days until Serena was back to her normal self. Mirjam and I had a pact with one another that if we noticed any odd behavior in the other that we would let her know. Upon talking to Fabian, I learned that after hibernation, he was not sleeping well and that he would go on long walks late at night. Mirjam told me that after her conversation with Fabian he let her know that Rachael had begun also having trouble sleeping.

Testing indicated that we all showed evidence to some degree that our cognitive alertness and concentration was below what the base line indicated when we began the voyage. Mirjam and Gabriele also had established a base line for each child when they reached one year of age. Serena and Fabian's test results showed the greatest variance. Mirjam and Gabriele ran diagnostic examinations on each of us and on each other. Imaging and blood tests indicated an imbalance in neurotransmitters. The younger team members showed no change in their base lines. Mirjam, Gabriele and I indicated little or no change in our base lines. Rachael showed only a modest change. Jabbar, Mirjam and Gabriele began research on how to restore the imbalances and after several weeks, they came up with a possible solution. They continued to refine the compound, and when they were satisfied that the compound was viable, they began the injections to each of us. After retesting, the results indicated that Serena, Fabian and Rachael each should receive two more rounds of injections. At this time, the doctors declared us all healthy. Mirjam confided in me that she hoped that there would be no reoccurrence of the cognitive imbalance in any of us, I could tell it had been unsettling for her and Gabriele.

It was not long after our recovery was complete that Serena and Gabriele, with the assistance of Mirjam and Rachael, were again planning the weddings. The four of us men were busy constructing two new apartments out of the remaining 3X3 meter modules. We were making each couple an apartment, under the oversight of the two grooms, which would contain a bedroom with a complete toilet area, living area and small galley. The newlyweds should be very comfortable in their new homes. It was amazing that this second phase took only three weeks; we could remember hearing of weddings on Earth taking months of preparation and all of us men were delighted that we did not have to waste that much time to make a wedding happen.

The women constructed two arches made from palm fronds and covered them with white orchids. They made flowing muumuus of linen fabric that we had made from the flax, grown on the farm, and cinched them at the waist with a wide sash. Each girl wore a red hibiscus blossom in her hair and carried a bouquet made of pink and red plumeria blossoms. Robert and Ravi wore their new tan uniforms with a red plumeria blossom pinned to their left chest. André wore his new tan uniform and served as best man for both Robert and Ravi. The younger children helped with the decorating and served as flower children dropping flower blossoms during the short ceremony. The double wedding ceremony was very delightful; however, quite emotional for the moms, OK, us dads also!

Mirjam prepared a feast of broiled fish seasoned with ginger and served with papayas, mangos, pineapples and coconut, accompanied with a vegetable curry, all served over rice. Following the wedding, which I preformed with a large lump in my throat, we ate the exquisite meal. The wedding cake was a fruitcake made with dried pineapple, apples, oranges and raisins, along with a variety of nuts from our miniature nut trees. After the delectable meal, followed by the wedding cake and our fill of fruit juices, teas and coffee, Serena, Jabbar and Gabriele entertained us with lovely, romantic music and we danced late into the night. It was a splendid and festive evening.

André was very excited for the couples that he had grown up with, but he felt disheartened and frustrated by the feeling that he was now completely alone. Now that his four companions were married, life would not be the same!

"What am I going to do now?" André asked his dad that evening. "Who can I marry or will I ever get married? Susanne, Faina and Lei are the only girls left, they are only nine, and I am sixteen. I have no one available. I will have a long wait until any of the girls will be old enough to become interested in me. Do you think I will be enticing enough to attract any of these girls? I already have my eye on one of them!"

"You have several years before you need to think about marriage," Fabian said, consoling his son. "You should spend your time studying and being a support for the others. You will be surprised by how fast the time will pass if you keep yourself completely consumed with your psychological studies and research, trust me; the girls will mature right before your eyes and at least one of them will want to snatch you up!"

André realized that the future of the colony depended on the younger generation and he decided that he would be a major part in shaping and molding the future, married or not. He began a tutorial program with each of the young girls and with the young boys, Aaron and Kian. They did not necessarily need tutoring but the girls especially enjoyed his attention; nonetheless, he became someone that they each admired. One evening I overheard Susanne and Faina talking about how wonderful André was and how much they liked him; they were discussing how handsome and brilliant he was. André seemed to be enjoying his role as an older mentor for the younger girls as well as for the two young boys. He also was beginning to notice that the girls seemed enamored with him.

The ship was functioning satisfactorily, Albert was contented, there were no small children to prohibit another hibernation cycle, and we were all tired and becoming very weary with the long voyage. I called a town meeting and posed the option of another hibernation cycle.

"I realize that the plan was for only two hibernation cycles," I said. "I have consulted Albert and he can discern no reason why we could not have another cycle. I am looking forward to finally seeing Kairos, at least on the monitor, and hibernation is a good way to pass the time."

"I am a little frightened about hibernation after what happened the last time," Serena said with concern. "How can I be assured that something dreadful will not happen again, and this time maybe to one of the children?"

"Serena, I am confident that the episode you had was due to a chemical imbalance brought on by hibernation," Gabriele said. Mirjam and I are convinced that our medication added to the mist will solve the problem."

Jabbar hugged her and reassured her that we had not overlooked anything during our process of checking and rechecking.

"All the chambers have been thoroughly refurbished, every tube and every clamp has been tested repeatedly," Jabbar said. "Eric, Fabian, Makoto and I cannot determine one thing that has not been consistently inspected and Albert is in complete concurrence."

Mirjam, Rachael, and Gabriele were all very sympathetic with Serena's apprehension about having another hibernation cycle, but they gave her reassurances that we had checked all of the systems and all the monitors and they reminded her that Albert was aware of all their apprehensions.

Mirjam explained. "We need to support the agreement to have another hiatus from this lengthy journey; we all are getting a little cabin fever!"

After a complete recheck of each of the hibernation units, we agreed to go for the third hibernation cycle. Because the ship's design contained only four hibernation chambers, Robert and Dorri were compelled to share our facilities so we constructed a petition that gave them some family privacy. Makoto and Gabriele made the same arrangements for Ravi and Miko, using the last of the units. Things had gotten somewhat more complicated with the marriage of our sons; however, they were becoming wonderful couples and we were looking forward to someday being grandparents. Albert would awaken us in time to prepare for the deceleration process.

I am secretly anxious about what could go wrong this time!!! I have not approached anyone about my concerns about Albert; we are all at his mercy. Perhaps when we awaken after this sleep cycle, I will be able to talk to Serena about my suspicions, but she is in no mental state for me to mention anything to her now, I will wait.

Grant Wickham

Log 2082-2

We were glad to hear about the plans at L5. It is an ideal location for such a venture.

It was Ann's dream to one day manage a five star resort there. I trust that she will have this

opportunity to fulfill her dreams.

After the second hibernation, we lost some alertness and the ability to concentrate fully.

Mirjam, Jabbar and Gabriele developed compounds to restore our mental imbalances.

Mirjam and Gabriele gave injections of this compound to each of us. Rachael, Fabian and

Serena needed additional rounds of two more injections.

The younger team members' tests indicated that they were unaffected.

They have added these compounds to the enzyme mist and we are planning a third hibernation.

Serena agrees.

Destiny

CHAPTER 35

Year 2088, Twenty-seventh year of voyage --

All had gone smoothly during our 'sleep' with no one having any mental or physical difficulties that we could determine; we were all very thankful. My apprehensions about Albert's trustworthiness had been totally unfounded, it now seemed.

We were wide-awake from our third hibernation, excited to get a look at the vastness of space surrounding Destiny and hopefully our first view of Kairos. The entire Destiny team: Fabian, Rachael, André and Faina; Jabbar, Serena, Lei and Kian; Makoto, Gabriel and Aaron; Mirjam, Susanne and I; along with the young marrieds were all gathered around the monitor. We were enthusiastically awaiting our first view of Kairos, not knowing what to expect, talking excitedly about what all the commotion was about, and in awe of knowing that our 'mission' was nearing an end. Aaron was the most animated of the five younger children. He had already exhibited an adventurous and curious nature, much like Robert.

"Will Kairos have the same number of moons as we see in our sky from the ship?" Aaron questioned. "Will there be any animals such as the ones we have learned about in our studies? I need to know what to expect, everyone older seems to know so much more than the five of us 'kids'."

"We do not know what kind of animals live on Kairos?" Makoto explained. "We are not sure what lives there although we are almost certain that something lives there."

"I have found it!" Fabian announced. "The bright yellow-orange star shining in the center is the star of our future home.

Finally, there was something to see other than the emptiness of space! We were still too far away to see Kairos. We had been waiting for this day for almost thirty years! There was not a dry eye to be seen anywhere, at least, not in the older adults.

"This calls for a celebration," I shouted.

After a period of exhilarated dancing, hugging, joyous laughter and backslapping, we finally settled down and surveyed our apartments and the common area to see if anything were broken or askew. Ravi and I scouted around the farm enough to determine that Albert and his robotic crew again had kept the farm in remarkably good condition during our last four years of hibernation. We were all feeling refreshed and ecstatic knowing that the journey was ending. Fabian, Robert, André and I inspected the orchards and gathered a large amount of fresh fruit for the evening's celebration. Makoto and Jabbar took Aaron, Kian and Lei to gather fresh vegetables for the evening meal.

We had a lot of work to do before we were to go into orbit around Kairos. While we were in hibernation, Albert navigated the ship to reverse our direction and fired the main engines to begin our deceleration. I was tremendously relieved that our repair of the second stage of the accelerator functioned properly. This maneuver would begin to slow the ship down for our swing around our new sun and eventually for us to achieve orbit around Kairos. Tomorrow Albert would begin the process of deploying the solar sail to assist the engines in our deceleration. It would be a very gradual process and we expected that its effect on us physically would be almost negligible, never the less; Mirjam, Gabriele, Jabbar and Rachael had prepared an anti-motion medication for anyone that felt disoriented. The thought of all of the packing we must complete before we could transport anything to the surface of Kairos was looming over us like an unending nightmare.

The evening was very festive; Jabbar did not drink fermented grains or fermented fruit juices so, as had become our custom, we all honored him by drinking only the juice squeezed from fresh fruit. The occasion was never the less a very festive celebration and no one had to worry about any hangovers during tomorrow's deployment of the solar sail. Our dinner cuisine was especially delicious and the after-dinner music was outstanding. Before our hibernation began, Ravi and André had fashioned a set of bongo drums out of a small mahogany tree trunk and covered them with latex heads made from the sap of a small ficus tree. With the help of Jabbar, they also had made a wooden flute to add to our musical instrument assortment. Our entertainment of melodic performances was always a joyful event. Plans were underway to develop more avenues of entertainment by Susanne, Faina, Lei, Aaron and Kian with the encouragement of Fabian and Rachael. Perhaps someday in the near future we would be able to enjoy stage productions and dance revues. Makoto would continue his lessons in martial arts and gymnastics as time allowed; he had determined that using his injured hand in martial arts and gymnastics was the perfect therapy for him. The after-dinner concert was especially relaxing and beneficial to us by preparing us for a normal night's sleep in our living quarters. I went to sleep thinking about the solar sail procedure.

As I was finishing my last cup of breakfast coffee, I heard Albert announce -

Section D3 did not open properly. I will try the deploying procedure again. The sail must deploy properly to achieve the necessary deceleration.

After we heard Albert's broadcast I gathered with the other men and we began discussing our options to decide on the best approach in solving the problem with the solar sail.

"Eric, Is your monitor in the proper location to tell if D4 deployed?" Fabian said with concern. "My monitor is situated at the wrong angle."

"I think I can see the sail clearly," I replied, "It still seems to be folded in the center."

D4 did not deploy. Manual deployment is necessary.

"Fabian and I will suit up and take the utility vehicles and deploy the sail manually," I said.

"I'll suit up also," Robert announced.

"All of the suits are individually fitted for the initial eight of us," Mirjam said, hoping that that would dissuade Robert from going. Have you discussed your decision to go with Dorri?"

"I have not discussed this with Dorri, Mom, but I am confident that she would support me in my decision," Robert replied. "I know the suits were made for a specific individual but surely I can find one that will fit me. I'll also be protected by the utility vehicle's semi-enclosure, stop being such a worrier, will you ever accept that I am a grown man!"

"Your Dad and Fabian are the only ones who have been trained in the use of the vehicles," Mirjam continued.

"Mom, I am aware of that, but before our last hibernation I had been practicing a good deal with the robotic harness," replied Robert. "I can handle it; also, they may need a third pair of hands, isn't that right, Dad!"

"We could probably use more hands," I said a little reluctantly. "However, keep your communicator on at all times and listen carefully and you should be alright."

The three of us began to suit up. We helped Robert, checking to see if indeed the suit's fit were O.K., then we put on our suits, checked our air supplies and inspected each other's connections. The utility vehicles were located near the back of the plasma drive between the drive and the fuel tanks. We each tethered to one of the monorail robots and Ravi, who stayed in the ship and positioned his arms and hands inside the robotic harness, directed the robot to move along the monorail until we arrived at the shelter containing the utility vehicles. The shelter platform contained footholds, which enabled us to maneuver the very short distance from the monorail to the vehicles where we again attached our tethers. We attached a second tether from the vehicle to the main frame of the ship. The ship's designers were very aware that we were not experienced astronauts so they had built in extra backup tethers. We maneuvered our vehicles past the large fuel tanks to the location where the sail attached to the ship's hub. We would be working near the plasma escape so our maneuvers had to be precise. It would take only a small miscalculation and we would be toast. The sail fanned out to form the shape of a concave structure with the engine at the center. The sail consisted of four large sections A, B, C and D. D1 and D2 had deployed properly, they were in good working order, but D3 and D4 remained folded together.

After several unsuccessful attempts maneuvering the utility vehicles, we finally succeeded by manipulating them up and to our right in reference to our orientation with the ship. We discovered that the utility vehicles maneuvered like a dump truck rather than a luxury sports car. Robert connected his vehicle to the inward portion of D4 nearest to the hub, I connected to the center portion and Fabian connected to the outer portion. We synchronized our vehicles and began to move D4 so that it uncovered D3. Everything was working as planned until Robert's vehicle tether tangled with the sail frame and snapped. Robert's tether entangled with the frame just as D4 was almost in position. We were applying a force against the sail to get it in the proper location. The movement of the sail, as it fell into place, pulled our vehicles forward. When the sail locked into place, it caused a sudden stop, which jarred loose our hold on the sail, and we began drifting away from it. That is when Robert noticed his tether was broken.

"Help me, Dad," Robert screamed.

That immediately got our attention as well as that of all those that were watching from inside. Mirjam screamed, Dorri screamed, Ravi screamed and I reacted!

"Don't move and just remain calm, Son, do not try to maneuver your vehicle, it could disturb your orientation with the ship, we'll rescue you as soon as we can reach you," I said trying to remain calm myself.

Even though we had no experience operating utility vehicles in space, our instincts caused us to react. Fabian and I disconnected our tethers, and Fabian maneuvered in position to intersect Robert if I missed grabbing the dangling end of Robert's tether. Our oxygen supply was getting dangerously low; we needed to secure Robert quickly. I recognized that Robert was exhibiting hyperventilation and knew that his oxygen was near depletion. I extended the robotic arm of my vehicle and grabbed for the tether. Our relative motion caused me to miss on my first pass. I instantly reversed my direction but now there was a considerable distance between Robert and myself. I shouted at Fabian that I was still attempting to grab for Robert's tether but was uncertain if I could because I was having trouble gaining enough speed to reach him.

"Fabian, get ready, you are going to have to intercept Robert if I cannot grab his tether since I have travelled a further distance away from him," I said with urgency.

"You can do this, Eric," Fabian encouraged. "I am readying myself into position if your attempt fails."

With my heart pounding and my muscles aching, I accelerated the vehicle, and with my robotic arm extended to the maximum, I was able to grab the end of Robert's tether just in time for Fabian to intersect his path. When we rescued Robert, we found him going in and out of consciousness, and his body was hanging limply in space.

"We must get Robert oxygen soon, and we have only minutes left," Fabian said. "When we were on the platform preparing to board the utility vehicles, I remembered from studying the diagrams that there is an oxygen supply connection on the platform."

237

We immediately moved to the platform and connected Robert's helmet to the oxygen supply. In a few minutes, he was breathing normally and soon he regained consciousness and began to ask what had happened.

"Robert, you reacted as instructed, but your oxygen was running out and you were becoming unconscious so we hurriedly rushed you back to the utility vehicle platform to an oxygen supply, and just in time," I said with relief.

"Thanks, Dad, you and Fabian could not have handled this task by yourselves; you needed the third utility vehicle to execute lifting the D4 sail from the D3 sail. Thank you also for trusting Ravi and me with this situation. Remember, you now know that we are able to be trusted and able to assume our duties like the original four of you men. Oh, yes, and thanks for saving my life!"

Now with Robert safe, Fabian and I went back to our utility vehicles and maneuvered back to D4 to survey the sail and we found that one of the latches had not completely locked. After we corrected the locking mechanism, we determined that the sail was in its proper position. I checked with Albert to confirm if our conclusions were correct, they were, so we headed for our ride back to the suit-up area and then home.

"I am so relieved now that they are headed back home." Mirjam said as she and Dorri watched on the monitor. "I didn't want Robert to go since he did not have the proper experience or the training for such a job."

"I know," Dorri replied. "I was terrified for him, but I also realized why he felt that he must go. Now that he is safe, I can start to breathe again. I am so proud of Robert; he is extremely intelligent and resourceful. He would not have wanted his dad and Fabian to handle the problem alone. I understand that you worry about him and so do I, he can be a little impulsive."

"Mirjam and Dorri, I understand your fears," I replied as I left the suit-up room. "But, you have to now know that Robert was capable of performing this task and I am convinced that I can count on him and Ravi when there is a tough job to be done. They both performed expertly, which proves to me that our colony will be capable of anything thrown at us. I am a very relieved and proud Dad."

Grant Wickham

Log 2088-3 (after 3rd hibernation)

Mirjam and Gabriele administered cognitive alertness and concentration tests.

New medication works – it was added to the enzyme mist.

Enclosed is a content list of the formulation for the refined enzyme mist.

Had problem with solar sail, details enclosed.

Trust that the sail problem was not another indication of sabotage.

Destiny

During the next few days, Gabriele and Mirjam scheduled each of our crew for a physical examination. Our harrowing experience with the sail had no long-term effect on any of us physically. Robert was in the peak of health as were the other young adults. During our physicals, Mirjam took blood samples from each person to check each individual's immunity system, in view of the fact that we had lived in a germ-free environment and she was curious as to how we would adapt to life on Kairos. She planned to obtain air and water samples from Kairos, to check for dangerous pathogens, and develop vaccines with which she would inoculate each of us before entering Kairos' atmosphere.

Kairos was appearing larger each day. The solar sail was causing us to decelerate at a very slow rate and motion sickness had not been a problem for anyone of us, although we each took the precautionary medication. Makoto, Fabian, Robert, Ravi, André, Jabbar and I spent the next day preparing the command center to accommodate our ten additional people. Everyone would need a seat to secure him or her for our major deceleration that would swing us around our new sun and eventually into orbit around Kairos. The four of us older guys took a nostalgic look around the center and we commented on how brave, however naïve, the eight of us were thirty years ago. We were so young, eager and anxious about our future. So much had happened since then. We all agreed that we had no regrets but that we were elated that the journey was nearing its destination.

"The extra reclining seats should be stored behind that panel," I said as I came back to the present and pointed to the panel on our right. The specifications for the command center indicate that there are recessed fasteners located on either side of the existing seats and provisions for a third row behind. Fabian, Jabbar and André located the fasteners while Makoto, Robert, Ravi and I removed five adult seats and five children's seats from the storage container. The seats were lightweight and easily carried by one person.

"It seems that we have spent a lifetime here," Mirjam said to Rachael, Gabriele, and Serena as she looked around the living area for the last time. "I am feeling rather nostalgic leaving our home where we have lived, our children were born here, we have raised them here, educated them here, had two of our couples married here, laughed together, cried together and done everything that families do together. Our lives are going to change in many ways when we reach Kairos. I hope we all stay as close and loving for the rest of our lives as we have been here."

"I know," replied Rachael. "A lot has happened while we lived here but I am very anxious to be able to soon set my feet on real ground."

"I feel the same," Gabriele added. "And once we leave, we will never see our home here again so we are going to have to work just as diligently to create even better homes on Kairos."

"I, for one have had enough terrifying experiences here and my dream is that our new homes will be peaceful and calm," exclaimed Serena. "I have had enough excitement for a lifetime!"

We arrived at the command center and the mothers instructed the younger children on how to secure themselves into their seats;

then they looked to see if their 'older children' had secured themselves properly. Moms would be Moms! I had anticipated that we had repaired the solar sail in time so that our deceleration was sufficient to take us around our sun. If our velocity were too great, we could escape the gravity pull and bounce off into space never to go into orbit or if our velocity were too small, we would go into orbit but not around Kairos.

CHAPTER 36

Year 2091, Thirtieth Year of the Voyage --The Year We Arrived

Kairos was real; it was finally within our reach, we could actually see our new home. This was almost more than we could comprehend as the planet continued to get larger and larger and finally fill the monitor. It seemed that we had spent half our lifetime getting to this point.

Fabian, Robert and I were preparing to send probes to survey the surface in order to have an enhanced close up view of the planet. We had been monitoring Kairos for several weeks to confirm the data given to us when we began the voyage. We were all extremely anxious to confirm that Kairos was as livable as the Earth's astrophysicists had assured us that it was. Whatever our findings would be, we had no choice but to be able to adapt to them. The results of our probes confirmed that the findings that we had received from the astrophysicists back on Earth were moderately accurate. Kairos had a livable atmosphere consisting of 23 per cent oxygen with no dangerous levels of methane, ammonia or other poisonous gasses in the lower atmosphere; however, it contained larger levels of ozone than were previously indicated by the scientists' findings. This would help shield us from the sun's radiation. The temperature at ground level at the areas sampled by our probes ranged from 10 degrees Celsius at the mid-latitudes to 50 degrees Celsius at the equatorial region. The humidity readings ranged from 40 percent in the mid latitudes to somewhat higher near the equator. It appeared that Kairos would be a great place to live, at least in the temperate zones.

The boost engines will fire in twenty minutes and there will be a rapid deceleration. You will experience three times normal gravity for the next two hours. You must remain in your seats during the deceleration process. Please take care of any bodily functions and any other needs you may have before the engines fire.

"We were able to repair the sail so our deceleration should be within the allowed tolerance," I said, reassuring Mirjam and myself. "The boost engines should be able to compensate for the small delay caused by our repairs."

"You sound a little doubtful, I am not sure I understand your concern." Mirjam replied.

I had not shared my concerns and their consequences with anyone, not even Fabian or Makoto; although, I was sure that the same trepidations had entered their minds and possibly several of the other team members. I had decided not to alarm Mirjam or any of the others; I just kept silent and crossed my fingers.

The firing of the engines caused a strong force, which pressed the original eight of us into our previously formed seats, and the other crewmembers' bodies formed their own impressions. All of us were still moving at near our cruising velocity but the ship was rapidly slowing down pushing against the back of our bodies. The sound of the engines and the force on our bodies, caused by the deceleration, was a little unnerving for everyone. The experience was not much different from what we had experienced on takeoff thirty years ago but, never the less; it was still unsettling especially to those born on the ship since they had never experienced anything to compare with this. We veteran space travelers reassured the others that what we were experiencing was normal and that there was no reason for them to be anxious. The novice crew, the fourteen and fifteen year olds, managed the deceleration without a major problem; however, Aaron and Kian both had a mild bloody nose during this time. What a mess, the blood formed streamlets from their nose to their ears, once the engines stopped, and we were in zero gravity, little droplets of blood floated above their heads like small red balls. It would have been a fascinating sight if it were not so serious.

"Don't breathe out of your nose until we can catch the blood droplets," Gabriele said. "We will need to catch every droplet so sit very still until we can clean you up and we have to carefully and slowly move around in this zero gravity so it will take a bit."

The two moms, Gabriele and Serena, returned to their seats after corralling all of the blood droplets just as we drew near to Kairos for our first close-up view. What a sight! Below us, was a blue sphere, which had tinges of green and light brown and, what appeared to be, hazy white clouds. We were still too far away to see details clearly. There was so much to take in that we were spellbound.

"I could only imagine this day, but now it is real," said Miko. "I have never seen anything as amazing as this. I have never seen a real planet; I can't even believe that this is real, my heart rate seems to be racing with the excitement."

"I agree, it is hard to believe," replied Ravi. "Pictures can give only a very limited perspective. Even the holograph three dimensional prints do not prepare you for the real thing, this view is spectacular."

"It looks very much like pictures we have seen of Earth, taken from space," Dorri added. "The colors are so brilliant; I can clearly envision an artist's painting of this hanging in our living space. Perhaps we could commission Lei to do a painting of this one day; hopefully she is capturing this in her artistic memory."

"I wonder if walking around on Kairos will be much different than walking to the lake," Robert said, reaching for Dorri's hand. "I still remember our first days of letting romantic thoughts come into our heads when we walked to the lake and the cautious excitement that I felt in letting you know what my thoughts were. Now that we are a couple, we can be free with what we say to one another and can begin to fulfill our every dream."

The engines had to fire somewhat longer than was originally planned in order to compensate for the small delay in the solar sail deployment. The longer engine burn required precious fuel that we would need latter. However, I had calculated that we would still have enough fuel reserves to maintain a stable orbit during the disassembly of the ship and the transportation of it to the surface of Kairos along with all of the on-board materials and equipment. The ship would serve as our source of building materials for the initial colony.

The ship will obtain a stable orbit in five minutes. The orbit will be slightly elliptical to conserve fuel.

The orbit moved the ship from 50 degrees below the equatorial plane to 50 degrees above the plane every ninety-five minutes at an average altitude of 425 km, which allowed us a fabulous view of the surface. Fabian and Robert were mapping our location as we made our first orbit. We were intently watching the monitor as Fabian called out our location.

"We are now crossing the equator and moving into the northern hemisphere," Fabian announced.

We had previously placed a north-south orientation to Kairos with respect to our new sun.

"I cannot see anything but water," Robert said nervously as we approached orbit. However, after a few minutes he added. "Now I can see three small green islands that appear to be of volcanic origin from the shape of the mountains in their centers, what a relief, I was beginning to wonder if we would have solid ground somewhere."

"They remind me of French Polynesia," Fabian enthused. "The middle island looks almost like Tahiti."

"Someday, Rachael, you and I will visit this island paradise, I promise," Fabian whispered in her ear.

A few moments later we saw a large land mass coming into view. It appeared covered with large trees surrounded by lush vegetation.

"This should relieve your dread of not having solid ground to walk around on, Robert," Fabian said as he jokingly jabbed Robert in his ribs.

"A large high plateau is coming into view now," Fabian said. "This might be a good landing site. It appears to be relatively flat and there is a large range of mountains to the north and a large body of water to the south."

As we passed over the 'Fabian Plateau', as Robert had named it, we became more and more interested in using it as our landing site. The plateau extended to the foothills of the mountain range to the north and dropped off onto a coastal plane covered with dense vegetation. There were two large rivers flowing from the mountains forming estuaries in the coastal plane. On our second pass, ninety-five minutes later, we scanned the area at various frequencies to determine the depth and type of soil and discovered that low vegetation, mostly grass-like foliage, covered the entire plateau. The area between the two rivers was flat and level and appeared be about 1,000 meters in elevation with a maximum width of 64 kilometers between the two rivers. The rivers began to cut deep canyons into the plateau approximately 30 kilometers from where it dropped onto the costal plane.

Leaving the Fabian Plateau, we then passed over a large expanse of steppe, which gradually converged, into what appeared to be some kind of coniferous forest with a large river flowing from the west and cutting an extremely deep and wide canyon as it flowed east into a second large body of water. North of the river and running parallel to it, we came upon an extremely high and rugged range of mountains containing several snow-capped peaks over 5,000 meters in elevation.

We were about to begin our third orbit and we were confident that the plateau would be the ideal location for our first human colony on Kairos.

The ship has achieved a stable orbit. Now decks A and B have gravitation restored, you may make your way to the transporters.

We continued to map and explore Kairos by making additional passes. The northern hemisphere consisted of a large ocean including a continent-size land mass. This northern land mass, surrounded mostly by water and which contained the Fabian Plateau, had a small isthmus connecting it to a second large equatorial land mass. The southern hemisphere consisted of one large land mass extending southward toward the South Polar Region.

During the next week, we were picking and freeze-drying or dehydrating provisions enough to last us for a season until we could plant a new crop and it could have time to reach maturity on Kairos. We had previously collected seedlings and seedpods from the farm crops and plants, which we used for preparing our medications.

Fabian and I sent the robotic probes, which Robert and Makoto had engineered to collect air and water samples for analysis, to the surface of Kairos and then to return these samples to orbit to rendezvous with the ship. As previously planned, Mirjam and Gabriele used the data collected by the probes' microscopic eyes and the returned samples to classify the types of organisms present and they endeavored to determine which ones might be harmful. Following their plan, they then used our blood samples to develop individual vaccines since during our thirty-year voyage we possibly had lost most, if not all, of our natural immunity. Their preliminary findings identified several questionable bacteria and viruses. They began at once to work on vaccines.

We continued with our data gathering, vaccine preparations and gathering supplies and maintaining a very busy and hectic schedule.

On the eighth day of orbit, I called a town meeting. "We need to select four individuals to explore our landing site. The purpose of the landing team will be to set up a base camp and survey the site. As a safety precaution, each one of the landing party will need to take an extra oxygen supply. The landing craft has a micro-fiber filter, which should scrub the air while they are inside the landing craft. In addition, each one will need provisions for three days, enough to last until we are in position for them to return. Serena and Fabian have developed a laser, capable of serving as a weapon, although our scans have not detected any major life forms; I would advise that the exploration party take at least one of the hunting rifles as a safety measure. I realize no one has had training or experience in operating a landing craft, much less in landing one. Albert has demonstrated that he is a very capable navigator and he has assured me that his expertise extends to the operation and landing of the craft."

"I would like to volunteer as a member of the landing party," Makoto said. "This is now our home. We must take ownership at all costs, for we cannot return to Earth."

"I will go also," Gabriele said enthusiastically. "I would like to collect some samples of vegetation; what's more, I want to share the excitement with Makoto. It is feasible that someone may need medical attention."

"Miko and I also want to go," Ravi said. "It will be exciting to finally set foot on solid ground. I am interested in beginning to explore and send back data for Fabian and Robert to begin mapping the surface."

"Thank you, all of you volunteers," I said. "You four will be heading for the most amazing adventure of your lives, we are all wishing we could come along, but that will come soon enough now and there is plenty of work still to be done here. Albert informed me that we would be in position to launch the landing craft at nine tomorrow morning. When you reach Kairos stay within sight of the landing craft and be diligent, we want everyone to return safely."

Ravi and Miko took a walk after eating a light dinner meal.

"I cannot imagine actually walking on anything that is not circular," Miko said.

"We will have a lot to get accustomed to, Ravi replied. "Tonight, I have so many thoughts running through my head about what lies ahead for us and our family, I am sure that sleep will not come easily."

CHAPTER 37

The next morning, launching day, I accompanied the landing party to the docking bay. We had not had an occasion to completely explore this portion of the ship although we were aware that the ship contained four landing crafts each capable of transporting 35000 Kg of cargo along with a crew of four. The craft, shaped like a large shuttle, had four stabilizer engines located underneath it capable of lifting the craft off the surface of Kairos, hovering over the surface and maneuvering in its atmosphere.

The landing party checked out the breathing apparatuses, which contained micro-fibers capable of filtering out microbes. They choose four of the individual oxygen supplies as their back up. Each landing craft came equipped with a similar filtering system and enough water to last a crew for a week. Makoto assumed the leadership of the landing party and following his lead, Gabriele, Miko, and Ravi buckled themselves into their seats. I operated the air lock while Albert operated the landing craft. The craft, controlled by small gas jets, dropped out of the bay, and as soon as it cleared the ship, its main engines fired, and the landing party was now on their way to becoming the first humans to set foot on a planet other than those in our former home's solar system.

The landing party was to keep in visual and audio contact with the landing craft at all times during the three-day exploration of our proposed landing site. I also reminded them to keep in audio contact with Destiny at all times and to keep their video monitors on at all times.

We watched as the landing craft took on the appearance of a meteor as it entered the atmosphere of Kairos.

"There will be a few minutes of ionization-blackout as the atmosphere compresses around the landing craft," I informed Makoto. "We are watching the landing craft's decent on the monitor. You are making quite a show."

"You have no idea," replied Makoto and the others chimed in. "We appear to be surrounded by a brilliant yellow-red glow. I certainly trust that the landing craft is not disintegrating!"

"The skin of the landing craft is made of flexible silicon-carbon fibers capable of withstanding temperatures in excess of 2000 degrees Celsius," I replied. "It sounds like a beautiful, unbelievable sight and I hope you are being able to get it all recorded for posterity. You're communication is beginning to break up," I answered with encouragement, but our ability to receive communication had stopped.

"This is so beautiful," Miko responded, when we were again able to receive communications. "There is a sea of green below us. The grassy growth appears to be tall and dense with stalks that have heads of grain much like wheat. From our approach angle, we can see the mountains in the distance to our left and the dense flora ranges from the foothills and continues until the plateau drops off onto the coastal plane. From our vantage point, we cannot see the water or the costal plane; however, I can see the beacon we sent ahead to locate a landing site."

Three days before, we deployed one of the robotic probes to locate a suitable landing site. The robotic probe consisted of a rover about one-and-one-half meters high and capable of surveying the landscape and sending video and meteorological information back to the ship. Albert used this information to locate the landing site, positioned near the larger of the two rivers and ten km from where the river dropped into a gorge. I had confidence in Albert's abilities and I was sure that the landing party shared my views. The landing craft slowed to a stop and hovered over the robotic probe and beacon, slowly descending and coming to rest a meter from it and 200 meters from the river.

"Touch down!" Makoto said loudly and with great relief. "The landing was smooth, and as predicted, the landing site is level and there is a gentle slope down to the river. The tall grass appears to be at least waist high on Ravi or me. We are suiting up in the breathing apparatuses. Ravi is taking a sample of the air as it comes out of the landing craft filter. It is clean and breathable although there is a slight musky odor, but not overly offensive. The temperature outside the craft is a comfortable 25 degrees Celsius. We are opening the hatch, which also serves as the airlock, and Ravi is first in line to exit. As you can imagine, our excitement is almost uncontrollable and we are wishing that all of you could have come on this first landing."

"Our first step onto the ground of the colony of Kairos, this will prove to be a monumental accomplishment for generations to come!" stated Ravi with breathless enthusiasm and a quiver in his voice as he reached his hand up for Miko to join him.

Ravi, being a thoughtful son-in-law, reached up and assisted Gabriele to the surface as Makoto was shutting down all the systems onboard the landing craft.

"Thank you Ravi," said Gabriele. "Isn't this the most fantastic adventure we have ever experienced, I feel as though I am a child in the largest, most incredible amusement park ever! Our new home is actually real after all, and I so wish Miko's younger brother, Aaron, were here to experience this now, but he and the others will have time to create their 'first' memories soon."

"This will be the perfect place to plant our first flag. Miko, be thinking of a design for a flag for Kairos, we can present the drawing to our crew members and ask for their input, I am confident that Lie can expound on your drawing," said Ravi as he and Miko were embracing one another as they surveyed their new surroundings.

Miko responded to Ravi's request by saying, "Ravi, I have been contemplating what the design for a flag would look like for a long time. I already have a design that I want to share with you. It consists of eight large stars surrounded by ten smaller stars; this represents the eight parents and their ten children. I have thought of the color midnight blue to represent deep space and a yellow-orange band at the top to represent the Earth's sun, and an orange band at the bottom to represent our new sun. I envision the stars placed in the midnight blue area. Of course, we will need to have input from the others, especially the gifted Lie."

"Miko, when did you have the time to work on this design?" asked Ravi. "You never cease to amaze me with your many and varied talents. The design sounds great, I am certain that the others will approve also."

Each of the members of the landing party were recording both video and audio and transmitting the information to the ship, and to Earth via devices attached to their helmets containing the breathing apparatuses.

"It is so difficult to keep audio recording," said Gabriele. "I find myself wanting to just take it all in; it is such a splendid and gorgeous landscape that my senses are on overload. I could never have imagined a place this fantastic except on Earth. I can hardly wait until the others can be here and see Kairos for themselves."

"Just put your recording device on automatic, Mom," returned Miko. "Describe what you are seeing and everyone back on the ship and on Earth will hear your descriptions; you have always been a great story teller and are so good with painting a picture with your vocabulary."

Deciding to do a small amount of exploring, each member of the landing party put on protective gear consisting of gloves, which covered the forearms and long leg coverings similar to chaps worn by cowboys in the American Wild West movies.

Gabriele, Miko and Ravi began collecting samples of the vegetation, including soil samples, while Makoto was collecting water and rock samples from along the river channel, which cut through a limestone layer. There were several different plants growing near the river that resembled ferns.

"Ravi, come take a look at this blood-red fern," Miko called to him. "I have never seen anything like this. The total plant seems to react to my probe when I touch the tip of any one of its fronds. The entire plant becomes rigid when I try to remove it from the soil and when I finally removed it, it withered and died and a red sap escaped from beneath each of the fronds."

"Have you tried to take another sample?" Ravi asked. "Miko, be extremely careful when handling the ferns, remember, we know nothing about these new species and some of them may be poisonous or otherwise harmful."

Miko exclaimed. "Ravi, I was being careful, but as I pulled up the plant, some of the sap got onto my upper arm above my glove. I tried to remove another fern but with the same results. You are right; maybe we should leave this species for study later."

"Ravi, hurry over here and examine my arm, the sap has left a stain and it is beginning to sting and look swollen." Miko urgently cried out.

Ravi hurried over to Miko as he called to Gabriele asking her to examine Miko's arm also saying. "Some of the sap from these red ferns splashed up onto her arm as she was trying to dig some out of the ground. She appears to be having an allergic reaction from the sap."

Gabriele rushed to the landing craft to retrieve her medical bag. She administered an anti-allergic ointment to her arm and gave her an injection of epinephrine and the swelling in her arm began to subside slightly.

"Look what I discovered!" Makoto said running over to where the others were collecting plant samples. "I found this fossilized fish embedded in the limestone near the water. At least we know that fish lived here at one time.

"Makoto, Miko is having an allergic reaction from some of the sap from those red ferns she was studying," cried Gabriele. "Help Ravi carry her back inside the landing craft, I am afraid she is beginning to develop a fever and she is getting weaker and dizzy and she can scarcely stand."

Makoto and Ravi hurriedly carried Miko back to the craft and once inside, they lay her down in one of the reclining seats and started giving her some water. Ravi stayed with her to monitor her condition as Gabriele went back to extract some of the fern sap for further study to ascertain what could have caused Miko's allergic reaction. Makoto went with Gabriele to assist in any way that he could.

Ravi asked as he felt her pulse. "Miko, how are you feeling now? Your heart rate and breathing has become even more rapid, your face is turning a brighter shade of red, is your head beginning to ache?"

Miko responded weakly as she was restlessly shifting her legs and arms about. "Yes, I am getting a headache and I have some nausea, what do you suppose I have gotten myself into?"

Ravi questioned her. "Did you notice any particular odor coming from the ferns as you pulled them from the ground?"

"Yes, I do remember smelling a slight garlicky odor," she responded, as she was becoming more and more restless, holding her abdomen.

It occurred to Ravi that this could be a cyanide reaction even though the odor was not as he expected. He retrieved a Cyanokit antidote from the medical bag and administered an injection of Hydroxocobalamin to counteract cyanide poisoning, if this were the cause of her reactions.

"Miko, I am giving you an injection of Hydroxocobalamin, if you are sick from cyanide poisoning, you should be feeling much better shortly," Ravi soothingly said to her.

Gabriele and Makoto returned with samples of the red ferns, in sealed containers, and found that Miko was feeling much better.

CHAPTER 38

Miko looked out of the landing craft and said to Ravi. "Look at the beautiful sunset to end our first day on Kairos. This day could have ended much worse!"

"Yes it is very beautiful," Ravi said. "I am so very thankful that you are feeling so much better. It seems as though we are as birds freed from their cages, just think, we can actually walk on flat ground and it seems to go on forever in all directions. Do you feel like coming out and walking around for a while with me and enjoying the sunset and these cool breezes together?"

As they were walking hand in hand, Makoto and Gabriele were arriving back at the landing craft as the sun was about to set.

"Ravi, will you help me set up a perimeter of sensors around the landing craft?" Makoto asked. "We have not observed much wild life but I am of the opinion that there is a lot that we have not seen. We should also place lights around the perimeter."

The landing party dined on dried fruit and vegetables reconstituted with some of the water and heated in the induction oven located in the small galley. Gabriele also had brought some of the bread that Mirjam had freshly baked the day before.

"Keep a watch during the night," I said as I contacted the landing party after their dinner. "We have no idea what lives outside the landing craft; therefore, keep your weapons ready and do not hesitate to use them. The landing craft should provide adequate protection but be watchful. It is wonderful to know that you, Miko, are feeling much recovered from your accidental poisoning. You are precious to Mirjam and me, as well as to the rest of our team, and we were all worried about you when we heard and saw the commotion that was going on. Congratulations on making the decision to use the antidote kit as quickly as you did, Ravi, you made us very proud of you. Our sensors indicate a bank of clouds to your west; in case of a storm, the landing craft should give you protection from the elements, but keep a watch on the weather. Keep a record all of the changes in the weather, whether calm or severe. Don't you think it's a good idea to start a log on everything happening on Kairos?"

"Will do, Dad." Ravi replied.

"Ravi and I set up a perimeter of sensors and the surrounding area is well lighted," Makoto informed the crew on the ship. "The weather is great now; we had a brilliant, stunning sunset, it reminded Gabriele and me of Hawaii. We are going to try to get some sleep now."

For the most part, the first night on Kairos was uneventful. Makoto awaked me during his watch at three in the morning reporting that the sensors indicated an intruder but that he and Ravi could not see any movement outside of the landing craft. I reassured them that the landing craft should be capable of withstanding any intruders.

I was relieved but excited that we had made the voyage to Kairos successfully, much to the disappointment of the Environmental Activists. Luckily, for us, their plans to destroy the ship had been unsuccessful and now that we were here, I could put them out of my mind. I would truly feel that we had accomplished our goal when all 18 of us were finally safely on the surface of Kairos.

The next morning Makoto and Ravi searched outside of the landing craft and reported that they could find only negligible signs of an intruder. They did, however find that one of the sensors directly across from the entry to the landing craft was missing and that the vegetation around it was slightly disturbed. They decided to set up visual monitors to see if anything else would be caught snooping around in the night with the added surveillance.

On the second day, as planned, the landing party explored the river channel downstream from the landing site. The river formed a series of rapids about 1000 meters downstream and approximately 1000 meters further the river plunged over a limestone shelf forming a series of waterfalls terminating in a gorge 300 meters below. The gorge apparently extended inland from the costal plane. Makoto and the others searched for whatever had attacked the water sample bottles the day before but without any success. The landing party spent the rest of the morning admiring the beauty of the waterfalls and lush vegetation covering the gorge below.

"I will visit this place again," Ravi said. "The next time I will bring climbing gear. I expect that we will find many interesting species in the gorge and costal plane. Miko, have you noticed all the birds that are flying over the treetops?"

"Yes, Ravi, I was admiring the way that they are swooping and soaring high in the clouds," replied Miko. "Have you been able to determine their size or shape?"

"I can't make out many specific details even with the telephoto lens," answered Ravi. "They seem to have brightly multicolored wings and heads. I am anticipating finding evidence of the birds' nests or home building materials further down on the costal plane when I return with my climbing gear, perhaps Robert and André will want to come with me."

"We will form an expedition soon," Miko added. "Rachael will be so excited to explore this place."

The landing party continued collecting samples on their way back to the landing craft. Makoto and Ravi were preparing to collect another water sample from the river when a large animal broke the surface and grabbed the sample bottle.

"What was that?" Makoto cried out. "Ravi, did you get a look at whatever that thing was? It appeared fairly large to me."

"It somewhat had the appearance of a large ell or serpent," Ravi replied. "I can remember seeing a large set of teeth as it grabbed the collection bottle."

"I will try netting it," Makoto said. Get one of the specimen containers ready and if I can capture the creature, I trust that I can manage it and that we will be able to coax it inside the container."

On the third attempt, Makoto pulled the net to the riverbank. It contained a large animal that appeared to be able to breathe out of the water although it had a set of double gills. It was approximately two meters in length with a shark like tail and no fins except for two protrusions on the belly below its gills, which it apparently used to move along the river bottom. Its teeth indicated it was carnivorous. Makoto and Ravi staked the container holding the mysterious specimen so that river water would flow through it.

"I will take samples of blood and tissue to examine," Gabriele said as she and Miko helped Ravi with the sample container. "Mirjam and I will definitely want to study this fellow further."

After collecting the samples, Makoto and Ravi released the river serpent back into the river.

"That is quite a specimen," Mirjam said over our communicator. "What other interesting samples have you collected?"

"I will have to fill you in on that later. There appears to be a large thunder storm approaching, by the look of the clouds." Makoto hurriedly said. "Ravi, we need to get all the collected samples into the landing craft before the storm arrives."

Ravi and Makoto replaced the missing sensor and secured the lights to protect them against the wind and any intruders. After securing themselves in the landing craft, Makoto asked me if the sensors were indicating the severity of the approaching storm.

"Makoto, the ship's sensors indicate that there is an abundance of air circulation in the clouds causing a disturbance, you are probably in for a turbulent night, I hope you can sleep because it will probably be quite noisy," I answered.

They spent the second night in the landing craft seats listening to the howling wind as it shook the craft. This was a truly new and frightening experience for Ravi and Miko, having only lived on the ship; however, Ravi reassured Miko by reminding her of some of their lessons about the formation and characteristics of storms. In order to calm the nerves of Ravi and Miko, Makoto mentioned that it would be a good idea to begin giving names to landmarks.

Ravi said. "That is a wonderful idea Makoto, let's name the waterfalls the 'Miko Falls' because they are so beautiful."

"In honor of my husband's fantastic discoveries in and around the river, I'd like to recommend that the river be named the 'Saito River'," Gabriele suggested.

Everyone was thrilled and happy that giving a name to these surroundings had been their honor.

Miko suggested. "The other river can be named the 'Deville River'."

Makoto and the others awoke the next morning to a bright sunny sky with only a lingering remnant of the previous night's storm. He and Ravi surveyed the landing craft in search of any damage the storm may have caused. It appeared that the storm was all wind; no moisture seemed to have fallen. They also searched the surrounding site for any intruders but apparently, the storm had frightened them as well. After collecting the sensors and lights, they prepared the landing craft to return to the ship. Makoto was communicating with Albert in preparation for their return when it happened -- all communication with the ship was lost!

"Makoto, what happened?" I said as I tried to establish communications with the landing craft. "Are you there? Can you hear me?"

"Ravi, please answer!" Robert said gravely with concern.

"Eric, can you hear me?" Makoto kept repeating, but there continued to be no response from Albert or the ship.

"We have a dilemma," Makoto informed the others. "Our window will close in another 15 minutes. We can manually fire the engines and hope that Albert can communicate with the landing craft once it is off the planet's surface. The alternative is to stay here and hope that communications can be resorted in time for our return. If not, our water supply should last until our next window appears but we will have to ration our food. What should we do? I am not a navigator."

< >

The atmosphere has developed clouds of ionized gas due to solar activity and has temporarily disrupted communication with the landing craft.

"Albert, how long will it be until the ionization cloud will dissipate and communications are restored," I asked. "I hope Makoto doesn't fire the engines with the hope that you can guide them home. We may lose them if he tries."

I do not possess the data to predict the duration of the ionized gas cloud. The solar activity is diminishing so it should not be long.

< >

"I vote to wait until communications are resorted," Ravi said, after analyzing the situation and his evaluation convinced the others to wait.

"We need to conserve our food and water," Gabriele said in response. "I suggest that we stay secured in the landing craft until we know more about what has happened."

"Makoto, can you hear me now?" I asked 20 minutes later.

"Yes, Eric, I can hear you," Makoto replied. "What happened, it gave us quite a scare?"

"Albert informed us that an ionized gas cloud disrupted our communications." I answered. "I am thankful that you didn't fire the engines manually. If you had, Albert would not have been able to guide the landing craft to dock with the ship. I presume that the on-board guidance system may have been able to get you into orbit but that would have been a great risk."

"We are conserving our water and food," Makoto replied. "It is cramped in the cockpit. We may venture outside but we plan to stay close to the craft."

"Keep communications open and we will meet you on the docking platform in three days," I replied.

While waiting for Makoto and crew to return, Fabian and I carefully packaged the solar panels, which he and Serena had created. One of our first industrial projects after we settled on Kairos would be to produce more solar panels. Our plan was to use the panels as our major source of energy.

"Eric, the night was uneventful for the most part," Makoto reported the next morning. "Our sensors picked up some movement outside the landing craft before dawn. We tried to get a visual but we were unable to do so. After daylight, I cautiously opened the hatch and looked around the landing craft. Whatever it was that paid us a visit last night must have been quite large because it trampled down the grass all around the craft. I made foot impressions for us to study on our return. This animal was much larger than the one the night before the storm. That night the intruder must have been small and light of foot."

"That must have been frightening as well as exciting," I replied. "I know that you and Ravi will want to make visual contact, but do advance with caution. Take the converted laser, I assume it will be powerful enough to use as a weapon against a large animal and, in addition, take the hunting rifle. We want to live in harmony with all new life forms but use your judgment. Keep safe and keep both visual and audio contact with us."

I monitored Ravi and Makoto following the trail left by whatever had disturbed the grass around the craft the night before. As they approached the river, the backside of a very large, brown, sparsely haired animal, lumbered slowly up the bank on the other side of the river. It was too far away to see much detail but it appeared to be the size of a small elephant and it moved into the grassy growth on the far side.

Makoto and Ravi did not attempt to follow because of the river's swift current and because they were still not certain what other animal life, the river might contain. They certainly did not want to meet one of the 'river serpents'. They returned to the landing craft and scouted around it looking for any scat, left by whatever it was that paid them the visit the previous night. They discovered footprints of at least three animals and plenty of fecal droppings.

The following morning, Makoto reported that they did not have additional visitors and that they were very cramped, very bored and most anxious to get back to the ship. Later that day, Albert contacted Makoto with instructions on preparing for the return flight. By that evening they were all back on the ship and we were getting a firsthand account of the six days on Kairos.

"Tell us everything, Ravi, and do not leave anything out," began Robert. "We have all watched the monitors closely and listened to Gabriele's narrative. It sounds like an interesting and exciting planet. What is your take on the weird vegetation? What do you think about the river serpent? Do you suppose that the hairy 'beasts' are migratory? Did they appear dangerous in any way? I have so many questions that I can hardly wait until another exploration can take place. Next time, brother, I am coming also!"

There were still many things unanswered and the crew had their own questions. We finally let the tired explorers have some dinner and each rushed the showers and their beds. Mirjam and Gabrielle asked Miko to report to the medical center after her shower for a check-up and some blood work, however.

The one thing we knew was that the analysis of the scat revealed that the animals that left it were herbivores and from all appearances, mammals. They must have been good swimmers because as they crossed the swift river currents they escaped by not being bitten or chewed on by whatever was in the river.

We had encountered our first life on Kairos and survived; I wondered what else could possibly lie ahead for us!

CHAPTER 39

I scanned the plateau on the next two passes over the site where Makoto and crew had landed in hopes of locating the large animals that had paid them a visit two nights before they returned to the ship. I made visual contact of a group of five animals at the north of my scanning range. They were too far away to make a definitive identification or to see any details even through magnification, but from Makoto and Ravi's descriptions, I must have been looking at the same animals that had visited them. They appeared large, strong, and perhaps they could be useful if our construction machinery malfunctioned or if we ran short on fuel.

Our immediate job, however, was to transport everything that we could salvage to the surface. We had four landing crafts and Albert's instructions would guide the crafts to the landing site.

"Fabian and I will take one of the all-purpose construction machines in landing craft number one," I said to Makoto as we approached the equipment storage hanger. "You and Jabbar use landing craft number two."

We located the two all-purpose construction machines and checked to see if the energy cells were still active after our long voyage. Each construction machine immediately came to life, so Makoto and Fabian moved them to the air lock located on the loading dock. Meanwhile, Jabbar and I went to the docking bay, the storage hanger for the landing crafts, and we moved them to the air lock, with the assistance of Albert's robots. Robert operated the air lock and Albert successfully docked the landing crafts. Makoto moved the large construction machine into the cargo bay of Jabbar's landing craft and Fabian did the same in landing craft number one.

A few hours later, we were on the surface of Kairos and we immediately began to unload the two construction machines. The entry into the atmosphere was incredibly exhilarating for me, and Makoto agreed that the second time was no less exciting for him.

"Fabian and Jabbar, can you believe this place?" I asked as we first arrived on Kairos. "It is going to be a beautiful home for our families, something we have all dreamed about for 30+ years. Our wives and children are going to feel as though they have arrived on 'Fantasy Island'."

"I know," replied Fabian. "Rachael and I have been dreaming and planning about the way we want to construct our new home in this *new world* after our colony has been established. I remember the promise you made to Mirjam back when we were at the estate. Our future will be very active, my friend."

"If we have no difficulty in completing the unloading of the two machines, the time we will spend on the surface should not interfere with an immediate return," I said.

We were in Albert's capable hands. We unloaded successfully and were able to return to the ship on the third pass. Everything went like clockwork. We would begin disassembling the large fuel tanks on the following day.

"The large tanks should be empty of fuel," I said the next morning. "Nevertheless, Fabian and I will suit up, and then we will purge them starting with tank number one. Robert, you, Makoto and Jabbar suit up and operate the utility vehicles that are equipped with laser torches."

Ravi put on the robotic harness and controlled the monorail robot to transport Fabian and me to the utility vehicle shelter. Robert, Makoto, André and Jabbar rode to the utility vehicle shelter with Ravi directing the second monorail robot. They tethered themselves to the utility vehicles and, in turn, tethered the vehicles to the ship. They attached the vehicles' suction feet to tank number one and began cutting sections around the circumference of the tank behind the frontal curvature. Each panel was 10 meters wide and 15 meters around the circumference. After purging the tanks, Fabian and I joined the cutting crew and by evening, we had cut and secured 100 panels.

During the following days, Ravi directed the monorail robot to disconnect from the rail. As the cutting crew finished cutting a panel, he collected and secured them in bundles of 40 for loading onto the landing crafts for transportation to the surface where we used the large construction machines to unload the craft.

After the panels were successfully bundled, Ravi's job became one of helping to prepare the medical center. Dorri and Serena decided to join the landing party and help with the construction project. André kept occupied by studying the three-dimensional map, which he and Robert had constructed from the data gathered from our numerous passes over the landing site. They had determined the best location to construct our compound and the land breaking for the first human settlement was proceeding as planned. Each of us had developed our individual construction specialties and each was accomplishing his or her tasks in an excellent manner. Without my prior knowledge, everyone had agreed that 'Ericsville' would be the name of our first settlement on Kairos. What an extraordinary honor!

The plan was to load and send two landing crafts at a time to the surface. We consulted with Albert as to whether it was possible to control two landing crafts at the same time. Albert suggested that we should stagger the departure by 15 minutes. This should still allow everyone to return to the ship before the return window closed. On the second cycle, Fabian and Makoto stayed on the surface to operate the construction machines for the unloading operation and they began preparing the site for the construction by building a temporary shelter. Ravi joined the construction crew and Jabbar and he would rotate with Fabian and Makoto every four days. If the weather cooperated, we should be finished with the downloading in a month.

After 20 trips, we suspended the operation and waited for a major storm to pass. The storm delayed the transport and the beginning of construction but finally we were successful in transporting all of the fuel tank panels and the panels cut from the tanks' interior supports. The flat interior panels would serve as the flooring and the apartment petitions for the construction development.

"Whew, this deconstruction project has taken some real muscle and time, I can identify every muscle in my body," I stated with relief. "How are the rest of you feeling?

"My workouts in the gym have not prepared me for this much physical effort," replied Jabbar.

"What are you old guys grumping about?" asked Robert jokingly. "All I need is a big dinner and lots to drink, I am famished."

"OK, ok, you've made your point, Son." I replied. "Let's all go back to the ship and eat and get a shower and a good night's rest."

During the time that we were engaged in dismantling and transporting the panels, Mirjam, Gabriele, and Miko were preparing the medical center for transportation to the surface. Rachael, with the help of the younger children and Albert's robotic army, was keeping busy by packing the pantry and frozen food supplies.

The following day we returned to the surface and Fabian and Robert operated the construction machines and began clearing the grass from the area that André had chosen for the administration building. The machines were multi-purposed. By using the land-removal attachments and laser-leveling technology, clearing the area for the structures progressed rapidly. Robert continued leveling the area ahead of us for additional construction sites while Fabian began moving and arranging the flooring panels. The high capacity-welding unit located on each of the machines made fast work of laying the floors.

Fabian held the curved tank panels in place while Makoto, Jabbar, Dorri, Serena and I used portable laser welding units to secure the panels in place. The panels were approximately one meter in thickness and constructed of a lightweight honeycombed alloy that gave the tanks both strength and insulation. A thin sheet of seamless titanium covered the tanks inside and out. The building took on the shape of an elongated Quonset hut, 28 meters from wall to wall.

While we took a break from the construction, I asked. "I have been thinking about how Albert interacts with us. Do we want him to continue to direct our lives?"

"He has helped us out of several dangerous situations," Jabbar said. "However, perhaps we could limit his involvement."

"You men are talking as though Albert is a person," Serena announced. "The HQ-3000 has personality traits but it is not a person. It can 'learn' to mimic human emotional traits and human logic."

"How does Albert know what we need and when we need it?" Fabian asked.

"Albert is programmed to pick up on our emotional feelings and thoughts through brain transmission," Serena explained. "The HQ-3000 is also programmed to single out our voice inflections and originally was to react only to a voice command."

"I think Albert has already become 'acquainted' with our older children by asking questions about their likes, dislikes, habits and reactions to different situations," I said. "He can read them just like he can read us. We may need to limit the younger children's close contact with Albert. They may not be mature enough for him to begin to communicate with them through their emotions."

"The sensors that pick up the emotional transmissions are built into Albert's 'being', Serena continued. "Distance is the only way to keep Albert from detecting one's emotional state although I do not know the sensitivity of these sensors so I don't know the range of the sensor's sensitivity. It is the old 'inverse square law'. But, Albert can determine a person's emotional state through the communicators at any distance."

"Do we still want Albert to continue controlling our lives?" I asked again. "As Jabbar had said, Albert has helped us out of several situations and his guidance has gotten us to Kairos. To what extent do we still need Albert's total involvement in our lives, we had governmental involvement on Earth and we were all weary of having to deal with it."

"Maybe Serena can rewire the circuits to eliminate Albert's ability to detect emotional transmissions," Jabbar said hopefully. "Serena, is there a way to use the vast storage ability separate from Albert's personality? We will need memory to store all of the administrative records and Albert does not need access to them."

"I believe that is a possibility, my dissertation involved work on advanced computer technology," Serena returned. "I'll work on a program to accomplish these goals."

By the time a window to return to the ship appeared, we were almost finished with the administration structure. Our water and food supplies were running low and we were immensely missing the company of the others. On our next trip to the surface, we would transport the solar panels that Fabian and I had previously packaged.

After several more weeks of salvaging, disassembling and reconstruction, we were able to report to our families that the apartments were nearing completion. The administrative offices occupied the northwest corner of the compound and faced to the southeast while the smaller adjoining structures containing apartments, ran north-south on the west side and ran east-west on the north side. The compound began to take on the facade of a fort out of the old North American Wild West. We constructed two large storage tanks behind the administration complex and a structure to house the nuclear-fusion-direct-conversion reactor.

After what seemed to be an endless number of treks between Kairos and the ship to transport the plants, seeds, food and our personal items, we were nearing the completion of our compound.

On one of the return trips to the ship, Mirjam announced. "Gabriele, Rachael, and I have packaged each of the delicate instruments which were in the laboratories. We have secured all of the medical supplies and pharmaceuticals in insulated containers, salvaged from parts of the ship."

I replied to Mirjam. "We will arrange to transport all the med supplies to the permanent medical center on our next trip. We are also about ready to transport the computer hardware to its permanent home in the administration complex. Serena and I will disconnect enough of the ship's sensors to set up surveillance around the perimeter of the compound to warn us of any unwanted visitors. I want to protect individual privacy now that we are almost ready to move permanently to our new home's surface. We no longer need 'Big Brother' to watch us. Serena will disconnect Albert's emotional receivers so Albert should become a voice-activated computer and large data storage unit."

"I have modified the transmitter from the command center and the one from your apartment," Serena announced as I returned from her laboratory with all of the extra chips, capacitors, coils and all the other electronic supplies that remained. "I have been able to design a small communication satellite from the electronics in the communication center. With all of these parts, we should be able to construct four communication satellites."

"All we need now is something to hold all of these parts together and something to receive a signal," Serena added, after we finished the four transmitters.

"I'll search for something to serve as the housing, I stated. "We have salvaged most of the solar sails; couldn't that serve as a receiver? I remember that I collected some corrugated tubing and some thin metal sheeting when we were in the process of salvaging and I stored those items in our apartment, expecting to utilize them for the satellite construction. I'll go get them and we should be able to engineer a receiving device and construct suitable housing for the satellites."

We modified one of the landing crafts and were able to load the four satellites onboard. With just enough remaining fuel, and Albert's navigation, we were able to achieve a geosynchronous orbit above Kairos and we positioned the satellites in the proper location to achieve complete coverage of the planet's surface.

When we were all on the surface, Mirjam and Susanne accompanied me on a tour of the apartments while the other families also toured the apartments. Mirjam and I were the first to choose the location of our new home and Mirjam chose the one nearest to the right of the administration complex.

"Mirjam, Sweetheart, this is not the house that I promised you," I said, as we inspected the interior of the apartment. "I will keep my promise; there are ample building materials available on Kairos to build us a very nice house."

"I am not complaining," Mirjam replied. "I am just very thankful that we have all arrived safely, healthy and alive. There have certainly been some harrowing situations to overcome. We are at the end of one epic journey and we are just beginning another unfamiliar phase of our lives!"

CHAPTER 40

It is now the seventh month since we arrived and we were all settling in; Kairos was feeling more and more like home. Fabian, Makoto, Jabbar and I chose apartments near the administration complex, with, of course, our wives' input and approval. The executive team was composed of our original eight. We had a government in the making. Next to the administration and commercial center was the school and library, at which André assumed the position of head master. The library contained the data bank of all of Earth's history up to the time Destiny departed the solar system. I had assumed the role of team historian and all of my daily logs of our journey were stored in the data bank for future generation's use. The research laboratories were located at the back of the large entry reception site that served as a common meeting area. The medical center was located across the common area form the library. Now that communications between Earth and Kairos were no longer a time-lapse problem, I communicated with Grant and The Committee on a regular basis.

All of the younger families and André wanted to be on their own and make their own decisions so they chose to live as far away from the administration complex as possible. A healthy choice we parents thought. Beyond their apartments was the open grassy plane that led down to the river.

A short time after we had settled into our apartments, I received a communication from Earth. I called for a meeting in the common area and after the community members had arrived; I announced that the colonization ship had left Earth around nine month ago.

"Chloe and her companion, Victor Matthews, are both graduates of the aerospace academy and are commanding the ship," I announced. "The manufacturing equipment that we requested has been loaded aboard along with two hundred colonists, several of which have special training in manufacturing techniques. The new hibernation chambers utilize the additional enzyme-mist discovery made by Gabriele and Mirjam. With these new developments in hibernation, the colonists will stay in a 'sleep state' for the entire trip. The colonists will receive nutrients directly into the body, and in addition, they will receive muscular stimulations daily throughout the journey. When they arrive, they will stay in orbit for a few days recovering from their long hibernation."

"It is unfortunate that technology has not produced a wormhole large enough for a small ship to pass through," Serena said.

"Perhaps someday soon," I continued. "Since there is no need for living quarters and therefore no need for artificial gravity, the ship is much more streamlined and the engines can continue operating throughout the trip reducing the travel time by 50 percent.

We had successfully transported the magnetic booster cores from the ship's plasma drive and decided to leave the remaining rocket fuel in the ship. This fuel would allow the stabilizer engines to keep a stable orbit with a small reserve for use when the colonization ship arrived. Albert still had control of the ship. The lamps, salvaged from the ship, supplied all of our lighting needs and the solar cells that Fabian, Serena and I made supplemented the energy. Eventually, we planned to convert the magnetic cores into turbines and harness the river's energy.

Robert, Ravi and André were egger to begin exploration of the river from the foothills to the falls where the river plunged into the gorge. Early one morning they packed camping gear and one of the hunting rifles, just in case of trouble, for an overnight stay.

"Keep your video-com on and operational," I insisted. "You have no idea what to expect. And be diligent, one of you should always be on the lookout."

"We will," Robert replied as they excitedly left the compound and headed toward the river. "We expect to complete an entire survey of the river before we return tomorrow."

"I am just being a dad," I said in a loud voice, with Fabian echoing my sentiments.

Wanting to be involved in what their husbands were doing and to remind them of their requests to watch for the unknown, Dorri and Miko followed the explorers past the end of the compound. Mirjam and Rachael also joined the send-off party, giving their own admonitions to be safe.

"Collect any plant life that we have not yet seen," Miko requested. "Look for additional blood ferns. And Ravi, do be careful, I would like to be going also but I am now at a critical point in the analysis and the classification of the blood ferns, this has taken longer than I expected."

"The 'be careful and stay safe' part goes for me to," Dorri said as she ran after him and gave Robert an adoring hug and kiss.

They had been gone no more than an hour when Robert buzzed us to get our attention.

"We are observing a large herd of the animals that Makoto and I tracked to the river's edge on the first landing," Ravi said with excitement. "They are grazing about 50 meters in front of us. The herd is on the same side of the river as we are and we need to either go through them or wait on them to move."

"We have decided to approach with caution," Ravi said. "I have not seen any fast movement from any of the animals."

"They look like a large overgrown mix between a musk ox and some kind of rhinoceros," André said. "If they behave like a rhinoceros, I am afraid that we will not be able to out run them, especially in the tall grass."

"The rifle may not penetrate the massive boney structure covering their head," Ravi commented as he removed the rifle from his shoulder.

"I will not ask you *not* to investigate," Fabian said. "But your mother is standing behind me biting her nails. Do be very cautious."

Robert, Ravi and André approached the herd very cautiously and fortunately downwind from the herd. The herd allowed our sons to approach to within 25 meters before there was any visible acknowledgment of their presence. One of the large bulls began sniffing the air and looking in the direction of André and the others. The alpha male began snorting and striking the ground and the other males of the herd positioned themselves between the herd and the three men.

"I think this is as close as he wants us to come," Robert said. "I am going to get the hypodermic rifle; I think that I can hit him from this distance."

"We should stand here and observe," André said. "If we need to run we will still have a 25 meter head start."

The large alpha male dropped a few moments after the needle penetrated the softer area of flesh at the base of his neck. When the alpha male dropped, the herd began slowly moving toward the river. One of the cows fell behind separating herself from the others and continued to graze near the fallen male.

"I want to see how close I can get to the cow before she notices me," André said as he approached to within 10 meters and then stopped. "I have the tracking devices on my belt and will staple one to the alpha male's ear while he is still out."

The cow continued to graze as though André were not there.

"I am going to see if I can touch the cow," André said as he moved even closer. "I think that 'rhinox' would be an appropriate name."

André approached the cow, which did not appear the least bit interested or aggressive, and patted her rump. He then collected the syringe, containing the tissue and blood sample, from the alpha male, and stapled the tracking device to his very tough ear. When the large male recovered, he and the cow rejoined the rest of the herd and the exploration team left as the herd crossed the river.

Robert, Ravi and André moved upstream continuing to map and survey and record the condition of the river and its surrounding countryside, using the three- dimensional-laser transit. As evening approached, they looked for a suitable sheltered campsite. As they approached the foothills, the river began to form a narrow valley with cliffs on the west side and they set up camp under a rocky overhang about 10 meters above the river. This afforded them an excellent view up into the foothills and out over the wide rolling plane across the river.

"Should we search for some kindling for a fire?" André asked. "I have read that fire is theoretically used to keep animals away."

"I am not sure that animals on Kairos have ever seen fire," Robert said. "Fire as a means of frightening night prowlers away might attract them rather than discourage any animal that might come our way. We do not need a fire to keep warm or to cook, and besides I have not noticed wood of any kind since we left this morning."

Ravi said. "We should take turns watching for intruders. Who will take the first three-hour watch?"

"I'll take the first watch," André replied.

"O.K., I will take the second watch," Robert said.

"There is another herd of rhinox across the river," André said as he looked out across the river and as he prepared for his first watch.

"It may be the same herd we encountered earlier," Ravi commented. "I will see if I can locate the alpha male we tagged."

As Ravi began looking through the magnifier attempting to locate the alpha male, a large, strange-looking animal came rushing out of the hills and attacked the herd. The males of the herd formed a defensive line between the attacker and the herd, in the same way that they had reacted to the team earlier. The massive boney plates on their heads were relatively effective weapons against their attacker. Eventually the attacking animal managed to grab one of the young rhinox in its massive jaws and ran back into the hills with his prey.

"What was that?" I asked as I called to the exploration team.

"Dad," Robert said still in amazement. "It is an animal about half the size of one of the larger rhinox and has extremely large and powerful shoulders and front limbs. Its head is massive with a mouth containing large canines about the size of a saber-toothed cat."

"How close are the three of you to where this beast entered the hills?" I asked.

"We are on the west side of the river protected by a rocky overhang," Ravi explained. "The herd of rhinox is on the other side and upstream approximately 10 meters. They are grazing near the water's edge and almost into the hills. The creature is very fast and it jumped out from behind a rock and retreated to the rocks carrying the young rhinox."

"We are keeping all lights off and each of us is taking a three-hour watch with the hunting rifle in hand," André added.

During the third watch, Ravi awakened Robert and André.

"Hurry, get up, we must head back immediately," Ravi cried out excitedly. "Dad just called and they are under attack by creatures that walk upright; he wants us safely back in the compound."

The young men hurriedly broke camp and began running along the river toward the compound. They stopped for a quick chance to catch their breath as the sun was coming up with brilliant colors in the eastern sky.

"Dorri, what is happening there?" Robert called with intensity in his winded voice.

There was no answer.

"Someone, answer me, we are stopped for a few minutes just to catch our breaths, anyone there, please answer," Robert continued.

Mirjam answered with fear and concern, "earlier this morning we were awakened by some unusual noises outside. The surveillance monitors only picked up a shadow, nothing distinct, only that they moved about upright. Makoto and Jabbar reset the sensors and placed traps next to the sensors with the expectation of capturing one of them so that we could have a chance to make an examination. Everything is calm now. Where are the three of you, how far away are you?"

"We are about 40 km from the compound," Ravi reported.

"Catch your breath and be cautious," Mirjam returned. "The excitement seems to be over.

The three continued following the river rather than cutting across the grassy plateau, which would make walking very difficult. They were still hurrying since they did not want the rest having to deal with any other intruders alone.

Shortly after sunrise, our sensors indicated that the trap had captured one of the primates. When the animal stood upright, it was over a meter tall with medium-short legs and longer arms with well-developed hands and feet. The head appeared to be primate-like with oversized eyes. We went out to retrieve our specimen from the trap when approximately 20 of the creatures attacked us, carrying long pointed sticks. They began to throw the sticks at us and as they got closer, one of the lances hit Makoto on the forearm that broke the skin. His arm immediately began to swell and turn red. Makoto began to stumble and could not focus. We hurried back to the common area, with Jabbar and Fabian carrying Makoto under his arms. Gabriele and Mirjam began treating Makoto while the rest of us retrieved the lasers and set them for a mild charge. I counted to see if everyone was safely in the shelter.

"Where is Faina," Fabian anxiously asked. "Has anyone seen Faina? She was right behind me when we left the traps."

"Faina, Faina, where are you," Rachael frantically cried, and called out as she ran through the common area!

Fabian, Jabbar and I each took our lasers and ran toward the open end of the compound. In the distance we saw four of the animals carrying Faina away, each one holding her by one of her limbs; she appeared to be limp and not struggling. Fabian ran ahead of us, his laser set on maximum. The other two of us followed closely behind.

"Mirjam how is Makoto?" I asked over my video-com as we ran in an attempt to catch Faina and her capturers. "Call Robert, and have our young men head for the water fall. It appears that the creatures are heading in that direction. We seem to be gaining on them. Ask the exploration team to keep in touch with us in case there is a change in plans. Tell Robert that the primates captured Faina."

A moment later Ravi called me. "Dad, we are over half-way back to the compound. Did I hear Robert correctly; Mom said one of the girls was taken captive?"

"Yes that is correct," I replied. "The creatures captured Faina and seem to be heading toward the water falls. Approach carefully; they carry poisonous sticks that can cause serious injury."

"One of the girls is missing?" André asked with concern, not having heard all of the conversations. "It cannot be Susanne, tell me it is not Susanne. I am very fond of her, we have been seeing a lot of each other lately, taking long walks together, and actually I am in love with her."

"Dad said that it is your sister, Faina," Robert replied. "Your dad and some of the others are in pursuit. They are heading toward the river so we are to go toward the falls and should meet up with them there."

"Not Faina," André anxiously replied. "She is so small and has always been so fragile."

Robert, Ravi and André started running faster, when they heard the news of Faina's trouble, and got to the cleared path between the compound and the river just moments after Fabian and the others.

Everyone was in constant communications now so André and the other young men headed down the river and were able to see us about 200 meters farther downstream.

As the primate-creatures neared the waterfalls and rapids, they disappeared around a large overhang. Fabian led the way into a cavern entrance at the back of the overhang. Fabian, followed by Jabbar and myself, entered the caverns carrying light torches and with our laser weapons at the ready.

As our eyes slowly adjusted to the darkness, we were astonished at what we saw. An enormous room opened up just inside of the cave entrance. The odor was disgusting, smelling of feces and urine. The walls of the room were dotted with dugouts, each housing two or three of the primate creatures. Faina lay on the floor of the cave with several of the creatures surrounding her, just watching. We cautiously approached but several of the creatures blocked our way by standing shoulder-to-shoulder, jumping up and down in place, fiercely showing their teeth and shrieking loudly.

Fabian, out of panic and fear for Faina, lowered his laser to stun the animals and fired, hitting the animal nearest to the entrance, causing it to lose consciousness for a moment. The other animals did not react because their companion recovered rapidly. Each of us set our lasers on maximum, just in case.

Fabian motioned to Faina and pointed back to himself. After several attempts to 'communicate' Fabian was at a loss as to what to do next. We could not win a battle against the poisonous lances.

"Do you suppose that they want to trade Faina for the animal that we captured?" Jabbar asked.

"Bring the captured animal to the waterfalls," Fabian said calling back to the compound, as Jabbar positioned himself near the entrance to the caverns to wait for the animal.

A few minutes later Dorri and Miko approached the waterfalls with the captured animal riding in a cage on one of the robotic rovers.

Dorri shouted. "We saw your laser lights, what should we do with this animal? Someone come and get it."

Jabbar came running to retrieve the cage and brought the animal into the caverns. He opened the cage as Fabian again motioned to Faina, then to himself, then to our captured animal, then toward the animals that continued to stand guard. After several similar attempts, the blockade of warriors backed away, allowing Fabian to pick up Faina and we all slowly backed out of the cave and then hurried back to the compound. Faina and Fabian rode in the rover, and the remainder of us followed closely behind as we kept our lasers on maximum. Jabbar brought up the rear, keeping a close look out.

On the ride back to the compound Faina began to awaken. She found herself in the rover sitting next to her dad with her head resting on his shoulder. She was feeling a little nauseous and had a mild headache but she was full of questions about what had happened to her. Once we were back in the compound Mirjam and Gabriele gave Faina a thorough check up and noticed a small, slightly swollen scratch on her neck, but most of the redness had dissipated. Mirjam administered an antihistamine as a precaution and if no residual effects from the poison remained, Makoto and Faina should feel healthy in a day or so. Faina was very happy to be back home, but immediately wanted to go and shower, feeling repulsed by the stench and slime on her.

That evening after we were all secure we met in the common area and celebrated the recovery of Faina and Makoto. We discussed our feelings of pride in our abilities in conquering our problems and relaxed by listening to a beautiful violin concerto.

Later that night, we were conversing about the frightening day that we had just experienced. We made a unanimous decision to use the 'buddy system' as a protective measure when leaving the security of the compound. I could not envision that this would be our last incident that would bring about unexpected and dangerous circumstances!

CHAPTER 41

Physically Makoto and Faina recovered quickly from their primate encounter since the poison proved to be short lived. Faina, on the other hand, had developed trouble sleeping and when she finally did go to sleep, the dreams of her capture interrupted her rest. André anxiously accepted the responsibility of treating his sister and she became his first patient and thus he began his psychological counseling practice. He had been studying psychology from the information stored in our extensive archives and from observing the techniques used in actual psychologist's sessions he was able to develop a style of his own and diagnosed Faina's anxiety. André had the ability to remember verbatim essentially everything that he read and observed. He was a good listener and was able to help Faina conquer her fears. After several sessions she stopped having the terrible dreams and with a mild sedative, administered to her by Mirjam, she was soon back to sleeping normally and returning to her happy teenager self.

As had become our custom, we all grouped together in the foyer of the administration building after breakfast each day to discuss our plans for that day.

Makoto announced, "now that I have recovered after several nights' of rest I would like to plan an exploration party up the river and into the foothills. That is, if I have clearance from the medical staff."

"You and Faina both should be fine," Gabriele said. "The poison was mild and seems to be related to the toxins found in the oleander plant back on Earth, but is not as potent. Mirjam, are you in agreement?"

"Yes," Mirjam said. "They both should be fine and I don't see an indication of any residual effects. You or Ravi should accompany the team on their exploration trip, however."

"Before any of us go outside the compound, especially into the foothills, we should take adequate precaution and be vigilant." I said. "Remember the incident when the three young men witnessed the beast attack on the rhinox herd. They were lucky to escape without harm."

"We could modify the rover used to carry the robotic probe," Robert said. "We do have another rover also, correct? And, I want to be included as a part of this exploration team that Makoto is planning."

"You're correct, we do have two rovers," I answered. "The rovers are platforms on tracks with over a meter clearance and powered with the same type of power system that is used in the construction machines."

"I would like to observe another one of the beasts that attacked the rhinox herd," André said. "However, I am now more interested in studying the primate behavior, but I still would like to be added to the next exploration to research the rhinox."

"Fabian, you are the senior geologist; you should go help locate possible mineral deposits." I added. We need to find building materials, these temporary shelters are going to become tiresome. You will need to map the entire area between the two rivers and extend the mapping into the foothills."

"I will need to go also," Rachael said. "I would like to be able to stretch my legs and look for other local plants; we have just scratched the surface of what this planet has to offer. I feel it is important to make field tests of the plants and send the data back for Jabbar to study."

We were able to modify the rovers by building a frame made of titanium tubing salvaged from the ship. In addition, we utilized the panels from the ship's apartments to construct the body of the rovers. Each rover contained four of the reclining seats from the command center, which would serve as sleeping lounges at night.

Fabian, Robert, Ravi and their wives rounded out our selection for the first major geological exploration of the plateau and the foothills. They took food and water for seven days, along with scientific equipment, typical camping equipment and survival supplies, along with one of the hunting rifles.

><

We had arrived on Kairos in the first quarter of the Kairos year, year number one. There had been very few storms and little rain since we arrived. The first project after setting up our living quarters had been to transfer the water treatment system from the ship. Our solution for an adequate water supply for our domestic use and for irrigation was a project to build a dam and lay a water line to the compound. We used the construction machines to move some large boulders to dam up the river and to dig a trench to lay the water line.

The first crops were maturing and with the help of the robotic farmers, under Albert's control, we were going to have an ample supply of food. From all the data collected before we arrived and from our observations, we should not expect a large climate change from summer to winter. The days were getting shorter so our winter was approaching. Subtropical fruit trees should withstand the winter on the plateau but our tropical varieties would need protection until we could find a suitable location to transplant those trees at a lower elevation.

I was confident that we could keep the compound secure. After the exploration team left, Jabbar, André and I, with the help of the teenagers set up a laser defense around the perimeter of the farm extending from the south wall of the west apartment wing to the east wall of the north wing. We also installed lights and motion sensors on the top of the apartments and administration complex, all compliments of our salvaging efforts.

While we secured the compound, André and Susanne began to study the primate's social behavior by placing sensors equipped with high intensity video and audio transmissions around the Miko Falls, with the assumption that the primates frequented that area for their water needs. The proof of their assumption occurred as it was becoming dark when they observed a hunting party of seven adult males using their poison sticks to throw at small lizard-like creatures near the river's edge at the bottom of the waterfall while others used the falls as a shower. The hunting party would pick up the stunned animal and puncture it through the head with a stick. Each hunter had his own collection of speared lizards. One primate had collected only three lizards while one of the larger males had collected seven. The one with only three ran over to the better hunter and grabbed two of his lizards. The better hunter started screeching and stomping to scare away the thief. This activity lasted only a short time but the crafty thief was able to keep his bounty. The hunting party of primates then returned to the cave but before leaving, several filled hollowed-out gourds with water.

While André and Susanne observed the primates on the monitors, I began noticing dark cloud formations building in the mountains to the north where the team planned to set up camp the first night.

"When was the last time anyone heard from the exploration team?" I asked Jabbar and the teens as we finished with the surveillance network.

"Mom called me about an hour ago," Faina said. "She said that they had set up camp along the Saito River as far into the foothills as the rovers could maneuver. She then said that Dad and Robert were going on foot to survey a rock formation a few hundred meters upstream."

"I will try and contact them now," I replied. "I'll update them on the weather; it is beginning to look very stormy and our instruments indicate a low pressure is building; they should be keeping their communicators on."

No sooner had I started to contact Fabian, than the ground began shaking.

Moments later I heard Robert faintly cry out. "Is anyone hurt?"

"No one is seriously hurt," I heard Gabriele reply to Robert. "We have a few minor cuts. But the violent shaking caused one of the rovers to slide into the river and the other one is covered by the landslide."

"What is the extent of your damage?" I asked after overhearing their conversation. "I'm thankful that no one was seriously hurt? We felt the trimmers here at the compound, but it sounds as if you were closer to the epicenter. The last we heard, Fabian and Robert were heading up the river to survey a formation cut into the mountain."

Fabian started explaining. "Robert and I were climbing the cliff on the other side of the river when the quake hit. We lost our footing and slid to a stop a few meters downhill, but the quake caused us to lose all of our gear along with our communicators. From the way the granite is uplifted we were on the fault line."

"The rover higher up the incline is not going anywhere with all these rocks on it and the river is not that deep so the one in the river should stay there for now," Robert said. "I suggest that we get out of this cold rain and enjoy a hot meal in the tent. It is getting late and we can survey the damage tomorrow when it is daylight and warmer."

The next day André was curious to see if the primates would repeat their early evening hunting activities. He and Susanne observed the primates going on their hunt as they had the day before; evidently, the quake had not interrupted their routine.

The exploration team awakened with sore aching muscles but in clean dry clothes. After a couple of cups of hot campfire coffee and some granola, each one was feeling much better. Makoto and Ravi began uncovering the rover while Fabian and Robert went in search of their gear and communicators. They also continued to survey the outcroppings in the cliff above the river.

"Makoto and I were able to uncover most of the rover which is stranded up here," Ravi said as we opened communication. "We will have to wait for Fabian and Robert to return before we can attempt to finish clearing the larger rocks and attempt to winch the rover up out of the river. We'll plan to spend another night here."

"Keep a communicator open, Son," I replied. "We are always anxious to find out how things are going, so keep in touch."

Early the next evening André and Susanne trapped some of the 'lizards' and tied sensors loosely around their mid-sections and turned them loose near the cave opening, with the expectation that the primates would capture them and take the lizards back into their cave. By the time, the primates returned to the cave with the captured lizards, two of the sensors had come loose and dropped to the floor of the cave. Immediately, two of the young primates grabbed them up and started chewing on them, as human toddlers would do, destroying them.

That experiment was not successful. André asked for Serena's expert assistance in manufacturing a very small remote controlled robot, including a monitor, which would transmit video images and audio sounds of the primates' behaviors. She was able to build the robot in a very short time, and André sent the device into the cave and he directed it to a secluded corner of the cave where he and Susanne were able to observe their daily activities.

On the third morning, the team loaded up the slightly damaged rovers.

"We plan to continue with the survey providing we can keep the rovers operational," Fabian said in his morning report. "We will keep in contact; we only have four communicators which are operational, however we are all eager to continue with the mapping and exploring. We should be back at the compound within days."

CHAPTER 42

The exploration party returned to the compound tired, sore and in need of showers and a good meal. After a good night's rest in their own beds, the explorers met with the rest of us for a community breakfast and they gave an account of their week of exploration.

"The Deville River extends much farther into the North Mountain Range than does the Saito River," Fabian explained. "It forms a very picturesque mountain valley. We took water samples and ran a qualitative and quantitative analysis and found that the Deville River indicated that there are ample deposits of copper, gold, tungsten, tin as well as traces of zinc, lead and molybdenum. In addition, the Saito River samples yielded zinc and lead.

"The plateau gradually descends to the coastal plane 100 kilometers west of the Deville River," Robert said.

"Several meters west of the compound we noticed that the plateau vegetation changes from the wheat-like grass which the rhinox use for grazing into a different variety of vegetation, which has a stalk amazingly like bamboo." Rachael added.

"We should see if this can be used in our house construction," Fabian added.

"I'll take the rover and go gather some of the bamboo-like plants for us to experiment with," said Robert. "I agree with Fabian that it looks like it could contain properties which we may be able to utilize in the construction of our homes."

We recorded and logged the report of the exploration team and forwarded the information back to Earth in my next report. I am certain that The Committee would be very pleased to hear of the mineral deposits we located.

Meanwhile André and Susanne continued their study of the primate behavior. They observed the primates going down the Saito River to gather fruit from several trees below the falls. The fruit appeared tropical in nature and we gathered several varieties and tested them for harmful compounds; finding that they contained none, we sampled them and discovered that they were very delicious. We, therefore, transplanted our tropical fruit trees, which were growing in the greenhouse, to the forest along the Deville River west of the compound. We utilized the rovers in moving the trees; and we are very thankful that they are still versatile in helping us with all the heavy moving and other demanding jobs we have.

After many trials using the mastic obtained from the 'bamboo' plants, we discovered that after refining it we could use it as an epoxy. We utilized the fibrous portion of the bamboo plant stalks by rolling, pressing and laminating them using the epoxy to form panels, which we used as partitions, in the construction of our houses and buildings.

We converted the landing crafts into haulers to transport marble slabs to our building site. With the four landing crafts' ability to maneuver in the atmosphere, eventually some of us mastered the agility to maneuver them sufficiently to and from the marble quarries, located in the foothills near where Robert, Ravi and André observed the attack on the rhinox herd. I carefully monitored the crafts during the marble hauling operation, hoping that they would last until we could finish building our houses and other buildings in our compound.

Our homes turned out to be beautiful and each one was extraordinarily different in design from the others. The houses each consisted of at least four bedrooms, a central family room/kitchen combination, lavatories and an attached storage area, which we could later convert into any number of a variety of useful rooms. The epoxy served as sufficient 'mortar' successfully bonding the precision laser cut marble-slabs. The slabs formed the exterior walls and the laminated bamboo furnished the other construction needs. The bamboo panels finished the interior design and with some modification served as a roofing material.

"Eric, our home is as gorgeous as the Chateau. The polished interior panels and marble used in the kitchen and lavatories are more splendid than I could ever have imagined," Mirjam said as we settled down for our first night in our newly finished house. "You promised me a castle when we were walking in the estate's gardens many years ago, and you certainly have kept your promise, thank you, darling."

"Mirjam, nothing is too great for you, I can never express what a wonderful wife you are to me and a fabulous you are to our children and soon-to-be Grand-mom to our grandchildren," I said as I enfolded her close to me. "This will work until the supply ship brings the manufacturing supplies and equipment, then everything can begin functioning properly, as a normal home."

Everyone assisted each other until each family's house was complete. We finished the permanent medical center, administration offices and library-school located north of the original landing site, now preserved as a National Historical Site.

Now that Ericsville was nearing completion, and we had some free time, I decided to lead an exploration team to survey the low lands and the delta formed by the Deville and Saito Rivers. By combining the fuel in the four landing crafts to assist the four plasma engines, I decided that there would be enough fuel to get as far as the delta, with the anticipation of getting partially home.

I spoke with Jabbar, Serena and Mirjam about the exploration I had planned.

"We need to pack survival supplies," I said as we discussed the trip. "We may need to hike part of the way back to the compound. I have calculated that we will have fuel enough to get to the delta but it will be a stretch to get all the way back."

"We really have no idea what we might encounter in the low lands." Serena commented. "We should pack camping gear and provisions. If we have to walk back, it will take us at least three days. And, we don't have any idea what may happen along the way."

"We each should take a laser weapon and one of us should take one of the hunting rifles, Jabbar added.

"All right, Jabbar, you are right, we will all take a laser weapon, you take the rifle, I will take a tent, and in addition each of us will take food for four days," I said. "Can anyone think of anything else?"

We discussed the trip for another hour and came up with a few other helpful items.

"Let's call it an evening," Mirjam said. "Tomorrow will be a long day."

We gathered at the craft after breakfast the next day. Everyone was there to wish us well.

"We will keep in contact with Fabian and he can give each of you a report." I said as we boarded the craft.

By mid-morning, we were approaching the delta and the expanse of water to the west. Just look at this view. I set the landing craft down on the north side of the delta and we disembarked. The energy cells in the crafts were getting low before we landed and I was afraid that they had finally stopped producing energy.

We headed west a few hundred meters and stopped on a pristine beach. After collecting water samples, we studied the fauna and collected several samples. The only wild life we saw were a few different species of waterfowl. Each was a little larger than a brown pelican, had a long beak lined with small sharp teeth and with sparsely fathered bodies.

By noon, I said. "Let's have some lunch here on the beach and study the behavior of these strange birds. We will have plenty of time before we need to get back to the landing craft. We can spend the night in the craft and as we head back we will undoubtedly have the opportunity to make several investigative stops along the way."

"Those birds are comedians," said Mirjam. "Watch them soar through the air, dropping their heads to search the ocean, then make a perfect dive and come up with a fish, tossing it in the air a few times, then swallowing it whole. Our future grandchildren are going to have a lot of fun watching these comics."

The next morning after breakfast I tried to start the landing craft but with no success.

"We must have pushed these landing crafts more than they were designed for; after all we have been using them like the old-fashioned diesel haulers in our transport work," I said to the others.

We had a long walk back to the compound so we unloaded the crippled craft and began our walk back. It was fortunate that Jabbar had suggested that we land on the north side of the delta so we would not have to trudge through any swampy delta wetlands.

As we were heading inland, the coastal fauna gradually changed and we found ourselves walking through a dense jungle. It was certainly a more difficult journey than we had in the landing craft. Luckily, we had brought two machetes and some torches. The sun could not penetrate the dense foliage, which seemed to close in on every side.

"The river is making a bend up ahead," said Serena. "Perhaps we should make camp here for the evening."

"Let's make a fire, hopefully that will protect us from any unknown searching eyes of creatures that might be lurking around our perimeter," suggested Mirjam. "It will be nice and cozy besides; this is a romantic setting, even if it is somewhat frightening."

I said. "Put your torches in a semi-circle between our camp and the jungle. This is still an uncharted area, and we need to be cautious.

I'll take the first watch, who wants to be next, we will schedule 2 hours per watch?"

Mirjam said. "I'll go next, Eric. I'm not very sleepy anyway; right now I feel sleep will not be coming quickly for me tonight."

"Thanks, Mirjam," I said. "Be alert and don't be afraid to call out if you need any help. Jabbar, will you be next on our watch schedule?"

"Sure, Eric, I'll be happy to and I am sleepy now, so see you later," said Jabbar.

Around 1:30 A.M., during Jabbar's watch, a noise startled him coming from the jungle and was coming from the direction behind their fire. The glow of the fire made it difficult for Jabbar to see, so he stepped into the shadows and saw a large animal that looked to him something like a bear. It was barring its teeth, making a low growling noise, with its massive head lowered to its shoulders, slowly advancing toward Jabbar. Jabbar screamed and shouldered his rifle just as I exited the tent. I started going toward Jabbar in slow easy movements as the animal lurched toward us. Jabbar fired the rifle as the animal kept coming toward us hurriedly. It grabbed my lower leg as Jabbar fired a second round into the animal's massive neck; and the animal dropped to the ground as it still had my leg gripped tightly in its jaws.

"Eric, hold still while Serena and I get this beast's jaws pried open so Mirjam can remove your leg," Jabbar yelled.

Mirjam, my very talented doctor wife, immediately administered an antiseptic salve to my injured leg, sprayed on an instant bandage and had me take two pain relievers. We all stayed awake after this frightful incident and were eager to start home as soon as daybreak.

Serena found a heavy-duty limb suitable for me to use as a crutch and we left for the highlands after a small breakfast and hurriedly gathered up our supplies, minus our tent.

"Fabian," Jabbar called on his communicator. "We were camped by the river last night and had an unwanted visitor. A bear-like beast appeared out of the darkness of the jungle and attacked us, grabbing

Eric in his jaws in a vise-like bite on his lower leg. He wasn't injured badly, there were no broken bones but he has a deep laceration below the knee. He will have trouble walking now that the landing craft is out of commission. Mirjam quickly treated his wound after Serena and I had dislodged his leg from the animal's grip. I had to kill the beast with the rifle, something we had not wanted to do, but I'm certainly glad we had come prepared."

Fabian said. "Keep your communicator on, I will use it as a beacon to help locate you. I will come for Eric in one of the rovers."

EPILOGUE

All the citizens of Ericsville were eagerly anticipating the arrival of the first colony ship under the command of Chloe and Victor, which was due to arrive in two weeks. The Committee had communicated to me that, as we had previously planned, a second colony ship had left Earth and was scheduled to arrive a year after the first. This arrangement would continue for enough years to establish Kairos as a thriving and productive planet. The future ships also would bring manufacturing equipment and supplies as well as people skilled in various trades. The Committee had conveyed their expectations that we should very soon begin to ship raw materials back to Earth. I had been keeping The Committee informed about the antiquated condition of our equipment and machinery and they had assured me that the colonists were bringing many new pieces of machinery and equipment specifically suited for our needs here on Kairos.

I would be an 'old man' of 69 when the first colonists arrived, although I looked and felt much younger, and so did Mirjam. We had established a stable working community and the citizens of Kairos had recently elected André as 'Head of State'.

Kairos had developed in many areas since we first set foot on the planet. The exploration and mapping of the plateau was now complete as well as most of the foothill region of the Northern Range. The 'rhinox', which we have now domesticated, resided permanently on the plateau. We also had discovered a migratory herd of animals that appeared similar to, but smaller than a North American Bison and with the agility of an antelope. We named these sable-brown, shorthaired, stocky, yet sure-footed animals, 'Kairos Bison'. They migrated between the mountains during the summer and the plateau during the winter.

Several small varieties of reptiles lived near the Saito River and served as a main food source for the primates. Makoto discovered three fish species in addition to the Saito River Serpent, which he had discovered on our first trip to Kairos. The fish looked remarkably like trout and bass species, found on Earth. Makoto collected specimens of the three fish species and after protein analysis, using a gas chromatography-mass- spectrometer and DNA profiling, Ravi and Miko determined that they were suitable for human consumption, making a delightful addition to our meals.

Mirjam, Gabriele, Ravi and Miko spent hours in the medical laboratory doing DNA research on the samples of blood and tissue, which we obtained from the rhinox and the bison. After several years of trial and error, they successfully were able to produce, by working with the frozen bovine embryos, one female in the artificial wombs. Comparative DNA of the 'bison' and the bovine embryos indicated a 98% match. The group continued to alter genetically the DNA and was successful in artificially inseminating the bovine female with the altered semen of a male bison. We now have a thriving herd of hardy mixed-breed animals capable of reproduction. Ah, steak once again, although the more Mirjam worked with the project, the more she was determined she was going to stay a vegetarian.

After arriving on Kairos, Robert and Dorri were the first to make Mirjam and myself proud grandparents. Our first grandchild, Samuel, now fifteen, the second was a beautiful girl, Ruth, who is now a blossoming twelve year old. André and Susanne had twins, which are now curious and intelligent ten-year old boys named Thomas and Andrew. Miko and Ravi have given us another granddaughter whom they named, Jessica, who is now thirteen and a grandson who is now an energetic seven year old named Joseph, (Joey) and are now expecting another son. Kian and Faina were a couple now, as well as Aaron and Lei and both couples are expecting. We were delighted that all the children had found compatible mates and seemed especially happy together. Our numbers would continue to increase; it was inevitable! Mirjam and I had discontinued our Bible story time when the children had gotten older. When we became grandparents, Fabian and I, along with our extended families, had begun a scheduled study of the Hebrew and Greek texts, searching for a pattern of worship found in the early Christian community. In addition to these studies, we renewed our Bible story sessions with the young children, whom have become avid readers and desire to study more ancient texts.

Life was good on the Fabian plateau. We had fashioned our homes after the estate, which we visited when starting this incredible chapter in our lives. The low foothills had an ample supply of marble and with the epoxy, made from the bamboo grass growing on the plateau, we were able to build our homes. Each couple had moved out of the temporary apartments to give room for the colonists when they arrived. We had discovered several strange species of flora and fauna and we were looking forward to organizing extended expeditions into the lowlands and into the mountains to the north. Kairos was a beautiful planet and a comfortable home for humans and we were all dedicated to keeping it as unspoiled and protected as possible

One spring evening as Fabian, Rachael, Mirjam and I were reminiscing about our lives and the soon to arrive colonists, we were astonished to hear a faraway noisy rumbling.

"That sounds like thunder," Rachael said listening to the low rumble in the west. "Fabian, we should hurry back to our home."

Looking outside, I said. "There is a plethora of lighting and an enormous black cloud forming low in the western horizon; it looks as though a major storm is forming."

There had been few solar disturbances, such as the one which was experienced by the first landing party, and no major thunderstorms since our arrival on Kairos, only the seasonal rains and snow in the higher elevations. Our average rainfall was forty centimeters per year and mostly in the winter. As Mirjam and I continued looking in amazement, the sky overhead became ominously dark and torrents of rain began falling. The thunder and lightning were more violent than we had ever witnessed. None of us had experienced such violent weather before. The rain kept coming with maddening speed and volume. As quickly as it started, it stopped. Immediately the wind became extremely violent, to the point of shaking the foundation of our home and the forceful wind ripped the roof off. Everything was as dark as a moonless night and the noise was as loud as a rocket blast. Debris was flying all around so that we could not see each other. I reached for Mirjam but she had vanished from my sight.

I awoke with a shape pain it my left shoulder. I could not move my upper body. I tried again to move my shoulders but the pain was too great. I pushed against something with my feet but I could move only slightly. Where was I? It was dark but I could faintly see a dim light above my head as I moved my head backwards. My memory began to return with a sudden flash-back, remembering the enormous wind and everything turning dark. I remembered trying to hold on to Mirjam by holding her in my arms. Frantically moving my head right and left, I could not find her. Suddenly I had a burst of strength, gave a shove with by feet, and pushed myself out from under the cabinet that lay across my chest. A couple more shoves and I was free. I continued searching in the darkness for Mirjam but I couldn't locate her anywhere. I managed to pull myself upright and tried to stand but that last push must have reinjured my left leg, which was wounded by the giant jungle 'bear' in the attack on our recent exploration. With the use of a broken timber as a crutch, I stumbled my way out of our house calling for Mirjam. There was no answer. After a few anxious moments, I saw Fabian struggling to move a portion of his roof and I began crawling over a mass of debris, as I called to him.

"Fabian, are you injured?" I yelled. "Have you seen Mirjam?"

"Help me, I need your help with Rachael, she is pinned under some of our roof supports," he called out in fear.

"Fabian, I'm coming to help you, but have you seen Mirjam?" I again shouted anxiously as I stumbled toward him. "I haven't seen her since she was swept away from my grasp during the storm and I have been shouting her name since I came to. She is nowhere in sight and is not answering me. I am so worried, I can't imagine where she could be."

I managed to get to Fabian and help him remove the roof supports and rescue Rachael, using my free arm. She was bruised and scrapped from the ordeal and had possibly suffered a serious head injury from the look of the laceration on her forehead. She was sobbing uncontrollably and quickly grabbed Fabian around his neck as soon as we removed the debris from her body.

"Oh, Fabian, I am so thankful you two are safe, where is Mirjam?" Rachael asked. "Has anyone else been hurt, how are our children and their families? I was so frightened that you could not find me and I was sure that I could not free myself without help."

"I haven't seen Mirjam since the storm struck and I am anxious to start searching for her," I replied. "I have not seen any of our kids or grandkids since the storm either, I am heading for their homes now to check on them and ask for their help to search for Mirjam."

I hurriedly left Rachael and Fabian and started toward the eastern edge of the compound. The younger families and their kids were out surveying the damage to their houses. None of them looked as if they were injured.

As I approached, Robert and Dorri were clearing some rubble from around the foundation of their house. The storm had not done extensive damage to the young families' houses. Fabian and Rachael's house and ours seemed to have sustained the most damage.

"I cannot find your Mom; she was blown out of my arms during the storm." I said with distress as my voice began to break. "Is anyone down here hurt?"

As soon as I had said that, the other younger families started showing up anxiously asking how we were, and not seeing Mirjam, they began asking about her.

"I have not found her," I answered. "I was holding her in my arms when the storm struck. The wind whipped her from my grip when it started escalating. We need to fan out and search for her immediately."

Fabian, Rachael and the others arrived shortly after I had gotten there.

Ravi, noticing the injuries on Rachael's head and seeing that I was cradling my arm, asked me if I were hurt too.

"I need to check both of you over," Ravi said.

He and Fabian transported Rachael to the hospital, which thankfully had not sustained damage. I declined any medical attention saying that my first priority now was finding Mirjam, so we divided into pairs and began searching for her.

"I'll go with you, Dad," said Robert. "Dorri, could you manage looking after the children while André and Susann help us search? Dad, we will find Mom!"

CPSIA information can be obtained
at www.ICGtesting.com
Printed in the USA
LVHW020804111119
636959LV00002B/277